THE HAND OF GOD

First Published in Great Britain 2011 by Mirador Publishing

Copyright © 2011 by Michael Davies

All rights reserved. No part of this publication may be reproduced or transmitted, in any form or by any means, without permission of the publishers or author. Excepting brief quotes used in reviews.

First edition: 2011

Any reference to real names and places are purely fictional and are constructs of the author. Any offence the references produce is unintentional and in no way reflects the reality of any locations or people involved.

A copy of this work is available through the British Library.

ISBN: 978-1-908200-58-7

Mirador Publishing
Mirador
Wearne Lane
Langport
Somerset
TA10 9HB

The Hand Of God

By

Michael Davies

Mirador Publishing
www.miradorpublishing.com

1

He stepped back into the dusty shadows away from the window and the pale silvery fingers of light cast by the gibbous moon as it approached the zenith of its monthly cycle. Small droplets of water still clung to the dirty cracked panes of glass from the downpour earlier, the tiny spheres of liquid capturing the moons eerie glow and transforming its pallid light into a tiny dazzling array of refracted coloured filaments. He took a further tentative step, retreating beyond the moons illuminating touch, stirring up the years of thick dust that had gathered on the creaking floorboards as he did so. He could sense them now, albeit faintly, but they were coming, their presence rode the atmosphere before them like the faint odour of mould and decay in the air. He'd patiently laid low for days now, living on scraps of food he'd managed to beg and steal, sleeping on a pile of old garments he'd gathered from the wreckage on the ground floor beneath him, waiting for them for he knew they would come, his troubled dreams had told him so. He closed his eyes furrowing his brow as he delicately caressed his forehead, yes they were very near now, he could almost mentally taste their presence like the onset of a migraine, a dark sickly pulse had formed in his head. He quickly shifted his focus opening his eyes hurriedly wiping the beads of sweat that had formed on his brow with the back of his hand, which he noticed was shaking slightly. HE was with them, dark and diseased his mind festered like an open wound.

There, still distant, the faint noise of at least two engines the noise carried by the stillness of the empty streets. No one dared to tread these streets after sundown, the militia (dubbed the "Hand of God") patrolled what remained of this ruined city, the survivors living in abject poverty drawn to this place with the promise of food, shelter and medical supplies, but recently these nightly patrols had increased plucking unwary travellers from the streets where they were taken back to the seat of " Heaven," to be recruited or executed no doubt. Tonight felt different though there was a palpable sense of danger and purpose prevailing in the atmosphere this cold autumn night. The Nefarious were accompanying the Hand of God on their nightly forays, they were on the hunt, searching for something or someone specific, but who or what?

The moon had ducked behind a lingering rain cloud shutting out the light temporarily, he took a cautious step forward peering through the dusty panes, in the absence of the moonlight he could make out the unmistakable beams of several headlights cutting through the gloom that had now enshrouded the murky scene outside. They weren't far now only a few short streets away, they were taking their time, methodically scouring the area for... for what exactly? He could now make out the purring of at least three diesel engines. Only the Hand of God personnel were authorised the use of automobiles, which were fuelled with what? He'd often asked himself, but as all technology and presumably the scientists behind the tech were all now relocated in Heaven then as always the privileged and the rich always get what they want! So even since the planetary shift some aspects of life still remained the same. The results of the planetary shift had, as been foretold by the ancient civilisations, been devastating, billions perished. Tidal waves, earthquakes and volcanic eruptions wiped out all the major cities but worse was the aftermath, the survivors holed up in remote mountain areas away from the worst of the flooding fared the best, escaping the worst of the natural disasters but thrown back into a stone age environment as a result, disease and starvation wiped out many more. Survivors gathered together like packs of wild animals foraging as best they could amongst the ruins that was once man kinds great civilisation. A new age of mankind had dawned one were only the strong and the murderous prevailed. As this current dark age of man had always been foretold in ancient texts and glyphs by prophets and spiritual leaders so our scientists and political leaders had prepared for this unavoidable catastrophe, now the Hand of God was the law, the central hub of all that remained. Rumours were abound amongst the dwindling populace that before the cataclysm befell our planet that the

The Hand Of God

worlds governments were conducting experiments secretly on the worlds populations. Chemical and ethnobotanical agents were being introduced via genetically enhanced foods and prescribed pharmaceuticals. These experiments were inextricably connected to the rapid growth in technological advancements, both physical and metaphysical. More and more of the populace fell under their " spell," it became the norm for the masses to swallow their prescribed pain killers and antidepressants, to conform and become sedated and compliable, comfortably numb to the disasters and atrocities that dominated our television screens, ingesting our prescribed dose of media to be taken daily with our colourful array of tablets our doctors and psychiatrists tell us will make all our fears and pains go away. Some conspiracy theorists believed that the experiments were far darker than even this. Stories abound of alien presences making appearances before the great planetary shift, some presumed they arrived to save us from our inevitable destruction but government documents and leaked video footage appeared to show what was the experimentation on our so called " saviours " and rumours of genetic engineering, of the splicing of human and alien DNA. The authorities quickly dealt with this leak and all photographic evidence, documentation and presumably the source of this information itself was erased and a convincing cover up story set up in its wake. Just increase the medication dosage... there's nothing to fear. For many the cataclysm was the end of all but for those who could afford survival they had planned ahead for many, many years. Secretly, away from the public gaze, huge solar towers had been constructed, using huge amounts of gold to cover these massive reflective panels, so much so in fact it depleted our stored resources from all global storage sites. Get cash for your old unwanted gold! These towers were anchored in space just before the Earth's polar shift, these were then connected using newly developed nano technology via massive cables that channeled the harnessed suns energy, which was then converted into electricity by hyperheating a vast underground water system, thus providing an unlimited energy source, at least for the privileged and elite. The hub of this power was old Antarctica, which after the shift was now seated on the equator. "Heaven" as the new elite populace had christened it. For decades this had gone on behind closed doors, preparing for the inevitable. Not long before the changes a subconscious shift in the populace, perhaps a result of the human psyche breaking free from the chemical and mental bonds enforced upon them, the human id recognising its inevitable demise. Riots and violence broke out globally, fuelled by increased poverty and starvation as natural disaster after natural disaster took their toll but the ruling authorities bided their time patiently, why waste resources on an inevitably dead population and so as predicted for centuries the apocalypse happened and everything changed. "Heaven" became the hub of the world, the seat of all power and the survivors became subjugate to "The Hand of God" a militia based organisation, led by the Nefarious, mentally enhanced individuals, gifted with psychic abilities, together they rule and dominate this mortally wounded planet for their own perverse pleasure.

Many decades had passed by since the polar shift only the children of the then survivors carry the history of our past. Several generations had passed rebuilding their lives again, interference by the Hand of God had been at a minimum or at least very discreet. Food parcels were delivered periodically and occasionally militia patrols were sent in to dispel any uprisings. The survivors found increases in certain psychic abilities over the years, probably a direct result of being fed mind altering drugs for years altering their DNA. These abilities ranged from simple psychic enhancements, manipulation of organic and inorganic material to more extreme physical mutations seen by some as abominations, such things should never exist but they do and their numbers steadily increased, trying to live their lives as anonymously as possible for fear of persecution. Now the Hand of God has set out to eradicate these " hostiles " by any means necessary. Unknowingly these evolved beings are at the forefront of man kinds future leading the way towards a peaceful world of equality, love and understanding of ourselves, our planet and of the universe itself. The bigger picture waits to be unveiled or will the bright canvas of our future become dulled and lost with the spilt blood of our true saviours?

The sudden re-emergence of the moons ethereal glow as it slid back into view startled him from his reverie, he quickly shook himself free of his thoughts and focused once again through the dusty window into the street below. He was on the first floor of a partially ruined building of some kind, the contents long ago looted or decayed, but it offered him a wide array of escape routes if called upon. He stepped further back into the shadows, he knew the darkness itself would not conceal him from the prying minds of the Nefarious but no invisible icy tendrils reached out searching, probing his mind and thoughts, no they had other dark business tonight. He leant forward just enough to allow him a glimpse of the small procession below, three vehicles, two sleek black saloons followed by an equally black off road vehicle, he could sense the Nefarious in the off roader. The trio slowly rolled down the deserted street like a funeral cortege, he was surprised they hadn't adopted a hearse as their mode of transport with HIM laid out in the back like the ghoul that he was. He smiled coldly to himself and let the shadows in the room swallow him up again. The dark procession slowly crept past, the earlier rain puddled on the road made a distinctive sound as the vehicles rolled by. Yes they were scanning the area alright but on their way where? He mentally cleared his head of all thought leaving an empty patch of darkness on the ethereal plane, just in case and sure enough he felt the scan briefly like someone passing the beam of a torch over his hiding place and just as suddenly it was gone. He remained in the same mental state keeping his mind empty until he could no longer hear an engine or the displacement of water on the road. He slowly exhaled, he hadn't been aware that he'd been holding his breath. What were they up to? And why was HE accompanying them, must be something important to warrant the presence of that black hearted bastard.

HE was the leader, the power behind the Nefarious, psychically sensitive individuals very adept at locating other Sensitives. Many had been "recruited" by the Hand of God, locating, tracking and capturing other gifted individuals. They were used, many against their will forced into compliance by HIM to find and covert or eliminate others of their kind. In close proximity they can enter a mind and reap it of all knowledge and memories leaving nothing behind but a living husk, an empty shell. These Sensitives were never meant to use their gifts for such dark deeds and the more they did the blacker their souls became, slowly losing their human appearance becoming pale and emaciated, their eyes blackening, their breath reeking of decay as the darkness rotted them from within for the evil crimes they'd committed on their own kind. They have become the Nefarious, led by the blackest heart of them all, Nekros. Accompanying them on their forays are the recruited militia, the Hand of God, men and women with hearts as black as his soul, motivated by greed, inspired by pain, driven by fear and rage and bloodlust, trained in aggressive warfare these individuals have no conscience, love was a completely alien concept to these factions.

Eve was scared and she didn't know why and that scared her more because she always knew, she could feel her fear balled up in the pit of her stomach, an icy knot of tension chilling her very soul. She'd been in her room trying not to listen in on her parents fevered whisperings for over an hour now, she knew they were scared too. The bleak cold nights offered them no comfort of late, autumn was upon them and darkness came early now. Her parents too preoccupied with their own concerns had ushered her upstairs out of sight, the Hand of God had darkened their door on occasion before and her parents had always sent her upstairs to hide until their departure but tonight was different there was a chill in the atmosphere an unnatural silence outside. Presentiment haunted the city this night. She was sitting cross legged on her bed, a simple wooden framework constructed by her father out of timber salvaged from the surrounding ruined buildings, her mattress was rather beat up and flat but was better than lying on the hard concrete floor where all manner of insect life scuttled and crawled as soon as the light dimmed. At the foot of her bed a small wooden box, inside a handful of neatly folded clothes and a pair of child's boots sat side by side, a hairbrush and a pair of rolled up bright red socks rested atop the sad collection of clothing, like a glazed cherry atop a cake. Staring out of the single cracked pane in the window that still remained, the rest had long since been boarded up, clutching her one-eyed teddy bear to her chest. She'd found him half buried on a foraging trip herself and her father had undertaken looking for still useable items, her father returning with her old mattress balanced on his head, she beaming with that old dusty bear under her arm, that had been a good day. She watched the moon as it slowly crept into view, the cracked pane giving it a split appearance. As far back as she could remember she'd always known things that she couldn't possibly be aware of, this scared her parents, particularly her mother who had reiterated on many occasions that she had never to tell anybody about her gift or what she saw, her visions would only instill fear in the heart's of others and no doubt bring the Hand of God knocking at their door. Although this adopted reclusive life herself and her parents led meant she very rarely encountered any other survivors anyway. She had recently turned eight and this dilapidated old cafe had been their home for the last four years, or there about . Very few buildings remained intact enough to offer shelter from the elements, the glass fronted building had been boarded up to keep the wind and rain at bay and the old place still retained its original open fire place and as electricity was for the residents of Heaven only, the wealthy and the powerful, at least they had heat and a place to cook. Regular food drops were made not far from here but far enough away to keep them out of the direct scrutiny of the Hand of God. Tonight though there was no fire aloud in the hearth and the cold gnawed at her fear, yes tonight they were coming and she was scared. Grasping her bear tighter yet she harshly blinked back her tears.

Leaning back against the crumbling old wall, seated on a bed of threadbare fabrics, so old and dilapidated now it was hard to tell what they once pertained to be. He rubbed his eyes with thumb and forefinger, pinching the bridge of his nose trying in vain to release the tiny knot of pressure seated there since his brief encounter with the passing Nefarious. No sleep tonight that was for sure, this vigil wasn't over yet. He closed his eyes and sent his thoughts after the small convoy, yes they were still on their mission and he had a gut feeling he was going to find out very soon what or who their quarry was...

Eve took a sharp, shallow intake of breath and held it there, her hand worrying over her bear subconsciously, she found she did this in times of high anxiety to comfort herself. Straining her ears as she did so, yes she could hear the vehicles approaching, they were here, she slowly and quietly let out her breath as if doing it too loudly would draw attention to herself. Her parents must've been aware of the approaching menace too as their voices had died away as the deadly entourage came to a halt directly outside their home. She heard several car doors open and the sound of booted feet make contact with the damp concrete outside, the Hand of God was with them. Several footsteps could be heard approaching then a moment of heart stopping silence before a loud bang on the door reverberated through the building breaking the silence then a moment later the unmistakable crash as a booted foot slammed open the door shattering the rotten wooden framework around it. "Nobody move!" The command was issued from a female clad in a black military uniform an automatic weapon raised in the direction of the terrified couple who sat cowering at a small rickety table situated in the far corner of the small room. She quickly scanned the darkened area for further signs of life, satisfied they were alone she stood aside allowing the rest of her team to enter the scene. Three other members of the Hand of God militia entered the room and spread out. A desperate, hard-bitten looking trio all clad in black, their highly polished boots and automatic weaponry glinting in what little light that entered the scene through the now ruined doorway. Their features hard to distinguish in the murky gloom. The female who had now approached the terrified couple was tall and athletic in appearance, her features pale and sharp, her black eyes sparkled in the near darkness, her hair pulled back sharply from her face and plaited into a ponytail, features that could be seen as attractive in any other circumstances. The muzzle of her weapon shone momentarily as it reflected the light. An emblem was vaguely visible on her lapel, a flat silver hand, held upright, palm out symbolic of peace, an indecipherable insignia barely visible on its palm.

The Hand Of God

Apart from the bellowed order on their violent arrival nobody spoke but all eyes turned to the doorway where several figures now loomed, pale and ghost like the tallest of the group glided forward through the entrance to the old cafe, the others remaining outside. He seemed to float appearing to make no effort to walk. Were his feet actually touching the dusty tiles that paved the floor? It was hard to distinguish in the sporadic light. His face seemed to glow like the moon that hung deathly silent in the night sky outside as he hovered over the paralysed couple who clung together as if one entity. He halted directly in front of the table at which they were seated and drew a slow but meaningful glance at the female at their side. She silently dipped her head and purposefully took a step back. He then returned his withering gaze to the couple placing his hands, palms down on the old furrowed oak table drawing back his bone-like fingers, his nails blackened and broken, scored the old wood like a cats claws, exhaling slowly and meaningfully through his nose as he did so. His face was reminiscent of a corpse recently exhumed, his almost transparent parchment thin skin clung to his bald pate allowing every vein and contour of his skull full prominence, his features sharp and drawn, his dark lips cracked and cruel and his eyes, black as death no light reflected there only an all consuming nothingness. Immaculately attired in a three-piece suit, a surprisingly crisp white shirt that reflected his pallid deathly complexion even more so and was finished off with a narrow black silk tie. He scanned slowly one then the other, his face cracked as those blackened lips drew back revealing blackened, rotten broken teeth, his breath hissed as it escaped his dark maw like deadly fungal spores carried on a dying breath. The couple were too petrified to utter a noise as Nekros leant forward and pierced their minds... It was like the cold hand of death reaching into their very subconscious, as freezing, cloying fingers grappled and explored every ridge and trough of their brains, a spreading sickness, a slow numbness encasing both their minds. Searching, feeling, raping memories, opening concealed doors as the terror worked its way through their very cortex. Tasting their fear, an invisible tongue, grey and decaying tantalizing like a lovers oral caress leaving a trail of burning, rancid fear in its wake, sucking its hosts memories clean as would a starving beggar suck the last of the flesh from a peach stone. Slowly, reluctantly withdrawing, his breath laboured as of a lovers after coitus, saddened, like that of a junkies return to reality after the ecstatic high. A small dribble of saliva oozed from the corner of his decrepit, wicked old mouth, grey and glistening he wiped it away with his index finger and smiling insanely smeared it over the lips of his victims, their features slack, mouths hanging open like lobotomised patients their eyes vacant, lifeless. Their breathing barely audible, his head cocked slightly as if listening to some distant voice. He then pushed his saliva wetted finger into the women's mouth moving it around, searching like a hungry leech for a bloody feast. Suddenly he stopped and his ghastly smile widened as he slowly turned his face towards the ceiling of the now sepulchral cafe. He slowly withdrew his finger from the women's mouth, trailing saliva as he did so. Straightening up, his cold dark gaze fixed unwaveringly overhead.

Eve froze, an icy chill crept up her spine and her blood turned to ice in her veins at the sound of the militias command from below, even though she wasn't physically present she remained motionless for several minutes locked in fear straining to hear the scenario unfolding beneath her. That feeling of dread didn't leave her as she slowly found the courage to move her frozen limbs. Still clutching her stuffed bear she slid from her perch on her bed lowering her stockinged feet to the floor, she momentarily recoiled as her feet met the cold stone floor beneath then forcing herself she placed her soles firmly on the bare floor and let herself slide quietly from the mattress and positioned herself under the wooden construct her father had built, huddling up into a ball her eyes squeezed tightly shut. Her heart beat so loudly she was convinced they would surely hear her below.

Nekros had returned his soulless gaze towards the black clad female again and inclined his head slightly toward the two gaunt empty vessels that still sat at the wooden table staring blankly into space and slowly glided towards the back of the small room where a set of almost unnoticeable stairs appeared from the shadows. His evil grin widened as

The Hand Of God

his gaze drifted up the gloomy stairwell which took a sharp right angle leading to a room above the cafes seated area and as if stepping onto an escalator he floated up the stone steps and was swallowed up by the darkness that dwelt there. The woman responding soundlessly to an unspoken command slung the automatic weapon she had been carrying over her shoulder and unclipped a side arm from her belt, released the safety catch and emotionlessly pressed the cold muzzle of the gun into the temple of the seated male...

Eve physically jumped in her foetal like position under the bed at the sound of the first gunshot and hot, burning tears clouded her vision as she heard the second the deafening sound ringing in her ears. Moments later she tried to stifle a sob as she heard the sound of the door handle to her room rattle briefly as it was turned and the door creaked noisily as it swung wide open. Almost too terrified to look through her blurred, stinging eyes she blinked rapidly to clear her vision and what she saw stopped her heart momentarily, a pair of immaculately buffed black leather shoes hovered several inches above the dull, grey floor shining eerily in the moonlight and above those the glimpse of a pair of clinically creased trousers. The shoes hovered for a moment before slowly floating toward the only piece of furniture in her room and her only hiding place. Her heart beat so hard he must surely hear her, the pumping of her blood filled her ears, deafening her, her eyesight clouded and her head began to swim as a result of all the emotion and trauma of the last few minutes.

Nekros hovered briefly in the doorway, the room was small and dark but the moon freed from its cloak of cloud illuminated the small space adequately enough through the single cracked pane situated above the bed. He grinned maliciously and floated towards Eve's hiding place. Halting at the bedside he slowly descended, his patent leather shoes making the merest whisper as they made contact with the concrete floor and then suddenly, almost quicker than the eye could follow, he swiftly stooped and reached under the bed with one grasping talon like hand clutching at the huddled form beneath and like a magician pulling a rabbit from a hat retrieved his prize. His ghoulish smile faded from his odious countenance and his face visibly darkened as the dark abyss of his eyes perused the one-eyed stuffed bear that hung lifelessly before him, swinging forlornly by one leg. His gaze once more returned to the bed and bending double, without stooping or bending his legs, placed his halloween mask face in the gap between floor and bed and peered darkly at the empty space beneath, revealing nothing but some recently disturbed dust and what appeared to be a few droplets of water. He reached underneath with his free claw and placed a single emaciated finger on one of the droplets. Retracting his arm he straightened himself and examined his glistening fingertip, it sparkled in the moonlight, rubbing the liquid between finger and thumb he brought it towards his face and sniffed at the salty residue left there, his brow furrowed. "Curioussss," he hissed to himself and still clutching Eve's teddy he once again levitated and glided from the room to rejoin his retinue below. Wordlessly he floated past the two lifeless figures of Eve's parents as they lay huddled together in a pool darker than their surroundings and exited the building. His attendants silently followed suit, remorseless at the events that had just taken place. Nekros paused briefly outside the cafe staring blankly up at the glowing form of the moon, no light reflected in those loathsome ebony eyes. He glanced down thoughtfully at the stuffed bear he still grasped and then seamlessly entered the lead vehicle and one by one they advanced into the night

About an hour or so had passed by since the funeral like procession had continued by on its dark quest. The moons nightly orbit through the starless sky had taken it beyond sight and was no longer directly visible through the small window from where he sat on his nest of salvaged bedding, only partially illuminating the area before him with its ghostly glow. His head lolled forward as he sat propped against the bare, cold bricks at his back his legs stretched out before him the worn scuffed brown leather boots that clad his feet lighting up periodically in the pale sporadic radiance that found its way into his secret place. He abruptly snapped out of his trance like state and stiffened, his eyes adjusting in the encroaching gloom as the light once again faded and blinked out, the moon hiding its sallow face behind a particularly

The Hand Of God

nebulous cloud. His head pulsed and his heart picked up its beat. Something was coming, had they finally back tracked and discovered his lair? There, a noise, like the displacement of air, a door opening quickly but silently, the ensuing draught being sucked into the space. He spun his head round trying to locate the source of this imminent arrival but the room he occupied was still empty, he the sole occupant, the heavy wooden door to his right still remained firmly shut. But wait, in the periphery of his vision he was aware of a dark shadow forming in the gloomy corner opposite him. Instinctually his eyes widened as his now throbbing head centred on the condensing shape that was invading his realm and with a barely inaudible gasp directed the sphere of pulsing energy gathered in the centre of his forehead towards this intruder. A split second before he released this ball of cerebral energy a child's weakened voice broke through the cloying atmosphere, quite unexpectedly, startling him. "Where... Where's Charley?" She gasped. Instinctually he clamped his grimy palms to his pulsating head locking the energy bolt within, its rhythmical throb filling his skull. Unable to free itself the accumulated energy exploded into a crackling electrical discharge that seared his brain, turning everything red. Momentarily before he succumbed to the encroaching darkness in his head he was dimly aware of the huddled shape opposite, now fully condensed, was that of a young girl, her breath laboured and panicky after her single utterance, before her slightly raised head thumped onto the dusty floorboards, unconscious. The apparently now lifeless figure was the focus of his attention as the invading darkness quickly obscured his sight and he was vaguely aware of a warm trickle spilling from his nostril, thick and salty. Then, his senses reeling he finally surrendered to the throbbing void that consumed his head like the seeping spread of an ink spill, his temple cracked audibly as it contacted the begrimed floor. Her scared little voice still echoing in his mind as he drifted into oblivion. "Where's Charley?... Where's Charley?... Where?... "

2

The misty, insubstantial tendrils wreathed and twisted reaching out for him, phantom fingers enveloping his mind, darting out intermittently, serpent like filled with purpose and intelligence. Caressing his mind, beckoning to him, guiding him, his wistful thoughts congealing, focusing on the fingers of fog that held him tightly in their miasmic grasp. He relaxed his mind succumbing and allowing this alien presence entry to his subconscious, floating effortlessly on a sea of delicate whispers and sighs. A figure enshrouded in the mist formed in the distance of his mind, his will grasping at the solidity of its being as the fingers stroked and cajoled his dream state body, solidifying and then bursting like elongated vesicles filled with pure white smoke stuck with a pin instantly losing their definition before slowly reshaping themselves. Coaxing him gently forwards toward the slender figure ahead, now gaining prominence before him. Undoubtedly female but slightly nonhuman in appearance. Her skin a pale sky blue, her tall slender physique clothed only by the white tendrils, a living cloak of mist, shifting and undulating constantly like a transparent robe disturbed by a gentle breeze. By now his passage through the ghostly mists had brought him close enough to this unknown being for him to be able to distinguish her features, which were most definitely human in a very alien way. Her long flowing hair, white blonde and luxuriant, trailed eerily about her visage like some beautiful Greek gorgon, swirling and gesturing, joining in with the miasmic shroud that clothed her giving her the appearance of being submerged in transparent crystal waters, the eddies and currents causing the fog and her hair to dance and swirl about her body as if performing some ancient, erotic dance, alluring and captivating, holding his attention, hypnotised by her alien beauty. She smiled at him as his astral body came to rest before this vision of beauty. Was she a goddess or an angel? Come to guide his aching soul into the light. Her perfectly white teeth shone between pale blue lips,

The Hand Of God

full and perfectly formed, her delicate bone structure revealed an elegant jaw line and high cheekbones. Her angelic heart-shaped face supported by an elegant, regal neck but her eyes were where his focus finally fell and was captivated. A myriad of sparkling blues and violets, glinting, soft and caring but filled with knowledge and compassion. Emanating love they hypnotically changed colour from the palest shades through to the darkest of midnight blues and violets constantly phasing and shifting like a kaleidoscope. He found himself filled with an ethereal glow, brimming with love and healing, a single dream tear welled up in his eye and rolled down his cheek. Her eyes smiled warmly at him and she spoke directly into his mind her cupid bow mouth unmoving. The warmth of her words filled his aching head, soothing his mind, like the opening of a window on a cloying summers day allowing the sweet, delicate perfumes of the season access, filling the stale room of his mind sweeping away the stagnant air making him light headed in his already fugue like state. Her unvoiced words whispered to him delicately, lovingly, he could taste her delicate scent, nectared and sweet. Inhaling deeply he drew her presence into his core allowing the feeling to course through his body, a tingling warmth, an overwhelming feeling of compassion and desire to be one with this heavenly presence before him. "The time is upon us, the Creatrix, the mother of all that is and will be, is calling for our return. Be strong and gather faith as the age of peace awakens. Follow your heart and others will follow." He gently returned from his rapture and focused once more on the elegant apparition before him, her tender smile and soft, wet eyes filled his heart with a strength and purity he had never known or felt before. She raised a slender pale blue arm in his direction, her delicate long fingers reaching for him, her index finger extended and touched the point on his forehead where his third eye was located. Her touch was soft and silky, the feeling slowly spreading like warm honey in his mind. His head pleasantly swam as her aura enveloped his being like some intense narcotic rush. "Find me... "Her final words brushed his thoughts carrying him off on a wave of bliss, like a return to the womb, safe, warm and protected.

"Tha... Thalia?" He murmured, his eyelids flickering in the harsh light, temporarily blinding him. His pupils quickly readjusting to reduce the excessive light filling the small room by the return of the sun which was high in the cloudless sky outside. Dust motes sparkled and danced in the air about the small figure that knelt before him giving them a magical appearance. "Thalia?" He questioned again.

"Who?" Came the somewhat confused reply. "Are you alright mister? You've been sleeping a long time. Is she your girlfriend?" She queried in return.

"No... Eh no... You, eh who's Charley?" He replied confused as well, his mouth was parched and dusty and he worked his tongue around his dry mouth generating some saliva and lubricating his speech slowly pushing himself upright into a seated position as he did so. His temple throbbed slightly and he winced as he gingerly explored the small lump there. Wrinkling his nose at the same time he could feel the dried blood that had escaped his nose cracking, he wiped at it with the back of his hand examining the dried, blackened flakes clinging there.

"Here," the child offered him a plastic bottle of water she had found lying on the floor next to him.

"Thanks." He accepted the bottle and unscrewing the cap took a small mouthful, swilled it around his mouth and swallowed, his vocal chords hydrated again he scrutinised the child that knelt before him. She only looked about eight or nine. Pale and thin, her short dark brown bobbed hair framed her pretty face which was somewhat grubby after her night lying on the dusty floor. Her eyes dark brown also and scared looking. She wore a holey pair of well faded denim jeans and an oversize maroon sweater, a little bit frayed at one sleeve. Around her neck she wore a delicate silver necklace on which was suspended a small silver locket. He noticed she wasn't wearing any shoes just a once white pair of socks. She sat hugging herself as she stared silently up at him. He offered her the water before screwing the cap back on when she declined.

"Charley?" He asked again, cocking his head in anticipation of her reply.

"Oh Charley he's my teddy bear, I must've left him be-

The Hand Of God

hind." Her eyes welled up with tears as she spoke, silently remembering last night's ordeal.

"Hey kid you alright? What happened to you and how the hell did you get in here?"

"I... I don't know I was hiding from HIM under my bed and then I was here. My mum and dad they... "She tailed off no longer able to hold back her flood of tears, drooping her head embarrassed at her involuntary show of emotion in the presence of a stranger. Embarrassed himself but deeply moved at her sadness he reached forward and stroked her awry hair soothingly.

"Hey kid whatever happened last night you're safe now okay we can go an look for your parents as well." Head still lowered she shyly looked up at him. He tried to smile reassuringly down at her coaxing a small half smile from her in return. She smudged away her tears with the heal of her hand and sniffing deeply introduced herself.

"My names Eve," she announced formally.

"Hi Eve, I'm Canova." He held out his hand extending the formalities smiling at her as he did so, she took it in hers and shook it.

"Canova? That's a funny name."

"Thanks a lot," he retorted and laughed aloud, Eve laughed with him. Still smiling, Canova, as he revealed himself to be, stood up slowly, grimacing as his temple throbbed, his eyebrows lowered into a frown his smile fading at the pain. Fully upright he stretched to his full height, throwing his arms out into a prolonged stretch removing the knots and kinks from his aching limbs and body after his night spent slumped on the floor. His neck cracked lightly as he twisted his head this way and that, finally shaking his head to remove the last vestiges of sleep from his brain but not aggressively enough to aggravate his throbbing temple more.

"You okay?" Eve asked concerned. Taking the opportunity to fully examine her new companion as she remained seated before him. He was quite tall, six foot or so she guessed, his build lean and wiry. He wore green combat trousers tucked into brown ankle length boots, which were badly scuffed and scored. One of the pockets on his trousers was partially torn and the loose corner was turned down revealing a fresh, rich patch of green material beneath. His black T-shirt hung loosely below the waist line of his combats, two dirty pink words emblazoned across the front read " lost souls." The brown leather of his jacket was well worn and broken in, almost worn away completely at the cuffs revealing the untanned hide beneath, the collar was furry and rather grey looking. His face wasn't bad looking, unshaven and grimy, his hair a messy shock of dark blonde, his eyes dark grey and rather serious looking and somewhat sad she thought but when he smiled down at her they twinkled magically. "You're a Psych aren't you?" She enquired finally standing up. "My parents used to tell me about people like you, my mum could do stuff too."

"Is that what we're called," he grinned good humouredly. "Yeah well suppose I am a bit mental and what about you, what do you do?"

"I just know stuff," she replied shrugging. "It's like I'm somewhere else," she tried to explain. "Like I'm not in my body anymore. I can go places and look around, listen to people and stuff." She concluded unsure of how to describe her talents further.

"And you say the last thing you remember was hiding in your room and then waking up here this morning?" She nodded.

"I just remember my head starting to spin like I was going to faint and... " She trailed off her thoughts going back once again to her parents and her eyes misted over involuntarily.

"A Porter, got to be," he concluded half to himself. "I've heard rumours of your kind. A natural mutation apparently, natural selection even but hard to track because of their abilities. So that's what they were looking for last night they're trying to catch themselves a teleporter," he concluded the pieces of the puzzle falling into place.

"A Porter, I've heard of that before I didn't think they existed I thought my dad was making it up, making fun of me." She paused. "Do you really think that's what I did?"

"It's the only explanation and it would explain HIM being with them last night and you say you've never done anything

The Hand Of God

like that before?" He quizzed her.

"No never, I used to just think I dreamt stuff until I started recognising people and places I'd been to. I told my mum but she got really scared and made me promise never to tell anyone not even my dad but I'm sure he knew he just never spoke about it. Do you want to see them?" She asked.

"Yeah sure." Realising what she meant when she touched the locket hanging around her slender neck which must contain a small photograph of them. Using both hands she carefully released the tiny clasp and opened the shining heart, raising it up so he could see the diminutive images more clearly.

"My dad found an old camera," she explained. "When we were scavenging, that's what my dad called it, he managed to get it working again using an old car battery he had lying around. It was one of those cameras where the picture comes out the front I can't remember what he called it but it only worked once, my dad reckoned the car battery was too powerful and melted the insides." Canova leant forward examining the two tiny faces. The images had been carefully cut from a larger polaroid picture, the remaining photograph discarded leaving the smiling faces of Eve's parents snugly fitted in the tiny heart-shaped insets. Even though the images were no bigger than his thumbnail he could instantly see the similarities. She had her mother's dark eyes and pretty smile. Her father was a proud looking man his cheeks ruddy, his smile wide.

"They look like really nice folks." He commented. "You got your mother's good looks." He complimented her.

"They are... or were." She finished sadly her features drooping as she closed the locket with a tiny click and laid it back on her sweater, her palm resting briefly over it for a second or two, protectively.

"I'm sure they're fine," he tried to reassure her but in his heart he knew that if Nekros was on the hunt last night then as sure as the sun was going to set then Eve's parents were already dead.

"It's okay," she lamented finally looking into his eyes. "I knew it was going to happen. He killed them both." She visibly shuddered at the memory etched in her mind. Poor kid, he thought to himself and brave too. Well it looked like fate had thrown them together for some reason and his thoughts returned briefly to his dream.

"Thalia." He whispered to himself absent-mindedly.

"Yes." She perked up instantly, anything to take her mind of the recent events of last night. "I forgot about that, you whispered her name when you were waking up, is she a friend of yours?"

"No, I... "He paused momentarily. "Don't know who or what she is. She was in my dream. My head. I don't know how but what I do know is that we have to find her," he concluded looking at Eve awaiting her reply.

"We?" She enquired.

"Yeah, unless you want to stay here?" She glanced around at the filthy room, nothing but dust and a pile of moth eaten old rags.

"You live here?" Her expression one of barely suppressed disgust, her nose wrinkling. He laughed.

"No I don't," he replied with mock indignation. "I don't have a fixed address I just move around from place to place." She grinned back at him.

"When do we leave?"

"Well it's decided then," he grinned back. "But we'll need to find you something to put on your feet 'cos you won't make it far like that." He indicated her stockinged feet.

"I've got shoes at home," she countered. "Food and clean water as well, you must be hungry." She commented.

"Do you live near here?"

"I'm not sure." She made her way to the grimy window and peered out into the brightly lit street below. The warmth of the sun shining through the remaining panes filled her with renewed energy. She shut her eyes for a second or two and basked in its brilliant radiance. Opening her eyes again she frowned as she examined the scene below before turning her head to face Canova. "I think I recognise this street, if I'm right my home isn't too far away."

"Okay then." The sun had passed its peak and would remain in sight for a few more hours only before darkness once again took dominion over the city. The Hand of God rarely patrolled the streets during daylight hours the Nefarious rarely if ever, the night was their element and they didn't want to be out in the open when the sun finally slid beyond the horizon. He stooped to pick up the water bottle and jammed it in his jacket pocket. "You be okay like that?" He pointed at her unprotected feet again. She looked down at her grubby socks and wiggled her toes.

"I'll manage," she smirked. Smiling at her response he strode toward the dark wooden door and turned the tarnished brass knob, opening it wide he bowed graciously gesticulating with his free hand.

"After you," he offered and together they left the confined space of the room and entered the murky corridor beyond.

3

The two unlikely companions stepped out onto the cracked rutted pavement basking for a few seconds under the steady golden gaze of the afternoon sun, its heat chasing away the cold chill still residing within their limbs, flushing them with renewed vigour and energy. Their stomachs grumbled in unison reminding them of their mission for today. They both laughed at the bubbling and growling that emanated from within. It felt good to laugh again, he hadn't had much cause for laughter of late. Spying a large puddle nearby, deep enough not to have been evaporated by the heat of the midday sun. Its surface shone mercurial like reflecting the suns glare. Making his way toward the pool, Eve at his side, he peered into the clear water, his reflection peered back at him with a mirror like quality. Crouching he scooped some of the cool liquid in his cupped hands and began to cleanse his bloodied nose and wash the grime from his face. Eve followed his lead, splashing the chilled water on her face, she shuddered involuntarily at its icy caress. Both felt refreshed and alert. Standing, they shook the sparkling droplets of water from their hands, Eve catching a lingering drop on her nose with the back of her hand. Canova turned to her, his face glistening lightly as the moisture there slowly dried in the cool air. "Which way then?" He asked her. She scanned the road ahead before finally settling on the pathway to their right, pointing.

"That way." She answered decisively. Canova looked in the direction in which Eve had indicated. Yeah that figured, he thought to himself, that was the direction the Hand of God had taken last night on their murderous quest and together they set off.

Judging by the distance the sun had traversed across the sky Canova estimated about an hour had passed by since Eve and himself had left the shattered remains of the building in which he'd been hiding out in for the last few days. So far they'd encountered no other survivors which wasn't surprising, most of whom had succumbed to the promise of food and shelter within one of The Hand of God's makeshift camps. A small gathering of corvines alarmed by their appearance rose noisily from their scavenging, the iridescence of their jet wings catching the sun, startling him. Even animal life was a rare sight these days most having fled from the cities returning to the relative safety of the hills and recovering forests. Only the more adaptable species surviving extinction during the shift, scavengers, rats, birds and crawling insects inhabited this empty city. During their trek through the city Eve had pointed out the way as she recognised ruined land marks. They made good progress under her guidance, Canova hoisting her onto his back periodically saving her unprotected feet from the worst of the rubble, shattered brickwork, shards of glass and torn, rusted pieces of metal that still littered the streets here. Eve had filled him in on the way with a brief biography of her life, chatting away amiably, happy to have someone with whom to talk too.

Her descendants, her great grandparents, had survived the holocaust hiding out in some mountain caves with several others. She didn't know where but they had clung to survival scraping out a meagre existence in the mountains living off what the land had provided but as mother nature herself had sustained just as serious a calamity as humankind many starved to death or died of exposure and illness during the harsh winters that befell them. When her parents had had Eve they mutually decided that her best chance of survival was to return to the ruined city located near the coast. A couple of travellers had happened upon the mountain refuge many years before spreading word of food, medicine and shelter magnanimously provided by this so called Hand of God. She was only an infant when her mum and dad had left their sanctuary and undertook the arduous journey ahead of them. The Hand of God had indeed provided camps for the survivors, regimented by the military, the whole appearance reflected that of a prison camp. Curfews were enforced, trouble makers swiftly eradicated and food rationed. Her parents had despaired as their golden path to a new and better life for themselves and little Eve had quickly turned to mud, the despair and oppressive atmosphere of the camp hung heavy about their shoulders. Deciding the return journey would be too much for them all to endure again they tolerated the camp site for many, many months until her father had crept away one night avoiding the militia posted to enforce the curfew and escaped into the remains of the city beyond. He'd soon stumbled upon a ramshackle cafe that still retained most of its structure. The shop windows shattered and gone during the many earthquakes that had shook the Earth violently during the planets magnetic realignment. Ever the optimist he'd returned for his family and he boarded up the old shop front with salvaged timbers and some old rusted tools he'd unearthed in the rubble. Her mother had cleared the interior of debris as best she could, initially sleeping on some rough grey blankets, liberated from the camp before they left, laid out on the floor at the back of the room where the counter had once sat which her father had broken up for fuel. The old cafe still retained its original sandstone fireplace now blackened and aged. The warmth and light filled them all with a new sense of hope and vigour. Her parents had given Eve the single room above the shop floor and her dad had fashioned her a bed frame from what he could find. Life had been simple but hard, her father had retraced his steps many times to the militia camp stealing food and clean drinking water and occasionally some items of clothing. It had been no life for an young girl but her spirit was strong. Canova smiled solemnly watching her skip ahead of him down a relatively clear stretch of path. She paused and turned her head about, calling back to him. "Hurry up it's not far now." Then continued down the street. He raised a hand in compliance and broke into a short jog slowing again as he caught her up, she gave him a sideways glance.

"So what about you? What happened to your mum and dad?"

"I don't remember much about them." He began, frowning as he tried to dredge up the few memories that still remained of his parents as the two of them continued on their journey. The sun's rays suddenly flickered out blocked by the remnants of some long uninhabitable terraced housing.

The Hand Of God

The shade offered there cold and damp still from last night's downpour. He gave a little shudder before bracing himself and relating to Eve what he could recall. His grandparents had survived the shift by taking refuge within a network of coastal caves, a considerable gamble amidst the earthquakes and tidal waves that ravaged the Earth but one that had paid off. They had remained in the vicinity with a handful of others, living off what the sea provided, combing the coastline for fish and shellfish which became their staple. Returning to the shelter of the caves to escape the harsh coastal weather. Enough wood was washed onshore along with all manner of flotsam, which fuelled their fires and kept them warm. Once the sea delivered too them some luggage escaped from some doomed ocean liner no doubt which provided them all with some much needed clothing some toiletries and medicine, including the now well worn leather jacket he wore which his grandfather had claimed for himself passing it down to his son and finally Canova. The people living there grew into a small community his parents meeting there and conceiving him. Christening him Canova, who he remembered his dad informing him had once been a great artist who had died many, many years before the changes. Unfortunately one particularly unforgiving winter disaster had struck the small community. Gales tore through the makeshift dwellings they had constructed, the churning, boiling sea rose smashing the shanty town and reducing it to splinters. For those that sought refuge once again in the caves disaster also ferreted them out. Huddled together like frightened rabbits the unrelenting force of the ocean drove deep into the heart of the cliffs dashing and breaking them against the rocks there. Only a meagre handful of disillusioned outcasts remained and together they abandoned their ravaged home, his parents hadn't been amongst the lucky survivors. The ragged band had travelled inland eventually joining up with others heading for the salvation promised them by the Hand of God and so he'd ended up interred within one of the camps as had Eve and her parents. No longer did the fresh salty breeze fill his lungs each morning, just the stench of filth and decay, spending most of the following years confined to one of the many grey tents that littered the site. The area had been stripped of rubble using enforced labour, which was in turn used to construct make shift walls around the site. All feeling of hope slowly evaporated, was this it? Had he been condemned to this life of drudgery, oppression and constrained quiescence, to die malnourished and diseased or worse. Hushed whispers infiltrated the populace of disappearances amongst them. The local militia uplifting them from this stinking swampy hell to be received rapturously into the Hand of God. "So one night I ran off into what was left of the city. I figured I had a better chance of survival out there on my own and well that's about it and I've been dodging about avoiding patrols, sleeping wherever I could an eating whatever I could find." His short tale complete he looked down at Eve grim faced.

"How long have you have been living rough like that in the city?" She asked.

"I'm not sure it's kinda hard keeping track of time. I reckon six, seven years maybe. Shit I can't even remember how old I am, at a guess... "He paused mid flow performing a mental calculation, before continuing. "Must be about twenty-two, twenty-three. I think!" He shrugged.

"You've been on your own all that time." She exclaimed aghast. He just nodded in return. "Well you're not alone anymore you've got me to keep you company now." She beamed up at him her infectious grin spread and he found himself grinning back. Then she put her pale little hand in his and tugged at him. "Come on just around this corner and we're there." His reluctance to follow her was immediately noticed and she turned frowning as she studied his expression, his grey eyes seemed glazed and far away. "What's wrong?" She sounded concerned and a little worried. He blinked his attention back towards her pale anxious face.

"They're here." He whispered. "I can feel them." Her face visibly drained further of all colour at his response and he could feel her trembling slightly through her hand as he clasped it in his own. "Don't worry I ain't gonna let anything happen to you, we were lucky that they took a different route this time or they might've taken us by surprise but now we've got the upper hand." He tried to smile reassuringly and winked at her. He held a finger up to his lips indicating that

The Hand Of God

they shouldn't speak for now and keeping their noise down to a minimum he led her by the hand towards a crumbling arched doorway in what remained of the wall over to the right. The wall turned the corner about twenty feet from where they stood heading into the street where Eve lived. They silently entered what remained of the shattered building through the archway, vestigial scraps of vegetation sprouted from the cracks in the old stonework the bright green foliage a welcome sight in this grey vista. He silently denoted she should ride piggy-back as the passageway up ahead was littered with debris. Lifting her up, her arms crossed lightly around his neck, he cautiously navigated the damp corridor, at the end of which was a set of stone steps. Water pooled in the worn concave stones, worn away by feet long since gone. He buoyantly leapt up the dozen or so steps, her slight under nourished frame almost weightless on his back. On reaching the top he slowed his pace and edged towards what had once been a window, the lintel long since gone. He lowered Eve gently onto a large block of lichen covered stone saving her stockinged feet from the dampness that clung to the stone floor. Canova then slowly made his way towards the near edge of the three sided window frame, all signs of glass or wooden framework long gone only cold stone remained. He leant forward, his heart and head pulsing in unison. One black clad uniform stood outside the cafe guarding the doorway, a black off roader was parked just past the entrance to the building. Projecting his thoughts he scanned the interior of the building ahead, only taking a few seconds he retracted his mind and drew back. Well at least the Nefarious weren't in attendance, although he'd never seen them venture out during the day on these excursions. He looked back at Eve who sat perched on her rock hugging her knees to her chest. He crouched down and in a whisper, loud enough for her to make out over the short distance between them asked, "You think you can do your thing. I can take care of them but I can't tell exactly how many of them there are or whereabouts. You think you can do that for me?" She nodded in compliance Canova giving her a thumbs up in return. Eve repositioned herself so she was now sitting cross-legged and closed her eyes, her hands lay loosely in her lap. She inhaled deeply and let her breath out slowly her head nodding forward as she did so. A few dark strands of hair fell forward partially obscuring her pasty complexion. A couple of minutes ticked by before Canova became aware of the rapid movement of her eyes underneath her closed lids. She raised her head back into an upright position and her eye lashes flickered as her lids opened sleepily still in R.E.M. The orbs of her eyes rolled back the whites staring blankly back at him.

Eve was sitting once more on her old bed. The sun beamed through the tiny cracked pane above her head, sparkling particles of dust floated in the light there. Her room was deserted. The door still sat wide open from last night allowing the sound of movement to filter upstairs to where she sat. She "thought" herself upright, not needing to use any physical exertion, she was a mere ghost in this world, an insubstantial glimmer of her true self. She allowed her conscious mind to carry her over the dirty floor noticing absently as she did so that her small box, that dwelt at the foot of her bed, housing her small wardrobe had been emptied unceremoniously onto the floor. A frustrated booted foot had scattered the contents during the futile search. She continued onwards through the open door and descended the dark stairwell entering the room below and viewing the scene that now confronted her. Two black clad figures hovered over a large bundle on the floor she couldn't quite discern. She noticed the guard outside, his bulk blocking the passage of some of the daylight from outside. She returned her attention to the two crouched figures to her left. Her spirit recoiled at the sight of the dark pool that surrounded her long cold parent's, the hands of the militia deftly searching the corpses for contraband or a clue as to where they could locate their missing daughter. Her dislocated mind reeled as emotion and shock washed over her at the sight of the gruesome spectacle unfolding before her.

She awoke from her trance gasping through her mouth deeply, tears welled up in her eyes and cascaded down her cheeks in great floods now unable to control the show of emotion at the vision of her parents lifeless bodies still lingering in her mind. Canova edged forward, concern etched

The Hand Of God

into his features and reached forward and clasped both her hands in his own. She looked into his face and saw it filled with genuine concern at the sight of her grief. She gulped back her emotions so she could relay the information she had gathered to Canova. "Three." She gently whispered, controlling her sobs she continued." Two downstairs towards the rear and the one guarding the front door." He squeezed her hands gently his smile tight-lipped and humourless, now it was his turn. He stood up releasing her porcelain hands and repositioned himself at the stone aperture once again peering through the gap. He projected his thoughts towards the building ahead and the unsuspecting militia. He gasped as the fire in his head escalated and condensed in his skull, building momentum as it twisted and crackled, it seemed to get more powerful each time he called upon it. Canova briefly touched on the minds of the three mercenaries, their positions revealed to him by Eve, envisioning them with his mind's eye, touching their thoughts delicately before unleashing the swirling power in his head.

"Did you hear something?" One of the militia in the building had asked his companion, slowly scanning the surrounding area as he did so. Before a sound was uttered from the other soldiers mouth a force simultaneously struck the three a bludgeoning force from within and silently, in perfect unison, the three slumped to the ground. The guard at the door toppled like a felled tree, breaking the fall unceremoniously with his face on the hard road outside.

Canova, at seeing the guards painful connection with the hard concrete, turned to Eve, who by now had regained her composure and was watching him with wet, sad eyes. "Okay it's done, let's go?" Hoisting Eve up onto his back once again he retraced his steps through the ruin back out into the street where he lowered her to the ground and together they warily rounded the corner and proceeded onwards toward their destination.

The gleaming off road vehicle looked strangely out of place, its highly polished liquid paintwork and glowing chrome features shone brightly as the sun continued its passage towards the broken horizon. The comatose guard outside the shop front lay unmoving and stiff, a small trickle of red glistened as it traced its way over the uneven ground. Eve looked up at Canova in disbelief and wonderment. "How did you do that?" She queried him looking down again at the prone figure laid out before them.

"I'm not too sure." He responded quietly as he knelt beside the guard. He touched a point on his neck below his collar checking for a pulse.

"Is he dead?" She asked. He remained silent for a few seconds as he searched for the weakened pulse there indicating the guards life was still intact.

"No, he's still breathing." Canova stood and turned to her." You don't have to go in there if you don't want to you know."

"It's okay I saw them in my dream." She sadly replied and with Canova leading the way entered her home silently. She pointed to a box sitting next to the blackened fireplace, its open hearth still housing the charred, charcoal remains of many past fires, some grey and white powdered ash had spilt out onto the tiled floor beyond. "There's food and water in that box I'll go and get my things." With that she ran quickly past the bodies of her parent's, now partially buried beneath the two unconscious soldiers and dashed up the stairs her stockinged feet silent on the stone. Canova watched her disappear and went to examine the contents of the dog-eared box which contained several silvery packets of military issue food supplies and some bottled water. He quickly scanned the rest of the room looking for something sturdier in which to transfer the contents of the box too. Seeing nothing that fit his requirements he returned outside and stepping over the prone figure there opened the rear door to the off roader and peered inside. On the backseat sat a small hold all, he grabbed it and returned triumphantly to the box and its contents. Unzipping the bag he unceremoniously emptied its contents onto the floor and sifted through the items strewn in front of him. Some ammunition, a couple of two way radios, some more food rations (which he stuffed back in the hold all) and a small zipped medical bag which he also returned. He was just fitting the last of the supplies into the bag when Eve appeared at his side, now wearing her boots the laces tied into neat bows. In her arms she carried a few items of clothing and a brush which she'd obviously just used as her brown hair was now neat and straight. He opened the bag wider and placed her belongings inside with the supplies filling the interior and closed the zipper. Canova slung the bag onto his back an arm through each handle wearing it like a rucksack. Eve looked forlorn and despondent, her eyes red and puffy. He gently put an arm around her slumped shoulders and hugged her tenderly.

"Come on its time to leave, we don't want to be around when these guys wake up." With his arm still protectively around Eve they left the cafe never to return. Eve peeked sadly over her shoulder as they made their way out passing the broken door which hung precariously on one rusted hinge before continuing on their journey, the atmosphere of death slowly dispelled by the last of the suns orange glow as its circumference touched the edge of the horizon. "We'll need to hurry and find somewhere safe for tonight, we don't want to be out on the streets when it's dark." Removing his arm he took Eve's hand, who's earlier cheerful demeanour had all but evaporated. Ignoring their hunger for now Canova took the lead this time and they swiftly made their way into the wastelands that stretched out ahead of them and the encroaching dusk.

4

Nisa and MacClure, Mac for short, had been keeping up a steady surveillance on the Hand of God encampment below, which had been set up in the square there for the last twenty four hours. Something was certainly going down as supplies and troops had been shipped in steadily since dawn yesterday. The contingent now consisted of about nine armed militia and several Nefarious who had now returned to the dark confines of the military style tent that had been set up, so as to escape the returning rays of the dawning sun. A four by four had recently departed the vicinity carrying three soldiers reducing their numbers slightly. "Hey Nisa you awake?" Mac nudged her into wakefulness.

"Fuckin' am now!" She crabbily muttered, rubbing the sleep from her eyes with thumb and finger. She yawned and stretched as best she could in her cramped position, located atop a three storey building that still remained surprisingly intact. The tiled roof had partially collapsed creating a cramped triangular tunnel in which the pair of them now lay pinned together, claustrophobic but warm and dry at least. Mac had knocked out some of the old crumbling brickwork allowing them a bird's eye view of the panorama in the square below. Mac was of a short stocky build allowing Nisa very little room in which to manoeuvre. Deftly wriggling backwards she freed herself from the confines of the self imposed stone sarcophagus. Finally freeing herself she painfully stood up to her full height arching her back and shaking the life back into her cramped limbs.

She was tall, over six feet and of solid build. Her physique showed through the black militia uniform she wore, the Hand of God insignia had been torn roughly from the lapel and discarded. The uniform donated by some unwary guard specifically chosen for his similarity in height and build, Nisa had deftly ended his life with no penitence for he surely would've done the same if she'd have given him the opportunity. Clad from head to toe in black, the leather boots

The Hand Of God

she wore had long since lost their shine now thick with dust and grime from hours of lying outstretched on the years of dirt that had accumulated in their hiding place. She brushed what she could of the residue from her pilfered uniform and stretched again her back cracking, she winced at the sound and kicked one of Mac's feet that protruded from his hiding place. "Any water left?" She asked sourly still petulant at her rude awakening. Without vocalising a response he rolled a half full bottle toward her. She scooped it up as it came rolling to a standstill at her feet. Flipping the cap she took a long draught before firmly closing the bottle and setting it down on the floor. She scrutinised her hands as she did so, badly scarred, a few recent cuts still showed but were healing quickly enough merging with the myriad of white scar tissue that crisscrossed the backs of her hands and knuckles. They were fighting hands and she knew how to use them. Her head was shaved, as was her companions, she was very adept with a knife, the hair growing in black and stubbly. She had a strong jaw line, her ears lay flat to her skull a small piece missing from one lobe. Her nose had been broken at some point in the past and never reset resulting in a small prominent bump on the bridge. A white scar was visible on her chin below her thin pink lips, her teeth stained one of the incisors slightly chipped. Her eyebrows thin and black, delicately shaped arched over her eyes, which were a breathtaking emerald green but cold and hard. "Hey Mac!" She kicked hard at his feet again.

"What?" Came his muffled reply noticeably irritated now.

"You formulated a plan yet 'cos I'm hankering for some action if you know what I mean." Mac carefully retracted himself from his observation point using his elbows to walk himself into the open space where Nisa stood waiting. When he finally cleared his head he knelt back and rocked himself onto his feet and stood in one fluid motion. He was several inches shorter than his comrade but wider and thicker. He also donned a militia uniform the insignia likewise removed. His neatly shaved head sat atop a thick muscular neck, his lips full and fleshy his stained teeth visible as he grinned at Nisa. His nose flattened like that of a boxer's, eyebrows dark and bushy, his pale grey eyes sparkled with mischief and humour. His large thick fingered hand grabbed the bottle of water and he gulped several mouthfuls before reclosing it and setting it down again empty. His gaze narrowed as he scrutinised Nisa the knife she carried sat bulkily in its sheath strapped to her thigh. They'd known each other for some time now and they made a good team both of them hardened and ruthless, someone he could rely on to watch his back. "Supplies gettin' low and we're out of water." Nisa commented nodding at the empty bottle. "So what's the plan?"

"We wait till sunset, those Nefarious fuckers'll be on the hunt tonight with a Hand of God escort no doubt. So we sneak in take out the fuckers still camped out and lie in wait an ambush the rest on their return, simple!" He concluded grinning widely. Nisa stared down at him coldly with those verdant eyes of hers, a lop-sided smile edged its way onto her thin lips and she shook her head slowly.

"So that's the master plan is it?" He looked up solemnly and shrugged. "Well it'll have to fuckin' do." She rebuffed, her smirk breaking into a full on smile. He grinned amiably back his eyes twinkling with anticipation.

Nisa owed Mac her life, saving her from a Hand of God cleansing team several years previously. Shifter's, as they'd been tagged for their ability to morph parts of their biological selves, the metamorphosis quite often being painful and emotionally induced. These mutations a direct result of DNA experimentation had been passed down through the generations genetically over the years. The Nefarious and the Hand of God had targeted and eliminated their kind ruthlessly since the global shift deeming these newly evolved human geonomes a growing threat and had determined that their kind be hunted down and eradicated until the brutal ethnic cleansing had driven them to near extinction. As a result of this relentless pursuit and extermination Shifters were an increasingly rare offshoot of the human species. Shying away from contact with others, seeking sanctuary with their own kind, never settling for any lengthy period in one location.

Nisa and Mac had become part of one such group of refugees taking shelter in one of the few buildings intact

The Hand Of God

enough to offer a rudimentary home on the outskirts of the city. Alas for most this was to be their down fall. No doubt, the Nefarious, led to their camp by an informer. The Hand of God had silently appeared one cold and misty morning which culminated in the Shifters near annihilation. Surrounding the building in which they'd inhabited the attack was swift and merciless, adults and children alike slaughtered. Grenades containing a deadly toxin were delivered from every angle filling the air with a thick deadly smoke killing the inhabitants swiftly and efficiently. The militia, protected from the now diminishing gas with full faced masks filtering the air they breathed, scoured the interior of the building eliminating any survivors within. This is where Mac's mutation came into its own. His biological chemistry could alter and adapt to harsh environments, his lungs quickly acclimatising to the poisonous environment rendering him immune to the cloying atmosphere. In his bid to escape he had stumbled upon the choking barely conscious Nisa struggling to crawl her way to freedom. He had deftly lifted her over his shoulders, his powerful limbs easily bearing her weight and barely slowing his progress. On reaching a ground floor exit he was met by a member of the masked militia. The two stood opposing each other surprised at each other's sudden appearance as they halted in their tracks. Mac regaining his composure first planted his square fist firmly in the face of the still stationary soldier smashing the transparent window in his mask and crunched satisfyingly into his face. The soldier dropped silently to the stony ground. Then carefully checking that the soldier had been alone Mac rapidly sped for cover his strength and stamina carrying himself and Nisa far from the killing site before finally lowering her to the ground hidden away in what used to be a small park, the plant life now rampant, left unchecked for years allowing the shrubs and trees full dominion over the small area which now resembled a small area of woodland. Mac hunkered down on his aching limbs his breathing now laboured.

Nisa's memory of the events had been vague. The sudden attack, the cloying, choking, deadly smoke. The bumpy flight hoisted over her saviours wide shoulders shaking her from unconsciousness periodically. When Mac finally put her down she fleetingly regained her senses, her emerald eyes focusing briefly on the figure looking down at her, the man to which she owed her life and from that day onwards the two allies vowed to destroy and disrupt the Hand of God by any means possible avenging their murdered friends and family.

The last vestiges of sunlight finally dipped below the horizon bruising the sky with purples and reds. Eve and Canova had taken shelter in a single free standing room, all that remained of the dwelling, little more than a large cupboard. Plant life had taken root where it could amongst the shamble of rocks surrounding the area softening the hardened edges, lichens adding splashes of yellows, greens and oranges haphazardly splattered around. Once safely out of sight they'd eaten sparingly, not knowing from whence their next supply top up would come from or when. The foiled packets once opened revealed their unappetising and unrecognisable contents but it quietened their protesting stomachs. After their sparse meal Canova had drifted off into a fitful doze his face full of nervous tics and frowns.

His dream was dark, distant lights twinkled like stars, each one sparking and burning out like embers the blackness encroaching even more as they faded away. His sleeping mind desperately clutched at the dimming scintilla searching for some guiding light to lead him forth from this all consuming pitch. His focus reached out to the one star that still remained unfading and as he did so its radiance slowly grew in luminosity, mesmerizing him as he was slowly drawn toward it. Or was it the star that sought him out? With a sudden rush of air, as if a tightly shut door had been opened onto a whirling storm beyond, the distant speck of light sped forth filling his sight and revealing its true resplendent form filling his very soul with warmth, his heart overcome once more with love and compassion. Thalia, the elusive blue skinned goddess, was once more the focus of his attention as her words caressed his mind tenderly. "The spirits of this world, both past and future, burn in the fires of their own lies and deceit. As the last of their dreams and aspirations flicker out like drifting embers carried on the wind. Their salvation lies in the hands of a few diminutive dissenters. Trust in each other for your faith is your strength. Find the others, for they await unknowing. The little one knows the way, trust in her." Her melodic voice faded gradually away in his mind like the lingering notes of some beautiful musical composition. His head swam from the presence of her aura as he tried to form a coherent question but Thalia already knew what his somnolent mind tried to articulate and answered him her voice now distant in his thoughts. "Our pathways will converge in short time but firstly rouse yourself to wakefulness for THEY come with murder in mind, the little one needs your protection... hurry... THEY come!"

With this warning still jarring his thoughts he jolted awake sitting bolt upright in the shadows where he lay, the sky outside was now illuminated by the moon the sun having completed its role. Eve jumped slightly at his return. "Oh you gave me a fright!." She exclaimed clutching at her chest but smiling relieved at his return to cognizance glad of his company once again. "I thought you were maybe going to sleep all night. Your were dreaming as well, of her again I heard you whisper her name." She waited on his reply hoping to gain more information on his dream and his clandestine meeting with this mysterious Thalia.

"They're coming!" Came his surprising reply and leapt up joining Eve at the entrance to their hiding place where she'd been staring up at the night sky. Canova strained his eyes and ears trying to pierce the night searching for some sign of their approach but for now the area outside remained undisturbed. Thalia's words still echoed in his mind and then remembering what else had been imparted to him he looked quizzically down at Eve. "Time to go I reckon, which way do you think we should head?" He asked her.

"Mmmm... I... don't know." She replied somewhat confused at his sudden need to leave their shelter.

"I know I'm sorry." He took a moment to calm his mind and took a deep steadying breath and hunkered down so he could look her directly in the eyes. "I really need you to try and project and see where you go, it's really important." Canova asked trying to impart the importance of the situation to Eve. She nodded.

"Okay I'll try. Is this something to do with your dream."

"Yes, yes it is but it's very important that we leave here now but more importantly we need to know in which direction to go." He took her hand and smiled encouragingly. Eve replied with one brave nod of her head, her dark hair swung loosely about her face as she did so and with a sharp intake of breath, her small hand still enclosed in his protective grasp, she closed her eyes and willed her imagination to leave her physical body and allowed her spirit to meander slowly forth into the night beyond.

Mac and Nisa had restlessly awaited the days sun to complete its painfully slow cycle across the sky. Dozing fitfully, they had they taken it in turns to crawl into the cramped space keeping a vigil on the scene below. As the sun finally dipped and the light began to dim the figures below prepared themselves for that nights operation. A designated team of three Hand of God militia and two gaunt Nefarious had marched solemnly from the makeshift camp and headed off in an easterly direction. The soldiers weaponry unslung and ready for any action they might encounter, two members leading the small team the third covering the rear of the party. The two Nefarious striding menacingly in the centre of the ominous congregation. Mac had noted the four by four that had left earlier hadn't returned to base camp that was definitely to their advantage.

Nekros' underlying, seething displeasure had been more than evident at the unexpected escape of his quarry the previous night. His dead eyes had bored into Stats' very soul leaving him chilled and nauseous as Nekros had vented his anger at their failure, which was Stat's failure also and was summarily shipped to the outlands to head this mission. Stats didn't scare or intimidate easily but that lifeless ghoul had the ability to fill him with dread, his heart overflowing with despair whenever he was unfortunate to be graced with his presence. He had learnt to closely keep check on his thoughts when around Nekros and his Nefarious as it wouldn't have been the first time one of his troops had been terminated for anarchic free thinking. Their jurisdiction, their laws, the Hand of God all but brain washed to comply unquestioningly or pay the consequences but the human spirit is a hard thing to control and manipulate. Most complied for fear of the deadly repercussions instilled upon them by their mephitic masters. So even within the imposed military host few had free will of their own, a dangerous thing to possess in these dark times and fewer still could be trusted. Another ranking officer within the Hand of God, Aleshia, was one of the few that shared his views and opinions, intelligent enough to guard her mind and elude the Nefarious's invading thoughts, their prying and creeping an everyday abhorrence, just an average day working for the Hand of God. Yes Aleshia was one he could trust, a true friend.

Stats' team cautiously approached an intersection in the street, a small thicket of self-seeded birch trees had found residence amongst the ruins there and a myriad of perennials had discovered sanctuary within the cracks that crisscrossed the road. Stats held up his empty hand, the other retaining its hold on his rifle, indicating to the other team members that they should halt their progress, since the lack of communication from the team deployed earlier that day the remaining soldiers had become increasingly apprehensive. The two Nefarious ignoring his gesticulated command proceeded unhindered toward the centre of the intersection before finally coming to a standstill there their skull white faces deliberately scanning the surrounding area before deciding on which direction to take, then in perfect unison they turned to the right and continued on their trek oblivious to the military escort that accompanied them. The pathway chosen soon led them into an open site littered with rubble, large blocks of weathered stone were strewn randomly around them. Sprigs of greenery showed up here and there as it slowly reclaimed the sterile vista before them, all signs of human habitation eradicated except for a small bunker-like dwelling in the distance partially obscured from view by the botanical camouflage around its perimeter. Stats registered the source of the Nefarious's attention and signaled to his subordinates to position themselves up ahead covering the bunk house. The soldiers hugged the shadows as they made their steady advance towards their destination. The Nefarious on the other hand strode meaningfully onwards undaunted their pallid faces glowing eerily in the moons radiance oblivious at what might lie ahead in ambush.

Mac observed the party of three militia and the accompanying Nefarious set off on their nightly excursion. He remained motionless only withdrawing once they'd disappeared into the shadowy post apocalyptic city. "That's our cue babe!." He whispered rolling his eyes in the direction of Nisa as he spoke. Her tall lithe figure barely discernable in the almost near pitch of their hide out. "Right let's get this done quickly, don't know when those fuckers'll be back. We got four armed guards, one posted at each corner of the perimeter, two guarding the tent and I reckon two Nefarious are still inside. Shouldn't be too much of a problem for us 'cept maybe the Nefarious." He concluded grinning coldly.

"Okay let's do this." Nisa held out a clenched scarred fist. Mac responded in kind and their fists meet solidly with a dull audible knock as their bare knuckles made contact. Then quietly they hastened from their post deftly avoiding the obstacles that lay scattered underfoot and made their exit from the building. Mac took the lead his eyes adjusted to the near darkness, his mutation allowing him a natural night vision. It was a shame the moon was out, Mac thought to himself, total darkness would've given them a distinct advantage tonight but time was of the essence and they needed to replenish their supplies badly. It only took them a few minutes to reach the ground floor and the exit from which they planned their assault. Flanking each side of the crumbling doorway they steeled themselves for the attack their eyes sparkling with anticipation and excitement as the adrenalin coursed through their veins.

Eve's corporeal self had floated dreamily and directionless at first before an invisible current had caught her in its embrace and with gathering haste drew her firmly toward an as yet unknown destination, her " ghost " accelerating through the darkened city as she went. Before long her attention focused on an open area up ahead and her flight began to slow as she arrived at the camp set up by the Hand of God in the cobbled plaza. Her essence yielding to the unseen force that beckoned her onwards and she found herself entering the tent pitched there, straight past the unsuspecting guards stationed at its entrance. The interior was dimly lit by a single battery operated light that hung suspended from a

The Hand Of God

canvas loop on the ceiling. Two cadaverous Nefarious were seated at a small collapsible table, a map covered its surface. The two ghouls looked up in unison, their psychically endowed minds sensing the presence of the unseen intruder immediately.

Canova's attention had been drawn away from Eve's flickering eyes by a movement in the shadows beyond the shelter. The creeping, cloying scent of the Nefarious filled his head like the onset of some contagious sickness. He closed his own eyes his remaining senses compensating for the temporary loss of vision. They were almost on them the touch of their minds was cold and loathsome. He estimated they only had two or three minutes left before the approaching enemy had visual contact but the Nefarious knew instinctually where their quarry lay concealed and there was only one way in and out, they were trapped. An eddy of swirling energy suddenly caught up his conscious thoughts unexpectedly distracting him from the unwholesome stalkers outside and like being caught up in a whirlpool of escaping water as it drained down a plug hole his mind was swept up as it was sent rushing in the corporeal footsteps Eve had taken. Moments later he found himself standing beside Eve in this new destination in the company of the two Nefarious. His transient disorientation fleetingly passed as he refocused on the new scenario that had unfolded before him. Canova gulped in a mouthful of the stale air that filled the tent, like a man close to drowning finally breaking the surface and gasping in a life saving lung full, giving his being substance, literally. He blinked now fully aware of Eve's physical presence at his side her small hand still enclosed in his own, her breathing tense and anxious. He gently squeezed her hand reassuringly as much for himself as for Eve. This was no hallucination or dream this was real, he was really here, somehow Eve had managed to draw his physical self to this point also. His conclusion was instantly verified as the two other occupants of the tent stood as one their ebony gaze fixed firmly on the intruders that had suddenly materialised in their midst.

Stats had tailed the two thin suited figures as they unerringly headed for the concealed bunker up ahead. His two men had concealed themselves opposite, kneeling in position their machine guns firmly held the barrels trained on the partially visible entrance awaiting further orders. As the Nefarious closed the gap ahead they slowed to a halt their heads turned keenly towards Stats, this was his unspoken cue to take the lead and scout ahead checking for a possible ambush. Half crouching he shouldered his rifle and retrieved the pistol from his belt, releasing the safety before stealthily edging his way past the silent, stationary pair, his skin crawled as he passed them by. He approached his destination at a slight angle hiding his approach from any watchful eyes up ahead. Then positioning himself behind a large slab of wall that still remained and silently counting to three he leapt up from where he crouched concealed, the pistol held firmly in both hands leading the way. The moonlight illuminated the area immediately inside the enclosed space ahead, he covered the remaining distance there in an instant and straining his eyes he tried to discern any movement within, swinging his weapon from left to right. Relaxing, he holstered the weapon, carefully engaging the safety first and turned to the Nefarious, who now slightly disturbingly, were now standing immediately behind him."It's empty, if there was anyone hiding in there there's no sign of them now." He relayed rather pointlessly as their sick minds would've felt any remaining presence had there been one. Abruptly the sound of sporadic gun fire could be distinctly heard in the distance. The sharp staccato shots ringing through the silent empty streets. Stats military training immediately took control and signaling to his men opposite he sprang past the unmoving ghouls, unshouldering his rifle once again as he did so and sprinted back the way they'd come, the two other militia close behind their booted feet sounding noisily on the hard ground underfoot.

Mac and Nisa had on a syncronised nod slid from cover and split up each of them targeting two of the guards posted at the perimeter of the open plaza. Using what little cover was available Nisa, her lithe physique quickly closed the gap between herself and the first unsuspecting guard, his attention was fortunately focused in the opposite direction. She slowly slid the blade she carried from the sheath strapped to

The Hand Of God

her thigh, the blade effortlessly slid from its housing the razored edge making an almost imperceptible chinging noise as the tempered blade was freed but it was enough for the distracted guard to refocus his attention on his approaching assailant. Too late though, as he spun round the gleaming blade glistened briefly before Nisa embedded it firmly in his chest. The guards eyes widened and his mouth dropped open and not uttering a sound he dropped to his knees before silently keeling over. Her hand still clutching the handle Nisa tried to tug it free but it was firmly lodged, embedded in the soldiers ribs. She released it realising the futility of her action and without pause broke into a run closing the gap between herself and her next victim. The second guard barely had time to realise his fate and unholstered his gun when Nisa's outstretched hand made contact with his chest, her fingers elongated into thin stabbing stilettos piercing his torso. He froze and his eyes rolled lifelessly back into his skull before falling dead like a felled tree, pin-points of glistening red bubbling on his chest where her dagger like digits had entered his body. Before he had even struck the cobbled ground she changed direction and made for the tent.

Mac's tactics had been equally as simple, taking out the first guard stealthily, twisting his head from behind and cracking his neck. Unfortunately the sound of bone snapping in the stillness carried to the other guards ears drawing his attention. Mac by now, realising his cover had been blown, was already lumbering towards him at full pelt. Hastily the guard had trained his weapon on Mac but had only managed to squeeze off one shot before Mac was on him. Knocking the muzzle of the gun aside with his left arm he planted a devastating punch on the soldiers chest his sternum giving way with a stomach churning crunch. The soldier coughed once as a result of the blow, spittle and blood sprayed from his mouth before he too fell lifeless to the ground. At the sound of the single gunshot the two remaining guards outside the tent sprung into action swinging their guns off their backs but Mac had grabbed the felled soldiers gun, who still held it firmly in his death grasp and squeezing the dead soldiers finger on the trigger using his own hand (the Hand of God genetically encoded all weaponry designated to each soldier which rendered them useless to all except those they were issued to) and took careful aim and accurately fired off two shots sending the two militia spinning to the ground, dead. Nisa appeared from around the side of the tent and waited until Mac joined her. They paused briefly and throwing back the canvas flap stormed the tent.

Everything had happened so fast his head swam. Canova took in the unwholesome pair ahead and instinctually conjured a ball of devastating energy in his skull and gasping with the strain directed it at the approaching menace. An indiscernible force connected with the advancing pair throwing their heads back, small trails of blood lingered in the air fleetingly as it escaped both their ears and noses, their blood dark and putrid. The force of Canova's will lifted them bodily from the ground and flung them mercilessly across the interior of the tent before the two of them descended crumpled and unmoving, a single leg twitched momentarily before shuddering into stillness, their bodies twisted together in a macabre embrace. With his head still swimming the ensuing silence was shattered by the sound of gunshots from directly outside the tent. Still holding Eve's hand he hauled the terrified child away from the tents entrance at which they'd materialised. Her face was now as white as the Nefarious themselves, muted with terror she offered no resistance as Canova pulled her out of the way just in time. Two black clad figures burst into the tent, presumably responsible for the affray outside. Having no cover from which to take refuge behind Canova and Eve stood wide-eyed and silent. Canova didn't know if he could muster another mind bolt so soon after the last, his head hurt and he felt weakened and nauseous. One of the new arrivals broke the deathly silence putting his mind at ease. "Well you ain't Hand of God and you sure as hell ain't Nefarious!" Mac proclaimed shifting his scrutiny from Canova and Eve to the two crumpled remains of the Nefarious.

"Hey Mac looks like we weren't the only ones with a plan tonight." Came Nisa's reply from where she now stood peering down at the two pale corpses. She kicked at them hard where they lay checking for signs of life. "These two'll not be causing us any trouble." She concluded returning her attention

The Hand Of God

to Mac.

"Who the hell are you people?" Canova asked finally finding his tongue.

"No time for questions the rest of 'em'll be back any minute now so I suggest we get the hell outta here fast." Mac replied and glancing over at the lifeless Nefarious continued. "And as it seems we appear to be on the same side you two better move fast too." Canova nodded his allegiance and hoisting the still trembling Eve onto his back the four exited the tent hurriedly. Nisa pausing at one of the fallen soldiers long enough to remove his pack which contained a few supplies and to her delight a small knife. Throwing the pack over her shoulder she picked up her pace catching up with the others as they sped from the open plaza and vanished into the night.

Minutes later the sound of military boots reverberated through the empty streets announcing the imminent return of the remaining Hand of God militia. Their pace slowing as they entered the plaza and the scene that presented itself before them, halting at the body of the first lifeless soldier they encountered. Stats cursed under his breath at the sight of the murdered soldier before him. "You two check the others." He ordered the remaining team. The two of them split up covering the area looking for survivors. Stats wearily made his way towards the grey outline of the tent knowing in his heart what lay in wait. He stepped over the two prone figures that lay sprawled not far from the entrance to the tent shaking his head grimly and on reaching the entrance he held back the canvas flap and hung his head in despair at the scenario that presented itself to him." Shit!" He expleted loudly through clenched teeth. He'd be lucky if Nekros didn't gouge his brain from his still living skull for this fuck up! He dropped his arm allowing the canvas flap to obscure the view of the slaughtered Nefarious within. Stats then became aware of the returning two Nefarious as they entered the square behind him and composing himself made his way towards the remaining vehicle parked close by, ignoring their reappearance. He'd better call in and report this mission failure, before they did and await his providence at the Hand of God.

5

Stats' report back to Heaven had gone as well as he'd anticipated. The Hand of God didn't receive failure lightly and the response was an order for his return to the Hub, a military helicopter had been sent for his immediate retrieval from his post at first light. This certainly didn't bode well for Stats and as promised an hour after the dawn of the sun a small black personnel chopper swooped into the open site of the plaza off loading two militia in a cloud of dust and awaited his immediate embarkation for the prompt return flight. He pondered at the inevitable reception that awaited him back at the Hub at the hands of the Nefarious and more particularly at the hands of Nekros himself, surely he'd be very lucky to escape his loathsome presence on this occasion with all his mental faculties intact leaving his employment a drooling imbecile incapable of a coherent thought. A long suffering sigh escaped his exhausted body his breath misting the small port-hole like window in the helicopter where he now sat awaiting his extraction back to base. The sliding door now firmly locked in place the rotar blades whirred once again into activity and the helicopter slowly ascended into the air, its cumbersome bulk pivoting as it did so in mid flight aiming for the direction from which it had come. The sound of the blades above had a soporific effect on his already fatigued mind and body and he allowed his aching head to nod forward coming to rest against the small window. He absent mindedly focused on the derelict scene below, the devastation becoming blurred and undefined as their altitude increased and before long the vista below changed to that of the expansive blue of the ocean far below. The distant waves shimmering under the steady gaze of the sun, its heat penetrating the aircrafts interior, warming and relaxing his body. The crossing of the vast ocean would take several hours to traverse and so he allowed the steady hum of the electric motor to lull him into a fitful sleep his eyelids becoming heavy as his head gently rocked on the warm glass

The Hand Of God

of the window.

Stats had been enrolled into the Hand of God on his sixteenth birthday as his father had been and his father before him as was expected of all males of the non-elite class. According to his grandfather before even the Earth's magnetic shift his family had always taken an active role within the military, serving and settling in South Africa his ancestors white South Africans born and bred. His upbringing had been a strict an unforgiving one as deemed by his father, a true military man through and through. His father had taken on the role of both parents, not very adeptly, since the advent of his mother's death, allegedly struck down by some mysterious and incurable illness when he had been but a young child. The details of this event had been rather vague, his father uncommunicative about the incident when Stats had questioned him years later about his mothers untimely passing, this led Stats to become distrustful of his father and introverted in his company. His upbringing, harsh and loveless, his father growing increasingly distant from his son, his childhood regimented and lonely. His inevitable enrollment into the Hand of God at his coming of age at least freed him from the constraints his father had bound him by making new friends amongst the fresh faced recruits. Many of whom over his long years of service had perished either during the many confrontations during the relentless hunting and eradication of the Bioshifters, Shifters for short, or at the cruel hands of the Nefarious, quick to punish those who failed and disobeyed. Stats had quickly received promotion after promotion finally being elevated to the rank of Field Commander for his outstanding conduct during those bloody years, his father's unquestioning subservience to his masters having influenced Stats' swift ascension through the ranks no doubt. Almost twenty years now had passed since his servitude to the Hand of God had been initiated, he'd lost count long ago of the numerous missions he'd led, the soldiers killed in action under his command, the innocents he'd murdered their blood spilled in the name of God, for his was a heavy hand that ruled. The ruthless ethnic cleansing amongst the remaining survivors being considered an ever present threat by the now ruling Nefarious. The Shifters all but eradicated their numbers dwindling to the point of extinction and then there were the " Witch Hunts." Beings created by medical science deep within the Hub, a mixed race part human, part alien, their powers and abilities both terrifying and beautiful. The Nefarious deemed these " Witches " an uncontrollable hazard, a threat to the world they had seeded and cultivated, condemned their creations to death, summarily ordering their immediate execution. A few escaped their incarceration in Heaven their alien abilities sanctioning a mass breakout amongst their kind which was countered by a focused hunt and elimination of their species. The few that still remained interned were harshly dealt with the others murdered during an operation that took the better part of thirteen years to accomplish. The mystical capabilities these individuals were endowed with bordered on that of being occult making them a formidable breed hence the protracted and arduous " Witch Hunts " that had become a class one priority for so much of his career. The Nefarious had been visibly nervous during those years and even to this day, the so called threat apparently resolved, a small team had been enforced with the task of a continued surveillance of the outlands, ever vigilant, awaiting the re-emergence of their old enemies. The Nefarious army, as it had now swelled to over the many years since the planet's shift rapidly infected the land like a plague, their numbers increasing with no sign of abating. The Sensitives succumbed, others complied out of fear, their dominion threw a dark shadow over what was ironically called Heaven, their inevitable ascendancy over the empire only a matter of time, their tyrannical claw crushing any resisting remnants of humankind.

Field Commander Kars Station, Stats as his fellow squaddies had come to tag him, was a well built muscular five foot seven, his military upbringing had kept him lean and fit, both physically and mentally. His hair light brown, kept short and neat befitting his position within the Hand of God. A light stubble dusted his face which was square jawed and weather beaten, his complexion tanned, his forehead lined through years of frowning, his eyebrows lowered in a permanent scowl shading his squinting pale blue eyes. His mouth was thin and straight, unused to laughter, his job didn't call much for the show of emotions and would've only been seen as a weakness by others. A prominent scar resided on the left hand side of his neck running from his jaw line to a point beneath the collar of his tunic, a souvenir from one of the many cleansings he'd led, getting too close to a Shifter on that occasion. A small pocket of turbulence caused the helicopter to suddenly dip and shudder shaking Stats into wakefulness. He reluctantly opened his eyes and stared absent mindedly out of the port-hole tracking their progress. In the distance he could behold the rugged cliffs of Heaven rising from the ocean. Antarctica as it had once been called its coastline now brushing that of the equator, its once frozen lands now freed from its icy embrace its surface now populated by the descendants of the then rich, famous, political and military top brass. The land fed by numerous underground irrigation systems creating a veritable paradise for the surviving populace, a true garden of Eden and at the centre of which lay housed the Hub, the point at which all of the orbiting solar towers were anchored and the harnessed energy converted and distributed. The Hub itself a large disc of operations where the Hand of God conducted their affairs. Housing the soldiers and Nefarious alike. The latter generally kept to the lower levels keeping out of sight they're growing numbers a mystery to most, conducting their experiments out of sight of the residing elite in Heaven lest they become suspicious of the events unfolding within.

The coastline increased in definition as his transport neared his destination, great cliffs towered into focus and those massive life giving umbilicals could now be seen, distant and hazy reaching far into the sky and disappearing beyond the range of his eyes. Specks of life could be seen swooping and diving around the coast line, gulls and other species of sea birds nesting within the rugged cliffs. Only a few species of animal life had been saved for posterities sake the majority left to take their chances with the unfortunate human populace. Those with status or vast bank accounts hid themselves in bunkers far beneath the Earth's crust, many of which were torn apart during the magnetic shift, there interiors filling with molten lava. Huge submersibles were launched seeking sanctuary deep within the oceans depths, many of these had also succumbed to the might of the many natural disasters that swept the Earth smashing the life pods breaking them open like eggs and spilling out the hapless passengers. All in all few had survived and this new Heaven and the other outlying lands were sparsely populated.

The land below, that Stats now passed over, was mostly dominated by young trees and shrubs reintroduced by scientists, carefully selected from the great seed banks stored deep within the Hub, small populations of primates had been saved and established within Heaven along with a variety of tropical birds and numerous species of insect life in an attempt to create a balanced ecosystem. Genetically enhanced crops ensured the continued survival of the depleted population, meat had become an unsustainable food source at least for those that dwelt in Heaven, for Stats himself and others posted for a time on the outlands had tasted occasionally of meat stumbling across some unwary bird or antelope. Even the animals on these land masses still capable of sustaining life had become a rare sight. Scientists had originally been flown out to these lands to evaluate the impact of the shift upon the natural world but the Nefarious soon condemned these scientific excursions as dangerous and unnecessary, the military escorts could be utilised in a more beneficial way. So before long these expeditions were outlawed, the scientific research incomplete.

The long flight over the ocean concluded the wealth of vegetation below reclaiming the once barren land becoming denser and lusher, a sea of green not blue this time filled the spectacle through the window, the trees barely past their infancy given the short period of time in which they'd been given to redeem this territory. Blocks of geometric housing were interspersed within the encroaching juvenile jungles constructed shortly after the Earth had once again settled. These dwellings consisted of only a few stories in height clothed in massive sheets of polarised glass, all facilities self contained. A network of access roads, strips of land cleared of vegetation the bare earth compacted allowing military transport connectivity to these residential areas. Only the Hand of God and the Nefarious were authorised the use of motorised vehicles, the small amounts of bio-fuel manufactured within the Hub barely being enough to sustain the small fleet of vehicles in operation, all boats and helicopters had been adapted to run on the substantial amounts of electricity generated by the solar towers. The vista of green below interspersed with blocks of housed residents stretched as far as his eyes could see through the small port hole, the inhabitants confined within these buildings blissfully unaware of the infernal goings on within the Hub and of the inhuman ethnic cleansing carried out by the Hand of God amongst the persecuted survivors still clinging to survival. The sprawling vegetation eventually came to an abrupt end giving way to large fields of crops. Genetically modified cereals, fruit and vegetables grew in great abundance surrounding the Hub, bees saved from extinction had been released allowing them to carry on the life giving pollination required and therefore sustaining the population. The Hub itself sat half-buried in the land like some huge donut encased in reflective heat resistant shielding keeping the interior and its occupants cool. Most of its vast bulk lay buried beneath the surface, the solar conduits, that also acted as anchors, pierced the centre of the Hub and penetrated deep into the Earth's crust. The Hub was where all military operations were conducted and accommodated those who served under the Hand of God. The lower levels housed medical facilities, science labs and holding cells for those unfortunate civilians awaiting further tests and experiments or if they were lucky execution. The lowest levels were the realms of the Nefarious where the source of their power was seated and only accessed by them, a greater power than Nekros himself the nucleus of all that existed above, something even more monstrous than his rancid black heart no doubt Stats had often speculated.

The regimented geometry of the crops sustained below soon gave way and a blacktop of military order filled the scenario. Military vehicles were lined up black and gleaming. Soldiers marched to and fro carrying out their orders as issued by their masters. The altitude of the helicopter had slowly decreased during its flight inland and Stats could make out the target at which the pilot was now aiming for, a large white " H " was now visible against the contrasting black of the tarmac below. He watched from his vantage point as a few soldiers hastily vacated the area below as the helicopter began its final descent, the downdraft created by the whirling blades sending dust spiraling into the air. Waiting on the periphery of the helipad stood an official looking welcoming committee. A slight jolt indicated touchdown and in response the whine of the motor slowly wound down the whirling blades quickly coming to a standstill. The commanding officer at the head of his welcoming party, at the cessation of the rotar blades, immediately made their way forward to greet Stats on his disembarkation. Stats stood up, stooping slightly, and grabbing the interior handle slid back the door. Even as the season of autumn was upon them the heated air outside was palpable being so close to the equator, beads of sweat formed on his brow as the warm dusty air filled the machines cooler interior. He stepped from the aircraft just as the officer assigned to meet him on his return approached and saluted him. "Good to see you back Field Commander." Continuing the formalities she returned her arm to her side and stood to attention.

"At ease Aleshia, there's no need for any of that formal bullshit with me." Giving one of his rare smiles happy to encounter a familiar face and a good friend on his arrival. "You're looking well," he continued. "Take it that old butcher wants to see me immediately does he?" He asked her getting straight to the point his smile slipping at the thought of his loathsome presence to come.

"Yeah 'fraid so." Came the predicted reply the pleasure at seeing her old friend again now marred by the mention of HIM. "Sent me to meet you personally and escort you to his quarters on your immediate arrival. Take it you know what this is about?" She asked frowning. By now the two had left the vicinity of the helipad, a grey overalled engineer pulled a thick black cable from a reeled housing in their wake and lifted a concealed hatch on the exterior of the helicopter revealing a socket into which he plugged the end of the cable. His job done he waved back to his associate indicating that he switch on the power and so charging the helicopters motor ready for its next flight. Stats and Aleshia made their way across the military base the half dozen militia who had escorted Aleshia tailing them as they did so.

"Reckon HE called me in so he could express his displeasure personally at his prize slipping the net yet again! Know what I mean?" Looking over at his companion with one eye before continuing. "But a Porter how the fuck are you meant to capture one of them? You've no idea when or where they're gonna pop up. This one's got some help too, took out some good men and a couple of Nefarious, not that I'll miss them," his tone was hushed as he concluded.

"A Porter? Really? Shit no wonder he was pissed!" Came her incredulous reply. "Imagine what the Nefarious would do if they gotta hold of one and isolated that gene?" The look on her face said it all, it didn't bare thinking about. Nefarious capable of teleportation, willing themselves to any location by just merely thinking about it. Aleshia shook her head despairingly having had the same nightmarish thought as he, her plaited pony tail swinging as she did so a few loose strands of hair floated lazily in the air. Her dark eyes narrowed further shielding her sight from the brightness of the sun, her almost black eyes squinting at Stats examining him for a moment before breaking the silence between them. "It's impossible to tell what goes on in Nekros's head," she purposefully lowered her voice afraid their entourage might hear too much. "Nothing good that's for sure. That murderous old bastard really makes my skin crawl and these Nefarious are increasing in number and becoming more and more like him every day. I really fuckin' despair sometimes." Shaking her head the initial joy at Stats' return gone from her expression. Stats gave her a sideways look, she was tall and good looking, he'd always thought that of her. Her years of enforced servitude had left her cold and hardened though but over the years they'd come to know each other well and he'd glimpsed the gentle beautiful soul of the person that dwelt beneath her military exterior. Finally they crossed the military encampment and approached a wide set of steps that led into the interior of the Hub, they mounted them two at a time Aleshia unfaltering at his side. Stats had been very aware of the underlying buzz of activity which seemed to intensify as they ascended the stairs, their escort finally peeling off their job done returning to their other duties. He frowned and raised a questioning eyebrow in response to the bustle around him cocking his head in Aleshia's direction. She sensed his attention and her dark eyes sparkled as they met his own pale blue stare. "Yeah I know," she responded. "It's been all hands on deck since last night, something on one of the outlands showed up, some glitch or hiccup or something picked up by the science team on one of their pieces of equipment." Stats stared at her wide eyed.

"You know what that means don't you? And it'd explain all this activity."

"Yeah reckon they must've found a Witch." Her reply short and to the point. "And I'd thought they'd wiped them all out years ago."

"Shit they must've known at least one of them had slipped the net otherwise they wouldn't've kept a surveillance team monitoring the outlands for all these years." His eyes gleaming his head buzzing with this new found knowledge. Stats turned to Aleshia as they made their way further into the cool interior of the Hub. "Well, well it's not over yet after all, let the Witch Hunt commence." Stats and Aleshia continued in silence each pondering the implications of the recent events. Stats barely aware of the hustle going on around them within the stark environment of the Hub. Materials had been transported to Antarctica and stock-piled since before the Earth shift in anticipation of the imminent disaster that befell the Earth all those years ago. The slow arc of the Hub was interspersed with numerous doorways leading to store rooms, laboratories and canteen facilities small windows set high in the wall allowed in some natural light. The black uniformed militia mingled with the white robed figures of the medical and science teams as they hurried about their business clutching sheaths of documents and pushing trolleys loaded with arrays of equipment. The two friends proceeded through the throngs of inhabitants until they reached a large open plan operations room, a scaled three-dimensional map of the Earth, as it was today, dominated the centre of the room, the locations of Hand of God teams marked with clusters of red lights revealing their positions on the outlands. Hub staff sat around the periphery of the holographic image making adjustments via the comput-

The Hand Of God

ers arranged before them. The two marched across the black marbled floor, the preoccupied staff all but ignoring their presence too concerned with their own tasks at hand. Stats and Aleshia came to a standstill in front of a set of elevator doors, the Hand of God insignia emblazoned on the ominous black entrance to the lower levels. The logo consisted of a golden hand palm out, a map of Antarctica, or Heaven as it had been renamed, sat in the centre of the palm several lines bisecting its interior a small disc marked the Hub itself. Aleshia positioned herself before a glass disc set to the side of the doors and an invisible beam scanned her retina confirming her identity. On completing the scan the elevator doors silently opened revealing its dimly lit interior, they both stepped inside and the doors silently closed shutting out the noise and activity of the operations room and with a barely audible sigh the elevator began its descent the passage of movement almost imperceptible.

The pre-ordained meeting with Nekros had gone better than Stats had anticipated. Nekros's seething anger at the escape of his object of desire for yet a second time was overshadowed by the re-emergence of his old enemy and did Stats also detect a note of fear visible on that cruel countenance of his? His corrupted mind distracted, fortunately for Stats, the only sound in the room the hissing of his fetid breath noisily escaping through clenched diseased teeth as he floated aimlessly around his quarters. The office was large and somewhat dimly lit by an arrangement of wall fittings evenly spaced around the room. A large desk was situated towards the rear of the office a small jumbled collection of items lay scattered on its surface, Stats could make out what appeared to be a child's stuffed toy amongst the items, barely discernable in the murk. Two large gold framed pictures adorned each opposing wall to left and right, each depicting detailed maps of Heaven and the outlands. The black walls and floor added to the oppressive gloomy atmosphere, Stats could feel it encroaching upon himself as he stood immobile and reticent awaiting the direct confrontation with HIM.

Stats knew very little about the ghoulish parasite that drifted to and fro before him resembling some automated attraction from some vintage horror film. He'd always presumed that Nekros had began his life a human Sensitive endowed with psychic abilities and as in all walks of society his ruthlessness and willingness to sacrifice others in his bid for power soon took him to the top of his bloodied ladder. Stats had heard the rumours that whilst he was still a servant amongst the ranks of the Nefarious he had been assigned, or volunteered, to the subterranean levels within the Hub, out of sight of the human population and jurisdiction. Survivors from the outlands were incarcerated there, the genetic experimentation conducted before the magnetic shift continued on in secret, the screams of the innocent victims absorbed by the very earth itself, the evidence of their corrupted remains reduced to ash in the furnaces of the lower levels. If the veneer of this artificial island paradise above was Heaven then those sunless unholy depths must surely be hell. Here Nekros resided for years discovering his true gift his poisoned soul luxuriating in the pain and hopelessness of others. Many Sensitive humans were captured and condemned to the lower levels to return brain washed, all vestiges of humanity erased from their minds and hearts another unwilling recruit for the Nefarious, now loyal and subservient, the unknown horrors they were subjected to at the cruel hands of Nekros reflected on their once wholly human features now returned from the fires of hell, phoenix-like their hearts now blackened and iniquitous, their souls charred by Nekros's depraved, polluted touch. The swelling of the Nefarious army had culminated with HIS return to the surface, arising like a demon summoned from his tomb his venomous mind infected beyond redemption. The Hand of God now fell under his jurisdiction, all seditious whisperings were quickly silenced, his harsh ruling hand and pestilent mind removing any who opposed his authority and in short time the Hand of God relented at witness to his mastery. The omnipresent psychological menace of Nekros and his host an ever increasing menace. Nobody trusted anyone through fear of being ousted for their beliefs, many had families their compliance gaining them protection, their loyalty earning them promotion. Stats' days of servitude were numbered he could sense it, like a freight train careering towards him unable to

The Hand Of God

move from its path patiently awaiting the inevitable outcome. Stats believed that one day soon all lives under the Hand of God would be forfeit as the Nefarious numbers steadily amassed, he doubted the existence of any remaining Sensitives outside Nekros's web. The essence of their very natures allowing their easy tracking and eventual capture and conversion at the hands of Nekros. One day their kind would dominate and rule this planet, all signs of humanity deleted, Stats had no doubt of that. Nekros now seemed to be slowing his pace, his agitated meanderings finally ceasing as he presented himself before Stats, the fact that he remained suspended inches above the floor and therefore loomed above Stats added to the already intimidating atmosphere.

"Well Field Commander Kars Station how glad I am at your safe return." The hissing sarcasm evident as it lingered between them. "Empty handed alas! Your incompetence hasn't gone unnoticed," his ebony gaze glanced meaningfully downwards. "Still Field Commander our elusive Porter, as you are no doubt aware by now of our little fugitives talents, is no longer of your concern. You have been allocated a new assignment and this time failure will not be acceptable." He paused, Stats could feel his loathsome intelligence seeping into his own mind.

"Yes of course I fully understand." Came his subservient reply.

"Good, good I'm glad we understand each other Field Commander. You will find your orders back at your quarters, your team has already been determined and deployed, you will depart tomorrow at your earliest convenience." Another pause, Stats could feel HIM retracting those psychic worms from his mind and before returning to his aimless wanderings concluded the meeting. "Be mindful Field Commander." The threat in his tone was unmistakable.

On his dismissal Stats turned about and as casually as he could muster stepped before the elevator doors which much to his relief were already beginning to open Aleshia awaiting his return in silence. Now safely within the confines of the elevator the doors mercifully shutting out the horror that was Nekros as he continued to haunt that sunless vault of his.

Stats and Aleshia had remained silent as they made their

way back to their quarters. A section of the Hub converted into basic single occupancy domiciles. On reaching their destination they each in turn stood before a retinal scan unit and having their entry authorised entered the accommodation section. A long corridor stretched out before them on the left hand side and on the right ground floor and first floor accommodation, the first floor accessed by a series of metal stairs that led to a walkway. Only when the access doors had fully sealed behind them did they finally break their silence. "Well how'd it go? As if I need to ask. "Aleshia picked up as they continued further into the complex.

"Coulda been worse, a lot worse. That's what worries me, he knows something that's for sure." Stats returned thoughtfully.

"An informant?" She countered.

"No I don't think so he's just gettin' too damn powerful I could feel him searching about in there." Tapping his temple with his forefinger as he spoke.

"Shit. Well I suppose it was only a matter of time before he suspected something and we ain't got any family, gives him no leverage over us, nothing to force our loyalty."

"You got that right, got me reassigned to some new bullshit charge and I reckon my retirement will be imposed upon my return, know what I mean?" His look serious as he matched her gaze. Aleshia studied his blue eyes for a few seconds before averting her stare at the implications of this last statement. She knew herself her days were numbered also, the force behind the Nefarious all consuming and unrelenting would eventually obliterate what remained of humanity, even the faithfully acquiescent would meet the same fate as their usefulness became obsolete. She nodded solemnly before returning to look once again at Stats as he came to a halt at her side the stairs to his upper floor billet located.

"Yeah I know what you mean I've sensed it too but what the fuck can we do? You don't know who to trust anymore." As if to reinforce her statement her eyes shifted from left to right reassuring herself there were no eavesdroppers loitering.

"Well one thing's for sure if I've to be placed into early

retirement, that's if I even make it back from this new mission, I'm goin' down fighting that's for fuckin' sure." His teeth clenched defiantly.

"Maybe your right but just the two of us? What kinda chance do you think we've got?"

"Less than none but at least it'll wipe the smile of that cretinous bastards face." Stats looked thoughtful for a moment before continuing. "Besides help can come in many shapes and forms." Winking surreptitiously he stepped onto the short metal staircase. "I really got to get some decent sleep now Aleshia I gotta be sharp tomorrow." The stairs mounted he strode towards his front door only a short distance along the elevated platform Aleshia keeping pace with him below, her own domicile located directly beneath Stats' own. She called up to him as he stopped to allow the retinal scan and gain access to his home.

"Give you an alarm call then? We can grab some breakfast together?" Stats raised his hand so she could see it, confirmation of their date tomorrow and wearily he entered the dark confines of his small home. He immediately sought out his bed and without undressing collapsed thankfully into a dreamless sleep.

6

Aleshia had woken early, the sun not yet breaking the horizon, her sleep had been fitful, disturbed by unremembered dreams and unnamed horrors. Lathered in a thin cold sweat she sat up and threw back her disheveled and dampened sheet and swung her legs over the side of her bed. "Light on," she commanded and a small dim light flickered into existence above her cot and she sat, her head supported by her hands as she gathered her thoughts. Her room, like all the others in the military quarters, was compact but adequate. Her sleeping area was combined with a small living space which housed a table underneath which were neatly tucked four plastic chairs. Atop the table sat a manila folder containing her latest mission orders, still unread, other than that the room was bereft of furnishings, a single framed photograph adorned one wall a colour image of her parents from happier times. Beyond this space a small kitchen facility containing a chromed sink, a refrigerator unit and tea and coffee making facilities, a sliding door led from there into a shower room, the amenities were basic but sufficed. The opposing wall to the entrance to her humble abode was sheathed with large slabs of polarised glass that could be manually lightened or darkened to allow for privacy.

Lieutenant Aleshia Kulak, her surname hinting at her distant Russian ancestry, had served the Hand of God since her eighteenth birthday, as did all female recruits. Her father had been an outwardly loyal servant to the cause but harboured a deep loathing of the Nefarious and their methods but remained reticent for fear of his families persecution and it was a proud father who had watched his little girl enrolled into the Hand of God that day tinged with sadness at what he knew lay in store for Aleshia. Two years after her enrollment her father had been killed in action during a Shifter cleansing. His body had been returned to Heaven, the funeral small and functional in the cemetery on Heaven, the Nefarious allowing such emotional whims to facilitate the continued compliance of their flock. Aleshia had been heart-broken, her father had been her world, her mother, a quiet, diminutive women who having suffered ill health throughout most of her life fretted deeply at the loss of her husband and lost her will to live two weeks following. The combined loss of both her parents in such a short space of time affected her deeply, scared and alone she threw herself into her work escaping the deep-rooted emotional pain she now carried within her. She quickly matured into an emotionless killer. Her sharp features, black hair and eyes combined with her height intimidated others she worked alongside, her coldness and authoritative air resulted in others obeisance and she was quickly promoted for her implacable service to the Hand of God.

During a tour of the outlands, capturing or eliminating any evolved humans, the remainder being rounded up and interned within the military camps that had been set up, she had met Kars Station. Stats as she came to know him by was ten years her senior and reminded her immediately of her father. A hard military man on the surface but with a good heart and a conscience buried beneath. They were both posted on several tours together which took them from the confines and conformities of the Hub for well over a year. The blood thirsty genocide that had dominated the previous years of their servitude forgotten for a while, the devastated population of evolved beings surrendered themselves or escaped far inland out of the grasp of the Hand of God, releasing Aleshia and Stats from the relentless killings required of them and they spent much of their time patrolling the camps together. During these more peaceful times they got to know many of the survivors at a more personal level, their role slowly changing from that of gaolers to that of aid workers, helping the sick and injured providing medical care and food for the inhabitants. Their short time spent within the camps together opened both their eyes and hearts once more to the horrors that had gone on for years previously, unchecked and unquestioned. Aleshia realising how her father would've reacted at the sight of these prison camps and at her own descent into denial and her mindless, bloody servitude brought all her past unresolved emotions to the surface finally releasing the feelings she'd kept chained up deep inside since the passing of her parents. Stats had been a pillar of strength during this transitory period during her life and now she felt the inner antipathy towards her superiors, the loathing hatred her father once fostered now became her own. Stats had recognised this in her and had confided in her of his own deep-rooted dread and abhorrence at what was to befall the last of the human race. Together they formed a strong bond hoping that one day others would sway to their rebellious way of thinking but others were reluctant, scared at what would befall themselves and their families should they switch allegiance. So Aleshia and Stats had hushed their minds and calmed their hearts, now filled with dissent and continued to serve, patiently awaiting the right opportunity in which to lead the revolt against their Nefarious oppressors.

Aleshia pulled her head upright and rubbed her tired eyes, she didn't feel good, that last execution she had carried out, as she had no doubt now that was exactly what she had administered, troubled her conscience deeply, her father would've been ashamed of her. This had had a profound effect on her, the couple she'd been silently ordered to kill by Nekros would've been around her own parents age, had they still been alive, innocent of any crime the image of their ruined bodies as they lay slumped on that bloody floor had haunted her ever since and was probably the cause of her nightmares, her subconscious reluctant to admit liability for those two guiltless souls. Aleshia finally stood up and walked over the cold bare floor pulling out one of the plastic chairs tucked under the table and braving the cold hard plastic sat down, she shuddered briefly at its touch. She stared down at the manila folder that lay before her and idly spun it around with her finger, pondering to herself before finally opening the folder and perusing its contents. She sped read through the majority of its contents only sifting out and storing the more important details she encountered. Well she'd been assigned the task of tracking and capturing the Porter, great! That'd be like trying to catch a ghost, an impossible task at best. The report suggested that the Porter was a minor, Aleshia's mind cast back to the night she had executed

The Hand Of God

the old couple and her heart felt heavy in her chest. Others were believed to be aiding the fugitive, other evolved beings. According to the autopsy reports on the deceased militia and Nefarious she was in no doubt that those that aided her were very highly evolved and dangerous. Trauma wound to the chest, the weapon of choice left embedded in the man's ribcage and had to be cut free during the autopsy, another having being stabbed by several fine sharp implements, a broken neck and yet another sustained a massive blow to his sternum crushing his heart and lungs. Could only be Bioshifters, Aleshia thought to herself, Shifters for short they were often endowed with super-human strength. She scanned further on through the report, two other militia shot dead, head shots both accurate and deadly, well nothing paranormal about that she thought. Finally she came to the report on the two dead Nefarious and slowed her hurried examination of the document opened before her. Both had been subjected to a massive cerebral trauma which had resulted in internal haemorrhaging and substantial damage to the brain tissue, no external injuries had been evident, had to be a Psych she concluded to herself and a powerful one at that. Aleshia browsed through the remaining report and at finding no further useful information there slowly closed the folder her mind distracted by what she'd read. She slowly stood up pushing back her chair as she did so and made her way into the kitchen commanding the light to turn on as she did so. The automated system responding to her order and filled the room with a dazzling radiance, causing her to blink several times as her eyes grew accustomed to the glare. She headed for the shower room and the door silently slid aside at her approach, a good hot shower should make her feel better and hopefully shake this feeling of dread that hung over her, she stepped into the small room the door soundlessly closing behind her.

After the hot invigorating shower Aleshia towelled herself dry and returning to her living area removed a fresh clean uniform from her built in wardrobe and quickly dressed placing her dirty clothes on her bed after first removing a small item from the breast pocket and placing it on her person carefully, the unseen domestics took care of all the military's laundry requirements, normally the wives and children too young yet for recruitment into the Hand of God. She began to brush her now unplaited hair, long, sleek and glistening with moisture when she heard a knock at the door. She interrupted the task at hand and made her way to the front door and after checking the identity of her early visitor opened it allowing them access. "Thought I was giving you an alarm call!" She commented as Stats entered her home at her request. He too donned a fresh uniform, his rugged countenance now removed of stubble his hair neatly clipped. Aleshia's smile broke the hard expression she normally donned and dimples appeared on her cheeks, her perfect white teeth flashing. Her loose hair swung past her shoulders alluringly and her black eyes sparkled behind thick dark lashes. "Eh you okay?" She asked interrupting his thoughts.

"Eh yeah, you?" Stats replied caught somewhat off guard by her appearance. "Slept like the dead but woke early you too I take it?"

"No, bad dreams I really think this jobs starting to get to me big time know what I mean?"

"Yeah I know the feeling." He agreed nodding in the direction of the manila folder laid out on the table. "You checked that out yet?"

"Uhuh, get a seat and I'll make us some coffee." She indicated the seat she'd vacated earlier and returned to the kitchen. "What about you what they assigned you to?" She called back as she prepared the drinks the sound of boiling water already reaching his ears.

"Just as I suspected got me headin' the Witch Hunt, the details were a bit vague at best but the science heads have narrowed the location down to about a twenty square mile radius at a point ten miles inland on one of the outlands, to be terminated on sight. Simple!" By now the aroma of fresh ground coffee had reached his nostrils invigorating his senses just as Aleshia reappeared clutching two steaming cups and placed one before Stats before pulling out a second chair on the opposite side of the table and seating herself, cradling her own cup between her hands enjoying the heat.

"Well it appears I've to take over from where you left off tracking down the Porter, bloody ghost hunt more like." She

The Hand Of God

quickly filled in Stats on her assignment and took a sip of the hot coffee. "As far as I can deduce," nodding at the folder that sat between them as she spoke. "There's at least one Shifter and a Psych tagging along too."

"A Psych? Don't hear too much about their kind these days thought they'd been mopped up a long time ago, surprised the Nefarious haven't tagged that one by now."

"Yeah me too, this one's talented too, took out the two Nefarious posted with you before they even knew what hit 'em"

"I did wonder about that." Stats pondered before continuing. "Didn't get much of a chance to check 'em out before gettin' air lifted outta there. Very impressive though I wonder what else our little band of fugitives are capable of?"

"Well whoever they are they really pissed off Nekros that's for sure, I'm kinda warming to them already," a smile crept back onto Aleshia's face.

"So what's your orders then a seek and destroy mission?"

"Being issued with tranquiliser guns he wants the Porter alive the others too if possible but if they make trouble deads just as good!" She shrugged taking another sip of her drink. Stats sat silent for several minutes periodically sipping at his cooling coffee. "You okay?" Asked Aleshia noticing his preoccupation with something.

"They assigned that cretin Szebrowski as my second in command and you know how I feel about him?" Aleshia nodded slowly in response. Szebrowski was a real brown noser the kinda guy that would oust his family to the Nefarious for the opportunity of a promotion and as if reading Aleshia's mind Stats continued. "A right brown nosed prick. Makes me wonder whether or not I'm gonna be returning from this little jaunt or at the very least nicely packaged in a body bag!"

"You really think he's been sent to watch your back? Make sure the job gets done and... "

."..And put a bullet in my head when no one's looking?" He finished."Yeah I do he's already posted at the designated location just awaiting my arrival." They both lapsed into silence for a while drinking their coffee both lost in their own thoughts before Aleshia spoke again.

"What you gonna do Stats?" Was all she could think of to say her concern apparent.

"Well I'm gonna make sure I pop that fucker first! And the Nefarious seem to be shit scared of these Witches as far as I can make out and I'm curious as to why that is and has anyone ever had any direct contact with them any communication of any kind? Could prove to be a powerful ally, let's face it any enemy of HIM and the Nefarious can't be all that bad." Stats waited to see Aleshia's reaction.

"Yeah you could be right but you be careful you're the only friend I got in here an' I'd hate to lose you." She placed a warmed hand over his as she spoke.

"You just watch your own back don't worry 'bout me the mere fact you're a known associate of mine puts you in a dangerous position." His concern was apparent.

"I know I'm aware of that but fuck it sooner or later I'm gonna die either in the line of duty or at the hands of the Nefarious got it coming to me sometime soon I reckon besides I can take care of myself."

"I know you can just follow your heart Aleshia and do what feels right for you. I know our days are numbered here, thank God!" He smiled ironically. "And when that time comes I'm goin' out with a fuckin' bang!" Stats sat back in his seat and downed what remained of his now lukewarm coffee and placed the empty cup on the table a large grin spread over his usually stern face.

"Well then." Aleshia followed suit and drained the last of her cup. "Shall we grab some breakfast then before we undertake another glorious day working for the Hand of God?" She replied her voice filled with sarcasm at the prospect of the day's work that lay ahead for them both. He nodded in acquiescence to her suggestion still grinning as he did so. They had nothing to lose now except each other.

7

Breakfast had been a solemn affair. Aleshia and Stats had sat opposite each other at one of the many stainless steel tables that lined the canteen preoccupied by their earlier conversation both deep in thought only distracted periodically by the comings and goings of the staff members within the Hub as they began or ended their shifts. Black uniforms mingled with the white coats of the science factions as they lined up at the counter collecting their trays of food containing a colourful mix of fruits and cereals which grew in abundance in Heaven, a far cry from the foil sealed packets issued them during their tours on the outlands. They were both aware of the furtive glances directed at them by some of the diners making them slightly uncomfortable and anxious to get away from the scrutinising eyes of their colleagues. Stats meeting some of the stares coldly until they shifted their gaze self consciously. Aleshia, head down, picked at the gaudy array of cubed fruit in the bowl set before her occasionally daring to sample a piece now and again her appetite stilled at the thought of what was to become of herself and her only friend. Finally she dropped her spoon into the bowl her meal unfinished and pushed it to one side looking up at Stats as she did so, he was scooping up the last of the milk sodden cereal, or the soya equivalent that substituted the real thing, in his bowl and shoveled it into his mouth obviously not enjoying the food but forcing it down anyway not knowing when his next decent meal would be. He had to maintain his alertness and strength on this what could prove to be his last and most important mission, his expression stoical as he finally chewed the last mouthful and looked over at Aleshia and indicated with a nod of his head towards the exit that they should leave at seeing her finished eating and eager to go. They stood in unison and casually made for the exit, heads turning as they did so curious eyes following their passage. They were both very aware of the looks, ignoring them completely but could feel the eyes boring into their backs as they finally traversed the length of the canteen and thankfully removed themselves from view as they rounded the corner of the exit. Aleshia threw Stats a knowing look as they made their way down the corridor, small rectangular windows set high in the walls allowed the bright sunlight outside to flood in, the warmth from the sun's rays felt good as they passed each opening the chill they'd felt from the perusal of their fellow associates quickly dispelled as they passed through the Hub's interior heading for the main entrance and the military transportation that no doubt awaited their arrival outside. As they passed the main operations room Stats glanced in noticing a member of the Nefarious scrutinising the holographic map projected into being by a bank of high tech scientific equipment, the intricacies of which beyond his understanding. As he did so the lone Nefarious turned his unwholesome countenance in his direction and his fathomless gaze met his own unerringly filling Stats with an unpleasant feeling of dread and foreboding, a cold prickly sweat broke out down his spine as he held the unfaltering stare only finally averting his eyes once he had cleared the door less entrance into the open expanse of the command centre. Thankfully he let out a sigh of relief as the ghoulish figure disappeared from view, remarking to Aleshia as he did so. "Things must be really moving it's not often you see them out on this level during daylight, could feel that fucker boring right into my "skull." He glanced back over his shoulder reassuring himself that the lone Nefarious hadn't trailed them on Nekros's orders.

"Yeah I can't wait to get outta here it feels like this whole place is gonna blow, know what I mean?" Aleshia seemed agitated and about ready to bolt for the exit the overbearing atmosphere pushing her onwards as she hastened past a likewise unsettled cluster of white gowned medical staff chattering hurriedly between themselves hardly even acknowledging the two friends as they brushed past them hastening in the opposite direction.

"Yeah it's kinda like sitting atop an active volcano just waitin' on it blowing its top." Stats stared down at the floor of the corridor his eyes narrowed contemplating before continuing. "There's something going on down there you can

The Hand Of God

feel it seeping through from the lower levels." He had become aware of an unpleasant sensation curling around his ankles which emanated from under the floor itself, a chill that wound its way around his calves, an encroaching and loathsome sensation that put him ill at ease. The look on Aleshia's face confirmed his own theory that the Nefarious horde below were gathering energy, the fetid gestalt activity underfoot leaching its way soundlessly upwards its invisible presence spreading like some deadly contagion. Aleshia felt the relief in her heart as the outlet to the surrounding military compound loomed ahead the large open doorway filling the corridor ahead with the suns golden glow. She picked up her pace at the sight Stats having to alter his gait to keep up with her long strides. Finally they reached the broad steps that led down onto the warmed tarmac outside. Her relief was evident, beads of sweat had broken out on her forehead the colour drained from her features.

"Hey you okay you look kinda sick?" Stats enquired of her knowing already the reason for her silent hurried exit his own feeling of apprehension lifting as they'd finally left the Hub the heat outside burning off the sickening feeling that had accompanied them from within. She nodded finally meeting his look, her black eyes looked panicked as she finally slowed her stride her breathing relaxing once again now she was freed from the confines of the Hub.

"Yeah, yeah I'm okay I just had to get outta there a.s.a.p., never felt anything that powerful before like standing in the company of one of THEM but magnified a hundred times. It felt like the floor was gonna crack open spilling THEIR sickness out everywhere. It's real close, THEIR emergence and take over I can feel it. You felt it too right? It's happening right now as we speak, this Witch Hunt, the Porter, once the last of the Witches are gone nothings gonna stand in their way and if they got hold of that Porter... "She tailed off her sentence unfinished Stats knew the rest she was right this was what the Nefarious had been waiting for the last Witch was all that stood before them and their complete takeover of Heaven, the Hand of God would fall before their growing might, the outland survivors would be mindlessly slaughtered and as Aleshia said the final stage of their plan would be the capture and absorption of the Porter, the gene allowing their physical bodies to migrate from one location to another almost instantaneously would be spliced to their own and then all of humanity would eventually yield and perish under their despicable rule.

"This is it alright, the final push. Well I for one ain't gonna let that happen as long as there's a breath left in my body. If this Witch is what's holding them back from completing their take over then it's up to me to find her before any of the others 'cos I reckon without her help we're all finished." Stats' attention was drawn by a soldier waving to them over the heads of the other militia as they crossed their path. He acknowledged the signal and aimed in his direction and their waiting transport.

"I didn't want to believe it, up until now but your right Stats you've got to find her I really feel now she's our only saviour and it's up to me to keep their filthy fuckin' claws of this Porter or shit it doesn't bare thinking about."

"We gotta be strong and focused looks like the survival of the human race has fallen on our shoulders but that Porters got some powerful friends in tow and we're gonna need all the help we can get. You up to this?"

"I ain't got no choice, we ain't got no choice, you can rely on me." She smiled humourlessly back at Stats the cold, focused look of determination was etched back onto Aleshia's face her dark eyes menacing, he knew she up to the challenge he had fought alongside her before and he had known her to be a ruthless and courageous soldier in battle but he still worried about her the Hand of God was her main concern at present and he voiced his worry.

"You watch your back when you're on the outlands don't trust anyone for all you know one of your teams already had orders to dispatch you on location. If you can make contact with these fugitives befriend them if you can an' then maybe we got some sorta chance." Nodding as she listened Aleshia smiled somewhat sadly he thought and she reiterated his words.

"You too Stats 'cos if your team manage to take you out and the last Witch too then no matter how I do then..." She paused searching for the right words, "then we're all

The Hand Of God

fucked!" She concluded.

"I'll be okay, promise," his pale blue eyes sparkling. "I got plenty of fight left in me yet and more experience than most if I can't get this done then nobody can!" Came his magnanimous response and grinned broadly. His own confidence filled her with a sense of hope his conviction and positivity bolstered her own dwindling faith and lighter in spirit they returned to their mutual silence as they approached the black military off roader that sat parked ahead off the soldier patiently awaiting their arrival opened the rear door for them at their approach. Aleshia jumped in first shimmying along the black leather seat allowing Stats to enter via the same door. The soldier immediately closed the door and saluted as their driver started the engine and engaged first gear. The vehicle slowly rolled forward and began its journey for Heaven's coastline where the Hand of God had a base located on the islands peninsula. Large operations required many recruits and transportation which were ferried to and from the outlands by huge electrically powered catamarans docked within a natural cove there. The journey wouldn't take long only a couple of hours the roads constructed to access the port straight and direct. Stats and Aleshia settled themselves down for the journey ahead their seditious conversation curtailed in the presence of their chauffeur.

8

The journey to the coast where the military harbour was based was rather tedious and uneventful the suspension on the vehicle easily absorbing the bumps sustained from the compacted stony highway, a wake of orange dust marked their passage obliterating the military base behind them, the Hub slowly disappearing from sight also as the islands jungle closed in once more the towering tree ferns obscuring it from view only the monumental cables that anchored the solar towers remaining in view their impressive size visible from any point in Heaven. Aleshia viewed the forest of greens and browns outside interspersed with shocks of brightly coloured flowers, oranges, purples and reds, a multitude of life was abound outside the stuffy confines of the vehicle. She'd always wished she'd been able to explore the veritable paradise outside the Hub and see for herself firsthand these wonders of nature. Her father had periodically returned from his many missions with a souvenir for young Aleshia, a colourful feather from one of the many exotic birds that flocked in Heaven, a beautifully fragrant flower sweet and iridescent or even once a shell its small delicate spiral shape and bright yellow markings fascinating her. She subconsciously placed her hand on her breast pocket were she had re-housed the small yellow shell earlier, she always carried it with her for luck and feeling its presence there filled her with a warm glow reminding her of past times, times she could never recapture. She blinked rapidly several times as her emotions got the better of her and returned her hand to her lap her mind straying once again to the multitude of shrubs, flowers and trees that rolled past as they continued on down the highway. If it wasn't for the ever present threat of the Nefarious and what was to come then this island haven would indeed be Heaven she thought to herself. The civilian residents unaware of how lucky they were living their lives ignorant of the many horrendous crimes committed by the Hand of God, the military segre-

The Hand Of God

gated from them keeping their influence to a minimum the Nefarious never seen to mix with the descendants of those past elite survivors, their appearance alone would probably plant the seed of dissention amongst the population. Televisions and all forms of communication were no longer necessary according to the new rulers, only for military use for even the Nefarious had no need of such things their psychic abilities connecting them as one, an amassing legion of parasitic phantoms sucking the very life and soul from the Earth and the people who dwelt there. Aleshia hadn't considered up until now what would befall the inhabitants of Heaven once the Nefarious's takeover was under way an eradication of all but the remaining willing participants left within the Hand of God she had no doubt of that their lives also becoming forfeit after their task complete their spilt blood merging with those they'd murdered. It was with a heavy heart she sat forlorn, missing her father more than ever wishing he was there to reassure her and tell her everything was going to be okay. She let the headrest behind her take the weight of her fatigued head heavy with the burden it bore and closed her eyes trying not to ponder on the upcoming events that could alter the future history of mankind.

Stats was deep in his own reverie, planning his own resurrection from his planned early retirement. An eight man team had been deployed already at the designated site, Szebrowski, the prick, the commanding officer until Stats' own arrival. Well he'd be the first to get it Stats promised himself there was no backing down now the outcome was inevitable and he was determined he would stand victorious at the end of this, no way was he going to be put down like some rabid dog. His curiousity about his quarry was whetted, even during the Witch Hunts of years ago he'd never got close one, extreme caution was always of the highest priority when dealing with their kind, he hoped that he could convince her of his new found allegiance or he might well face death at her hands and not that of his own men after all. The Nefarious had been understandably reluctant to leak much useable information on their old adversaries perhaps afraid that the human denizens would realise the truth and overthrow their bloodthirsty lords. These so-called "Witches," so named to provoke fear and distrust towards them amongst the people, created by medical science as far as Stats was led to believe, a mixed race their talents and abilities at best a vague conglomeration of whispered rumours passed down through the generations since the Earth's shift. Fearing that which they did not understand the Hand of God unquestioningly undertook the task of eliminating their existence at the decree of the Nefarious their localities pin-pointed by a specialised order of the Nefarious, tracking them, the Witches powers when used left a distinct residue on the ethereal plane, these energies tagged "spells" were the only means by which they could be located. Their unusual appearance led the escaped survivors to seek out solitary refuges far from the Hand of God and survivors alike. Allegedly they were capable of minute alterations to the current time line rendering them invisible to the search parties that swept the outlands seeking them out existing in a bubble out of time and out of sight but the persistence of the Nefarious prevailed and up until now all had thought their species deceased. Apparently all their kind had been female as well Stats didn't recall any mention of a male Witch and they were generally mute this man-made breed communicating solely through psychic interaction. Stats' ruminations were cut off in mid flow as a colourful display of birds took to the air as the transport that carried them disturbed their feeding. Stats followed the rainbow flock as they soared above the canopy of vegetation and dove for cover again further in the forest their alarm calls fading as they settled down to feed once more. Stats sensed Aleshia also following their progress through the sky and he turned meeting her gaze, he clasped her hand in one of his own and squeezed it comfortingly, they had almost reached their destination the jungle thinning as the coastal base slowly dominated the view through the windscreen ahead, a hive of activity at the ensuing conflict about to commence.

The four by four finally came to a standstill as they pulled into the dock lands, the dusty cloud that accompanied their arrival was quickly dispelled by the fresh coastal breeze and Stats and Aleshia breathed deeply of the cool salty air as they disembarked the vehicle. The harbour was dominated

The Hand Of God

by several large black catamaran's, their hulls sleek and streamlined built for speed, the hold of each designed to carry military personnel and transport to and from the outlands. Each sat docked a massive umbilical of electrical power connected to each feeding the huge motors necessary to power such large vessels. An arrangement of tinted glass set atop the boats indicated the location of the cabin which housed the navigation systems and pilots alike. The whole construction smooth and enclosed to protect the interior from the elements, the imposing Hand of God insignia positioned upon the prow of each. The stern of each boat had been reversed into the dock and a ramp connected each to the concrete mainland, a procession of men and machines slowly boarding and disembarking, Stats's own boat was readying for departure as a grey overalled mechanic disconnected the power supply and sealed the socket making it water tight. "Well looks like this is it." Stats broke the silence between them, "time to head our separate ways." His heart was heavy at the separation that was to come.

"Yeah well this is it. Good luck Stats." Aleshia strained to keep her composure intact realising that they may never see each other again and her eyes misty at the prospect. Stats, struggling with his own emotions, enfolded Aleshia in his arms and gave her a hug.

"You give 'em hell kid. I'll see you soon okay?" He whispered to her as they embraced. She returned the hug uncaring of the attention it attracted by the nearby militia, her fingers digging deep into his uniform reluctant to release him.

"Oh I will," she promised."You take care, I'll see you again when this is all over one way or another." Aleshia added not convinced herself of their reunion but attempting an air of optimisy for the sake of them both. Stats released her from his clasp and the two friends took a step back and formally saluted each other and with a final nod Aleshia turned about her black pony tail swinging as she did so and headed in the direction of the boat designated to carry her to her location, her jaw clenched barely suppressing the tears that burned behind her cold gaze. Stats watched her depart following her progress through the many workers amassed at the docks until he lost sight of her as she blended with the other black uniforms. Taking a deep steadying breath he pivoted where he stood and viewed the boat onto which he was to board as the last vehicle was chained securely within the hold. This was some operation he thought, a military camp was to be set up on the coast at their designated disembarkation point from where he was to be transported inland to join his Witch Hunting team. He steeled himself in anticipation and marched up the ramp and into the hull of the waiting boat. Once onboard a waiting dock worker raised an arm knowing his signal would be picked up by a pair of watchful eyes from within the control room of the catamaran and in response the ramp began to slowly retract sealing the hull. Stats stood watching as the space narrowed closing out the docklands from his view and silently prayed for Aleshia's safe return but in a world where God's bloody Hand ruled at the order of the Nefarious who did you pray too?

9

The four fugitives continued their unfaltering escape from the city. Mac now burdening Eve on his back, his own and Nisa's stamina far outstretching Canova's own as they persevered relentlessly through the ruined streets and collapsed buildings. Their passage revealed no hidden surprises or ambushes along the way their escape route illuminated by the moons glowing presence making progress easier. Mac and Nisa's knowledge of the city guiding them through the hostile environment in their bid to be free of the oppressive environment surrounding them at present. Under the burnishing light of the silvery satellite overhead Canova couldn't help but marvel at the scale of the devastation, he'd only explored a small part of the city since his escape from the militia camp he'd been interred in staying close to the heart of the city where he could still find sustenance. Blocks of stone had tumbled into the streets revealing the torn, twisted skeletal structures of the metal beneath. Collapsed walls revealed the cell structure of the once inhabited homes and offices inside, the exposed walls crumbling away as a result of the years of wind and rain. Cracks and fissures crisscrossed their pathway forcing them on occasion to scale some of the piles of rock to avoid the larger chasms, the scale of some of these apocalyptic monuments of stone leaving Canova gasping for breath as he struggled to keep pace with is new companions. Plant life had randomly taken root amongst the debris their roots holding fast the loose brick and stone underfoot. Mosses carpeted vast areas and lichens clung to the walls vying for the best positions awaiting the return of the life giving rays of the sun. Colourful fungi blossomed clustered together on decaying wooden beams. Ferns bushed from cracks within the still remaining walls, their feathery fronds dancing in the night breeze and here and there a tree had successfully germinated, its seed carried here by some winged propagator. Flowering plants were a rarity in this part of the outlands at least, insects and in particular bees had taken a great loss amongst their kind and in consequence the plants in need of their pollination for their continued survival had suffered in turn, only species that relied on the wind to carry their spores and those carried by birds and bats had managed a successful comeback. The displacement of rubble under foot and Canova's own laboured breathing the only sounds as they progressed on their route through the city. Eve resembling a rag doll as she clung to Mac's back jostling this way and that as he lumbered tirelessly onwards, Nisa bounding ahead her long legs and natural agility covering the obstacle course with the confidence and nimbleness of a mountain goat. Canova became increasingly aware of the encroaching vegetation as they neared the outskirts of the city, natures dominance over the grey and black stone becoming more and more apparent, his feet at last finding comfort from the cushioning growth underfoot. Their pace now gradually decreasing to a more leisurely trot as the cityscape fell behind them. Nisa altered her course at this conjecture aiming for a copse visible in the distance the shrubs and grasses there stretching waist high at points. They continued onwards for about twenty minutes before she finally checked her gait as they neared the patch of dense shrubbery the canopy of the trees offering them shelter from any aerial pursuit that may be out hunting for them. Once within the relative protection of the copse they finally came to a halt, the dappled moonlight filtering through the trees above shone patchily on their faces the accumulated sweat from their exertions shining brightly. Nisa was doubled over her upper body supported by her hands that now rested on her knees gasped in controlled lung full's of air slowing her heart rate, Mac, who had now lowered the shaken Eve to the ground the dense plant life here reaching almost to her shoulders, was lathered in sweat his heavy breathing slowing to a more normal rate in a surprisingly short period. Canova himself collapsed bodily into the grasses, the soft greenery cushioning his fall his legs unable to support his weary body any longer, his body shook uncontrollably, his gasping breaths like that of someone returned to life. Eve sat huddled beside him, her forehead resting on her knees, she hadn't spoken since before their materialisation in the tent. In rec-

The Hand Of God

ord time Mac and Nisa had regained their composure. Nisa searching through the pack she'd removed from the dead soldier and recovered a dark grey blanket and opened it out with a shake then stomping an area of vegetation as flat as she could manage laid out the blanket indicating that they should all be seated the blanket offering them a little warmth and protection from the damp ground. They arranged themselves on the small space as best they could and Nisa handed out food rations to each of them followed by a bottle of water as much to slake their thirsts as to wash away the unappetising flavours residing in their mouths after they'd eaten. Eve immediately curled up at the backs of the others where they sat talking, she was soon lulled asleep by the comforting sound of their whispered voices and the heat from their combined bodies. The other three remained awake awhile chatting and listening to the insects and other nocturnal life that had ventured forth once more after their noisy arrival, calling to each other in their own unique languages. "So what's the story with you and the kid?" Nisa finally asked Canova, his limbs had finally ceased their quivering his breathing now calmed.

"Her parents were murdered by the Hand of God last night at her home and well she just appeared right out of thin air where I was hiding out, for a second I thought the Nefarious had finally tracked me down. Hell came as a big surprise to me."

"You mean she's a fuckin' teleporter! Shit no way!" Exclaimed Mac incredulous joining in the conversation, staring back over his shoulder at the sleeping child. "Didn't think they were for real, you know just rumours, stories." He returned his attention to Canova obviously impressed keen to know more.

"Yeah gotta admit I'd always thought the same till last night. That's who Nekros was really interested in her parents were just in the way."

"Nekros! Shit! This just gets better and better, makes sense though a teleporter no wonder he was out making house calls personally." Mac exclaimed in disbelief. "They're really gonna be on our asses now like flies on shit!" He chuckled amiably, a grimy thick finger poking at a point in his mouth trying to dislodge a piece of his bland meal from between his teeth with his nail. "Well fuckin' bring it on that's what I say, the more the fuckin' merrier ain't that right Nis?" And he nudged his companion playfully, ignoring Mac's jibe Nisa's attention was still focused on Canova and his accomplice.

"So that's how you the two of you appeared in that tent back there, we'd been keeping a vigil on that camp and was sure neither of us would've missed seeing you two enter the scene."

"Yeah we'd been hiding out deeper in the city but the Hand of God were onto us, had us trapped, they had a couple of Nefarious in tow as well, didn't think we had a chance but Eve got us both outta there just in the nick of time."

"So who took care of the Nefarious back at the tent, you?" Nisa countered. Canova nodded in affirmation. Nisa raised her eyebrows encouraging a more detailed explanation behind the demise of the two Nefarious.

"I can summon this energy in my head when I need to and direct it at whoever I want, can give 'em a headache to remember, knock 'em clean out or probably much worse, although I've never done that before."

"Oh yeah those two you hit were definitely dead when I checked them out." Nisa confirmed. "First time you've taken a life huh? Well I can assure it ain't gonna be the last."

"Well we could certainly do with some of that kinda mind shit on our side." Mac piped up slapping Canova on the back solidly with his shovel-like hand. Canova winced at the force of the friendly pat. "By the way I'm Mac and this here's Nisa." Nisa nodded at Canova at her introduction. "And you are?"

"I'm Canova and that there's Eve."

"Well Canova looks like our little ragged team here ruffled a few feathers tonight, no doubt the Hand of God will be out in force at first light tomorrow looking for our asses especially if they know we got a Porter with us." Mac took in the sleeping form of Eve again before continuing. "So what other hidden talents you got?"

"I can sense the presence of other psychically endowed people especially the Nefarious, can smell them like rotting meat, can almost taste 'em. The militia are harder to pick up I gotta know where they're located before I can isolate them and enter their minds. Once there though I can sift through their memories, steal information even control them mentally for a while. Almost got taken out a while back by a Hand of God patrol I got sloppy sleeping out in the open during the summer woke up staring down the barrel of a gun. The fucker had purposefully woken me up, thought he'd intimidate me a bit before blowing my brains out, big mistake, got into his head, convinced him there was nobody there and sent him on his way. Used that trick a few times over the years got me out of a few tight spots but that one was a bit close for comfort." Canova filling in his captivated audience happy to have company to talk too.

"Sounds to me like you're still developing your talents. I've seen it before abilities increasing in times of high emotional stress. Invading another's mind and being able to manipulate their actions that sounds like an advanced form of sensitivity to me. The Nefarious would love to get their claws into you as well no doubt." Nisa pondered for a few seconds before asking. "So in theory you could remove us all from the picture so to speak convince them we're not really there?" Her piercing green eyes held his gaze unflinchingly awaiting his response.

"Yeah well I suppose it's possible, never tried with a group before though but once I'm out of their presence I can't control them any more,"

"Well I'd never heard any stories of a Porter carrying a passenger before either but here's the proof." Mac interjected his mischievous eyes twinkling in the moonlight.

"Yeah I think the more you use these powers the further they evolve." Nisa added. This time Canova took up the role of inquisitor.

"I take it you two are Shifters then?"

"Yeah not too hard to figure that one out." Mac chortled. "Nisa here well she can, well just show him babe." At Mac's request Nisa held out her right hand extending her fingers as she did so and with a wry smile the ends of her digits extended into razor sharp points at least the same length again as her fingers. She playfully tapped the lethal tips together before slowly retracting them absorbing them back into her body. "Cool eh?" Mac enquired of Canova as he watched entranced at the display.

"Wow! I mean I've never seen anything like that before, does it hurt?"

"Na you get used to it." She replied casually. "And there's a good chance you won't see anything like it again if the Hand of God have anything to do with it. Most of our kind have been exterminated over the years I'm lucky to be alive, I'm only here thanks to Mac." Mac took up the story at this point filling in Canova on the massacre that took place wiping out their fellow Shifters all that time ago. Canova, head bowed, listened in earnest as the story unfolded, the short tale complete he raised his head deeply moved at the image of women and children alike gassed ruthlessly as most of them slept.

"I'm really sorry you guys, for your losses, it must've been terrible." Mac just nodded sadly at the memory of that fateful morning. The tale of Nisa's near end concluded, rescued by the man that now sat at her side she spoke up adding.

"So you don't want to get on the wrong side of Mac he could punch a hole in a wall." Her chipped tooth showing as she beamed in Mac's direction elevating the sombre mood that had descended. Mac nudged her slightly embarrassed at her praise.

"You know it babe." He retorted and placing his square fists in front of his face in a boxers block threw a couple of mock punches to demonstrate, then in good humour kissed each of his fists. "Yeah these babies got me outta a few tight spots."

"Takes a lot to put Mac down." Nisa continued her appraisal. "Fast healer too and as you already heard can adapt to harsh environments, excellent night vision too. Don't know what I woulda done without him." Her gaze softened as she looked at Mac affectionately.

"Hey always watchin' yor back Nis." His round cheeks now notably flushed at her attention. Mac swung one of his hefty arms over Nisa's shoulders and hugged her protectively adding, "well we'd better join the kid 'cos we got some

The Hand Of God

ground to cover tomorrow an' dawn can't be far away." Mac calculated turning his attention towards the moons position overhead.

"Yeah you're right we'd better get some rest." Nisa yawned as she spoke and huddled up to Mac who sat stoically in position, eyes closed his arm still around Nisa's shoulders.

"Any ideas on where we're headin'?" Canova asked no one in particular as he curled up into a ball on the blanket.

"Nope was kinda hopin' you'd take care of that." Mac answered one eye opening as he spoke a playful grin touched his broad lips before his eye closed once again. Canova didn't reply instead he yielded to the tiredness that lurked inside his head, his aching eyelids thankfully closing. He felt his sore muscles slowly relaxing one by one, his jaded mind and body finally giving in to sleep as he drifted soundlessly into his visionary dream world.

Canova's disembodied mind drifted aimlessly through the ether glad to escape the ordeals of the waking world for a time. His calm, languid mind was gently swept up by invisible currents and there she was once again, Thalia's whispered words distant at first touched on his sleeping mind, her delicate voice almost imperceptible at first grew in clarity as he focused on her words. "Faith will be instilled once again amongst the peoples of the Earth elevating them into a peaceful, harmonious new existence. A world where class and hierarchy have no place. A world where thought carries weight and love creates." Her contact once more filled his soul with a glowing warmth a smile crept onto his sleeping countenance as she continued. "Our time fades quickly, the final hunt is underway. This must be my final communication for they know who I am and where I lay concealed until now. Together we are this worlds last hope.The dawning of the sun will herald a new beginning for us so be strong of heart and lead us to salvation." Her voice was faint now, the delicate tones ringing in his mind like the chiming of exquisite crystals resounding off each other their vibrations gradually fading away to nothing.

She was the last of her kind, a mixed race born in the laboratories of mankind, her sisters hunted to extinction by their own detestable creators, hounded and persecuted till all but herself remained. The Earth and its true inhabitants last hope of redemption, her passing would plunge this world into a dark abyss of screaming horror from which there would be no retrieval. Remaining hidden for many years deep within the outlands, concealed amongst the flora that grew unchecked there since man kinds almost complete demise in the wake of the magnetic shift, surviving on what nature herself provided, berries, edible roots and fungi sustaining her life awaiting her call to return to the place of her birth. Her physical presence veiled from prying eyes and minds by charms and "spells" awaiting those who would accompany her, aiding her in her life's task and finally lead this world into salvation. But now the time of change was almost upon them and she had dared to break her silence, communicating psychically with the one who would lead the other survivors into the light awaited their arrival, knowing that those blackened souls may also hear her call but it was a risk she had had to undertake, forgoing her own safety for the greater good of all. Weakened by her recent efforts, her defences lowered she had sensed the dark, fetid minds of those that would lead this world into perdition as they scoured the outlands that she had called home for so long now. Barely avoiding the rancid touch of their thoughts as she broke her silence to reach out to him. The hunt had commenced and it would surely be only a short time before one faction discovered her location. Thalia knew this for sure for it had been predicted by the Creatrix herself.

Thalia, as she had chosen to call herself, sat at the mouth of a small cave that overlooked a picturesque river that coursed through the landscape. The ground leading from her haunt to the shingled banks of the river beyond a gradual incline, rocky and wild, a scattering of towering pine trees clung to the slope their browned needles littering the forest floor in dense springy mats, bright red-capped fungi grew in small clumps amongst the litter. She idly listened to the calls of the songbirds as she sat and watched their colourful passage as they flitted from tree to tree as they went about their business. Since the destruction of man kinds many industrial achievements the pollution imposed upon the planets water ways and atmosphere had been completely ceased and in its absence mother nature had reaffirmed her reign once more. Thalia's thoughts sought out the animal life that thrived here in relative safety with which she found a natural affinity with and she gently smiled to herself. Her normally immaculate appearance had become disheveled and unkempt as a result of her years living in the wilderness. Her pale blue skin seemed to have faded further reflecting her weakened state, the last traces of her energy slowly diminishing as she continued to maintain the "spell" that prevented those unenlightened beings from uncovering her whereabouts. She closed her eyes and entered a trance-like state, her heart rate and metabolism slowing, conserving her stamina, as she patiently awaited the advent of her saviour. For she knew he would find her for it was his destiny. Thalia had endured much anticipating the coming of the one named Canova over the years but she maintained her faith, he and his friends would come of that she was sure.

10

Canova awakened to the sounds of nature inhabiting the woodlands that surrounded him. The relaxing rustling of the leafy canopy above stirred by the gentle breeze sending occasional orange and red tainted leaves spiraling to the earth as the deciduous trees prepared for autumn, the uppermost branches swayed softly and the long grasses that surrounded his bed filled his nostrils with their delicate sweet scent. He lay silently for a while enjoying the chirruping of the insects and the songs of the birds that inhabited the copse where he lay. Small rays of sunlight touched his face as it filtered through the shimmering foliage and he smiled to himself, it'd been a long time since he'd felt this relaxed, freed at last from the confines of the city that had been his home for too many years now out of reach from the oppressive Hand of God but not for long he thought as he recalled the events of the last couple of days, soon they would be tracking himself and his companions, in fact he'd be very surprised if the hunting parties hadn't already been deployed their orders received and were right now hot on their heels as he lay sprawled on the grey blanket amidst the dense vegetation. He finally opened his eyes realising he had the blanket to himself the others departed. He sat up stretching and peered above the long grasses that enclosed him on all sides but the others were nowhere to be seen. For a few minutes he surveyed his surroundings in more detail until he finally detected movement through the trees up ahead. He focused harder and was aware of the others making their way back through the thicket towards him, their figures gaining definition as they closed the distance between them. Canova finally stood up plucking a few stalks of vegetation from his clothing that had lodged there as he had slept on. With his vision now elevated he could now clearly make out Mac and Nisa's imposing figures striding through the undergrowth towards him, Eve playfully bounding through the jungle only her head and shoulders visible. At seeing his emergence from

The Hand Of God

the greenery she waved at him and picked up her pace. He smiled widely at the sight of their return and waved back. Obviously the night spent under the trees amongst the flora and fauna had done her the world of good, himself also, his spirit lifted. She beamed back, her smile wide her brown hair bounced wildly about her face as she closed the gap between them. "Morning sleepy head." She called out to him when she was within earshot. "Didn't think you were ever going to wake up," she teased. "We've been picking breakfast," she explained finally meeting Canova as he strode through the grass towards her. She was carrying the knapsack Nisa had liberated and she opened the zippered compartment allowing him to view the contents herself, Mac and Nisa had gathered whilst he had slept. He perused the contents, a colourful collection of fruits, berries and mushrooms.

"Mmmm looks delicious," he commented, "How long have I been sleeping for?"

"An hour or so," Mac enlightened him as himself and Nisa caught up with Eve. "Thought we'd just let you sleep on a while, looked like you needed it. What d'ya think?" Mac asked him referring to the contents of the bag. "Better than that military issue shit eh?" Eve giggled at Mac's use of language.

"You sure do swear a lot," she laughed.

"You better fuckin' believe it kid," he retorted laughing with her. Canova shook his head smiling, well at least Eve seemed to have regained her cheery self once again after last night's close call.

"Well then shall we eat?" Nisa suggested her emerald eyes sparkling in the morning light as she returned to the spread of the blanket.

"Yeah I'm starved." Mac added and with that they arranged themselves around the outer edge of the blanket and sat down, the contents of the bag emptied in the middle, its previous contents had been carefully packed away with the few supplies that remained, Eve's handful of clothes and hairbrush and the first aid kit were packed together in the hold all Canova had found in the off roader. He examined the fresh produce spread before them, half a dozen green apples, blushed with patches of red, a mix of red and black berries, that looked succulent and juicy and a mixed assortment of fungi. He selected one of the mushrooms, twirling it between thumb and forefinger.

"Sure they aren't poisonous?" He asked of Mac and Nisa, looking for verification before sampling the small yellow mushroom he'd selected.

"Yeah they're cool." Nisa answered popping a brown-capped variety into her mouth and chewing. "Mac can tell can't you?"

"Yeah I just eat 'em an' see, my body can cope with the toxins I just sweat out the poison so I've learnt over the years which ones are safe for others to eat, handy eh? So no sweats equals no poisons!" He grinned as he chomped into a particularly large fungal bract. "Those ones are real nice," he indicated the brown-capped variety Nisa had chosen, "they got a real nutty flavour." Canova selected one and popped it in his mouth, its juices filled his mouth with the most amazing nutty flavours as he chewed and he nodded his appreciation. The four companions remained silent as they finished their breakfast, their appetites now satisfied, their fingers stained red from the juices of the ripe berries.

"That was so good." Eve voiced her appreciation. "I've never had mushrooms before."

"Me either." Canova added, "never knew which ones were safe to eat always afraid I'd end up poisoning myself."

"Yeah always best not to try if you don't know what's good an' bad." Mac agreed knowingly.

"Well we'd better be thinkin' 'bout makin' a move soon." It was Nisa that brought them back to reality reminding them of the danger that was surely tailing them by now. The city they had recently vacated was distant now, only a few ruins were distinguishable through the encroaching vegetation but still close enough to remind them of the peril they were in at the Hand of God. "Times gettin' on so which way we headin'?" All eyes turned to Canova which made him slightly uncomfortable.

"Eh well." He pondered not too sure himself. The contact with Thalia in his dream last night still lingered in his mind, the memory swelled as he recalled the meeting. One thing was for sure they had to find her and fast. He concentrated

The Hand Of God

aware of the others awaiting his answer. A stream, no a river, something about a river surrounded by trees. He stood up scanning the landscape ahead through the trees as best he could. In the distance a range of mountains peaked above the tree line, their slopes green with pine forests, scarred periodically with bare rock and loose scree. The location at which the sun had risen that morning spilling its warmth over the countryside. "That way!" He finally answered pointing confidently. "She's hiding out in those mountains somewhere." Nisa frowned as her eyes followed the direction in which he pointed.

"She? Who's she?" She asked somewhat confused.

"Not quite sure she comes to me in my dreams like an angel, a blue-skinned angel..." He tailed off somewhat embarrassed.

"A Witch? Really?" Mac asked his interest piqued. "Wow thought they were extinct, only breed persecuted more than us Shifters." He glanced over at Nisa as he spoke. "Those Witch hunts were brutal man, took the heat off our kind for a good few years though." Mac stood joining the others hoping to gain more information on their elusive quarry.

"Can't really tell you much more I just know that it's real important that we find her before the Nefarious do, an' I got a real strong feelin' that she's our last hope of overthrowing Nekros and his army. Sorry that's about as much as I know." Nisa appeared deep in thought before adding.

"Makes sense otherwise why the big push years ago to wipe 'em out there's gotta be a good reason for that. Reckon the Nefarious are scared of 'em for some reason and that makes her a powerful ally in my eyes." She finished her green eyes turned to Mac awaiting his approval.

"Yeah I agree, we bumped into each other for some reason an' I reckon your right Nis with a Witch on our side we might just be able to get the better of those Nefarious bastards!" I'd love to be around to see that day." Mac wore a determined look on his face as he held out a clenched fist in Nisa's direction, she followed suit and their fists met, their equivalent of an agreeable handshake.

"Well it's decided then, we're in." Nisa spoke for them

both as she returned her attention to Canova who smiled in response, the thought of these two warriors accompanying himself and Eve on their journey filled him with positivity.

"Well then," he added, "so our own Witch hunt begins. I just hope we find her before THEY do."

"We will." Eve piped up confident and excited at the prospect of meeting a real live Witch. Nisa stooped and picked up the remaining uneaten apples and stowed them away with the rest of the supplies, then grabbing two corners of the blanket she shook off the debris that clung there before folding it neatly and storing it away in the empty knapsack. Mac claimed the two bags and slung them over his wide back and with that the four allies turned east and began the long trek that lay before them, their spirits enlivened after their delicious breakfast. The city receding further into the distance behind them as they ventured further into the wilderness.

After last night's fevered evacuation of the city Mac and Nisa undertook a more leisurely pace enjoying the air here filled with the scents of nature and crisp golden leaves as they tumbled toward the ground. They meandered through the woodlands in which they'd camped taking the path of least resistance, large patches of thorny brambles and wild roses made some routes impassable and they had to skirt their boundaries until they found a less formidable path. Occasionally large trees felled by the earthquakes all those decades ago crossed their path, their rotting bulks now home to a myriad of tunneling insects and fungi feeding off the dead wood, they were easily traversed, clambering over their prone bodies or ducking beneath them. They periodically paused to fill the near empty knapsack with the succulent mushrooms that grew in abundance on the dead wood. Small clusters of berries were eaten on the move. Eve skipped happily from one patch to another returning to the others her hands full offering them their share of the sugary sweet delights her hands and lips dyed red by the oozing juices. Periodically they startled a solitary deer or other small mammal as it ventured into the thicket to gorge on the feast of fruits and berries, the tall thick grasses shaking as it hurriedly made its escape. Bird calls escorted them on their way, flitting from perch to perch as they watched these unusual additions to their home. Finally the trees thinned into open grasslands the vista ahead occasionally broken up by a lone tree. This environment stretched ahead until the shallow slopes of the mountainous regions in the distance. At least a day's travel, possibly more. The group stopped to gather their thoughts on the periphery of the woods. "Well I reckon a day and a half till we make it to those woodlands on the other side of this savannah," Nisa estimated. "Must have about three hours of daylight left and I don't much fancy bein' out in the open. We've been lucky up until now, so we either camp here where we still got some cover or we aim for one of those trees ahead an' pitch camp there. What d'ya think?" She asked no-one in particular her hands resting on her hips as she spoke to her companions.

"Well I think I'd rather aim for one of those trees ahead, problem with campin' here is if they are tracking us, which they will be, they can use these woods for cover too. At least out there we'd see 'em comin'." Canova voiced his opinion nodding back the way they'd come, the dense thicket offering numerous hiding places for the enemy. Mac nodded in agreement.

"Good call I'm with you let's get out into the open a bit, good all round surveillance we'd see 'em comin' a mile away." The three adults looked at each other in turn and nodded in mutual agreement. Eve oblivious to the decision making was captivated by the flutterings of a delicate pale blue and orange butterfly as it fed on the nectars of the brightly coloured flowers dotted about.

"Hey Eve." Canova called over to her. She looked up and bounded over as he beckoned to her to rejoin the group. Once she'd returned Nisa spoke again.

"Right then guys we're gonna be right out in the open here, there's no canopy to hide us from above so be vigilant, keep your eyes and ears open for any aerial patrols, shouldn't be too hard to spot them and we should hear them coming from miles away but stick together now and no wandering off." She looked meaningfully down at Eve who nodded in compliance.

"Don't worry I won't."

"Okay then we'll continue for another couple of hours

then make camp under one of those trees out there." Nisa scanned the open grasslands ahead. "It'll be a full moon tonight as well which'll aid any hunt they got goin' on so we'd better choose our cover well tonight." Mac had been rummaging about in the hold all and retrieved four of the remaining apples, one for each of them, handing them out before taking a large bite out of his own, juice spilling down his chin.

"Better than that bottled water." He commented spraying fragments of apple as he spoke his mouth full. Eve giggled at Mac's manners and likewise chomped into her own fruit the other two following suit as they set off into the open, the shadows of the tall trees finally falling behind allowing the last few hours of the sun's rays to fully embrace them.

"Hey I just thought." Canova ventured after a few minutes as he followed in the wake of Mac and Nisa, the tall grasses crushed flat in places as they marched onward.

"Yeah what?" Mac called back over his shoulder throwing his apple core far ahead with a casual toss.

"Well if they do come looking for us this way we've just made a path for them to follow probably stand right out if they fly a helicopter over."

"Shit yeah never thought of that!" Mac halted his progress for a second and turned about viewing the visible pathway of broken and damaged vegetation they'd just created. "Shit be as well paintin' a big fuckin' red arrow saying here we are!" He exclaimed, "well not much we can do about it now what d'ya think Nis?" Nisa had also stopped to examine the pathway in their wake Eve looked up at them worriedly her small hand seeking out Canova's.

"Like you say Mac there ain't much we can do about it now we just gotta hope that they don't send out a chopper at least until we got some sorta cover even if they do send one out at night the full moons gonna show 'em the way. We'll just need to keep a watch out tonight in case they sneak up on us."

"Agreed." Mac nodded. "Right let's move," he narrowed his eyes and scanned ahead his vision adapting and refocusing on a point the others were unable to see at this distance. "Okay I got a spot up ahead, few miles yet, two to three, a handful of trees, they'll give us some good cover," he reported.

"Lead the way then." Nisa offered and with Mac heading the troop Canova still holding Eve's hand followed closely behind, Nisa bringing up the rear keeping vigilant, scrutinising their back and the skies above for any signs of unwanted company.

11

The journey to the outlands aboard the catamaran had been a painfully slow crossing. The hollow hull of the craft that housed the vehicles and militia alike reverberated loudly with the sound of the powerful electric motors that sped the boat over the choppy ocean. Aleshia braced herself as she felt her stomach lift before the craft slammed back down making contact with the ocean once again, her seatbelt holding her in place. Just as well she'd eaten frugally this morning or no doubt she would've showered her comrades with an assortment of partially digested fruit by now. The hold in which she sat was absent of windows and was lit by a series of fluorescent tubes fitted along the ceiling. The space within was long enough to house three military vehicles, basically four by fours kitted out with highly advanced communications and tracking systems their boots laden with weaponry no doubt, as yet to be issued and programmed. The vehicles were parked along the centre of the boat allowing for stability, heavy chains were wrapped around the large off road tyres securing them in place for the duration of the crossing. On either side of these sat the Hand of God militia, two dozen aside, chatting aimlessly amongst themselves, likewise strapped in where they were seated upon a long uncomfortable metal bench. Towards the aft of the boat a small but steep staircase led upwards, at the top of which resided a solid looking door which led to the cabin, the crew housed there guiding the boat onwards towards their destination. She gritted her teeth again as she felt the crafts bulk lift completely from the surface of the water bracing herself once again anticipating the bone charring impact that was to inevitably follow, the whooping of some of the soldiers filled the cramped space obviously enjoying the rollercoaster ride. Aleshia had no idea how much time had passed since they'd left Heaven, she'd never worn a timepiece in her life, but she looked forward to them nearing the coast and escaping the choppier waters of the open ocean. She wondered

The Hand Of God

how Stats was doing, wondered if she was ever going to see him again, she hoped she would with all her heart, maybe even under better circumstances once the Nefarious had been removed from power and Nekros slain as surely he deserved. She immediately quietened her mind realising that the Nefarious may well be accompanying them on their excursion secreted away in the upper cabin. It would be below them to be seen to mix with the soldier's. She steeled herself yet again as she felt her stomach lift at yet another wave, she couldn't wait to feel solid ground beneath her feet once more.

Stats was similarly uncomfortable, strapped in at the very stern as he'd been the last to board, a four by four blocked his view of the seated recruits opposite. A few curious faces had leant forward further down his line during the early stages of the journey staring in his direction. Stats had quelled their curiosity with his cold hard gaze, unflinching until embarrassed they sat back in line hiding their identities. Fuckers, he thought to himself, if only they knew what the future lay in store for them, then they wouldn't be so fucking smug, the smiles would soon be wiped from their subservient faces. He clenched his teeth, his fists bunched. Yeah in kind of a sick way he was looking forward to the confrontation that was to come at long last after all these years. He hoped he was still alive to witness the fear on Nekros's odious face when he finally realised his reign of terror was at an end. Oh yes now that was certainly worth fighting for. He closed his eyes and tried to relax, shutting out the external chatter as best he could as he endured the ocean crossing.

Finally Aleshia became aware of the hum of the electric motors slowing their pulse as their passage across the vast expanse of water gradually slowed, the rollercoaster ride easing, the passage of the boat becoming gentler as they neared their destination, now rocking to and forth, like sitting aboard a train as it rolled over uneven tracks. The conversations of the men and women onboard increased in volume, their voices blending into an unintelligible babble as they also sensed the journeys end. Aleshia took several deep breaths, relaxing her tense muscles and calming her rolling stomach. Almost there now, her mission was to subdue and capture a Porter, a Psych and at least two Shifters if possible, if not they were to be eliminated. Not if she had anything to do with it. It was time the balance was shifted and she had inadvertently enrolled herself as a major player in this small but significant rebellion that was to come but maybe it had always been destined to be that way she ruminated to herself. A two person rebellion at that, at least for now, until then every man and woman holed up with her were just as potentially dangerous as the Nefarious themselves.

Stats composed himself, focusing his mind on what could well be his ultimate mission as he felt the crafts engines burst into life once again indicating their arrival at their appointed destination as the catamaran was reversed toward the dock outside. He had to locate the Witch and protect her at all costs, the lives of the troops under his command forfeit on this occasion unless they switched allegiance, even then could he really trust any of them? And then what? He really hoped the Witch would take it from there but knew in his heart that if he accomplished his task then a return to Heaven and the Hub with his "secret weapon" would be inevitable as would the final confrontation with Nekros, but no need to worry about that yet he first had the task of locating her. The engines thrummed once more before slowly dying away, the boat finally coming to a complete standstill, they'd arrived. A soft electrical whine cut through the subdued chatter on board. The troops ceased their conversations at the sound anticipating what lay ahead of them on the out lands. A small crack appeared where the ramp joined the hull, the bright sunshine slowly flooded in illuminating the interior once again, a fresh, slightly chill breeze accompanied the sunlight invigorating Stats with its salty taste. Shielding his eyes with his hand allowing them adjust once more to the natural light, awaiting the scene outside to slowly unfold. He released his safety belt with his free hand and stood up arching his aching back after the hours he'd spent seated. He raised his head as the ramp was lowered enough to finally allow him a glimpse of what lay beyond. Tree tops came into view breaking up the solid blue of the sky followed by a dense jungle of vegetation below. No military port here, just a simple dock constructed from heavy duty timber beams

The Hand Of God

met the ramp with a dull clang, the wooden beams nearest shook briefly with the weight of the metal ramp before settling themselves. A small itinerary of militia awaited their arrival. Beyond the wooden jetty a rutted track road led into the greenery beyond. Somewhat surprised, Stats had expected an imposing military base making its mark on the landscape as he strode down the ramp leaving the others to release the chained vehicles onboard. One of the stationed soldiers saluted at his approach, recognising Stats' rank by the gold insignia on his lapel, the saluting soldiers uniform bore a lower ranked red insignia. Stats followed protocol and saluted back as his feet made contact with the weathered wooden beams. "Good morning sir." The soldier welcomed Stats returning his arm to his side stiffly.

"Morning soldier, at ease." Stats absently replied and continued past the small welcoming party and onwards over the jetty until he reached the solid ground of the track beyond and stood to one side awaiting the disembarkation of the first vehicle. He peered down the route the track took trying to make out what lay beyond but the dense forest there obscured his vision, towering bamboos mingled with the oranges and reds of the broad leafed autumnal trees. A small brown spotted snake slithered for cover, disturbed from its basking in the sun at Stats' arrival, he watched its retreat, its reptilian grace captivating him, the wonders of nature had never ceased to amaze him. His attention was drawn back to the catamaran as the engine of the first vehicle turned over and burst into life. A militia member stood on the ramp guiding back the driver as he slowly reversed onto the jetty, once there the gesticulating soldier stood aside allowing the four by four ample room to continue. Once on the track beyond the driver deftly did a one hundred and eighty degree turn before halting awaiting Stats to board. He opened the front passenger door and leapt into the empty seat, he nodded a greeting at the driver and closed the door behind him and without a word the driver selected a gear and followed the dirt track into the forest.

The journey took about twenty minutes, Stats bracing himself periodically as the vehicle navigated the deeper ruts, their depths hidden by the muddied waters that had collected there forming small pools. The vegetation was dense on both sides and insects flew across the pathway ahead disappearing once again into the lush shrubbery on either side, beams of sunlight burst through the trees periodically lighting up the dirt road ahead with bright golden beams. Within a short period of time the narrow track opened up into a large grassy site its surface heavily scored by tyre tracks, another off road vehicle lay parked to the left of the clearing and to the right a large operations tent had been pitched, two soldiers stationed on either side of the entrance. Beyond this clearing lay another area separated by a single row of eucalyptus trees, a helicopter sat immobile at its centre. Stats' driver pulled in alongside the parked vehicle and engaged the handbrake before turning off the ignition. He opened the door and stepped outside at once aware of the humid atmosphere here away from the cooling coastal air, the abundance of plant life here maintaining a warmer, moist environment. Taking a deep breath he turned about and headed in the direction of the tent aiming for the open entrance, ignoring the soldiers posted there. "Szebrowski, it's been a while," Stats coldly acknowledged his second in command as he entered the tents cool interior.

"Yes indeed it has Stats, what about eight or nine years ago since the last of the Shifter cleansings?"

"Yeah gotta be about that and what have you been up to since then?"

"Just doin' my job Stats, serving the Hand of God an' following orders." Came the equally cold reply, Szebrowski's eyes bored into Stats searching for a chink in his armour a weakness from which to gain an advantage over his old adversary. Stats had never taken to Szebrowski, he'd always been a little bit too willing to follow his masters orders unquestioningly, reguardless of the consequences and during those cleansings of years ago Stats had bore witness to his blood thirsty nature, taking perverse pleasure in the torture and murder of the evolved humans their masters had sent them to eradicate. A man who could not be trusted and Stats had made a mental note never to have his back turned to this one when out in the field as he was sure Szebrowski had had his orders reguarding Stats' "retirement."

The Hand Of God

"Yeah and here we are again following orders, this time a Witch hunt, who'd have thought it, this should be very interesting." Stats' attention left that of his nemesis as he took in the others inhabiting the tent, half a dozen militia stood to one side, automatic rifles slung over their shoulders, a table was set up in the middle of the space a large detailed map unfolded on its surface. Szebrowski's enthusiasm for the up and coming mission was plainly visible. At the mention of the ensuing Witch hunt his eyes had sparkled filled with glee and murder no doubt as he repositioned himself at the table and indicated a small red circle on the map, his attention to Stats averted temporarily.

"Yes it should be very interesting," he agreed. "The science team and the Nefarious have narrowed down the location of the Witch to about a twenty mile square area. We're here," he pointed to a circle that showed their current position. Stats made his way around the table and joined Szebrowski as he examined the map. "They're pretty certain she's hiding out in this valley here." Stats followed his finger as it traced a line from the circle into a river valley not too far from their current position. "The terrains not suitable for vehicles so we're on foot from here on in. Two teams will be deployed, one each side of the river." Szebrowski pointed out the meandering blue line that passed close by to the militia camp site before meeting the ocean beyond. "Four men per team, we've been issued with two-way radios so we can remain in contact at all times" "Eight of us do you think that's sufficient? I've heard these Witches can be quite a handful."

"According to information received this one's weak, they reckon the energy she must've consumed maintaining her invisibility all these years has left her seriously depleted so she shouldn't be too much trouble." Szebrowski's attention once again returned to Stats trying to gauge his reaction in response to his own greater knowledge of the mission but Stats remained impassive not giving anything away.

"Good, good should be quite routine then," he beamed at his second in command which unsettled Szebrowski considerably.

"Yes quite but we should exercise caution though 'cos

you never know eh Stats?" Szebrowski averted his stare the infliction in the comment wasn't missed by Stats as his second in command attempted to tip the scales once more in his favour.

"Yeah wouldn't want to catch a stray bullet now would we, eh?" Stats added jovially. "So when do we depart?"

"Immediately, we were only awaiting your arrival." Szebrowski appeared a bit perplexed at Stats' buoyant mood.

"Well then let's get kitted up shall we I'm itching to get this over with." His pale blue eyes narrowed and he smiled humourlessly at Szebrowski before examining the map once more, committing the immediate area to memory. As Szebrowski seemed to have the heads up on this mission at least the forest through which their route would lead them would offer him some sort of cover from which to steal an advantage.

Aleshia's arrival on the outlands had been an altogether different affair from Stats' own. She now stared solemnly through the mud splattered window of the off roader as they made their way through the civilian encampment, which began from almost the point at which the catamaran was now berthed, stretching for about a mile along the coast and about half a mile inland. The route they took,carrying Aleshia and three other militia members, bisected the depressing scene outside. Pale, unhealthy faces peered up at them as they passed through, their limbs emaciated and malnourished. Aleshia's gaze scanned the seemingly endless town of grey tents pitched in the brown mud churned by the trudging of feet over many years. Nothing grew here except fear and loathing for their suppressors. She guiltily averted her eyes as she became aware of one particularly grimy looking child as she caught her eye as she stood at the side of the track, her pleadings for help going unanswered as the vehicle continued unchecked. As she was seated upfront she focused her attention up ahead, averting her gaze following the meandering trail through the shanty town and beyond into the city. Aleshia and her team of six, the others following the lead vehicle in a black military van which also contained the necessary equipment and weaponry needed for the mission. They were to be dropped at the point at which the Porter had

The Hand Of God

been last reported, presumably at the plaza site from which Stats had been air lifted from only the day before. The journey across the camp had been quiet and somewhat tense, the cloying atmosphere filled the interior of the four by four and Aleshia was glad as they finally left the miserable environment behind them and entered the ruined city beyond, she pressed the button that opened her window allowing a two inch gap to appear. The fresh air flooded in and she breathed deeply of it cleansing her head and her thoughts and focused on the task ahead.

A couple of hours had quickly passed by since leaving the relative safety of the woodlands behind them. Eve's initial enthusiasm at natures many wonders she'd encountered along the way had slowly dwindled as they trudged through the long grasses, hidden rocks and twisted exposed roots a constant hazard. Her thin frame was weakened and she was noticeably exhausted as a result of the many miles they'd covered. "Hey Mac!" Canova called waving him to a halt as he looked back, catching up with him he continued. "How long till will reach our campsite? Eve's exhausted an' I could do with a rest myself." The four had now regrouped. Mac looked down at Eve, she looked tired and about ready to keel over.

"Yeah well we've made good time today that's for sure, looks like maybe an hour or so of daylight left anyway." Mac cast his eyes over the landscape ahead. "'Bout half a mile to go till we reach that cluster of trees, give us a bit of cover for tonight at least. You okay kid? We ain't got far to go now." Eve smiled up at him somewhat forlornly.

"Hey it's not far to go now I'll carry you the rest of the way." Canova offered, she nodded tiredly and he knelt down allowing her to climb aboard.

"You okay?" Mac asked Canova as he stood up bearing the fatigued Eve.

"Yeah sure I'll be fine it's not far anyway." Mac nodded and they set off once again, the only sounds the rustling of grasses, the occasional snapping of a twig or branch underfoot and the chirruping of unseen insects. Nobody spoke for the rest of the journey and they reached the trio of trees Mac had located in no time at all. Relieved, Canova set Eve down and she immediately repositioned herself at the foot of the largest tree its canopy a shimmering golden red. Resting her back against the smooth, mottled trunk she closed her eyes retracting her hands into the sleeves of her jumper for warmth. The largest tree offered a wide canopy thirty or forty feet above their heads, the other two barely half the height sat on the periphery of the others shadow providing good camouflage from any aerial surveillance. The grasses here were far shorter, the roots of the trees showing above ground here and there restricting the growth of the other low lying plants. Nisa had carefully chosen where to lay out the blanket, an area that offered most cover from above and where the ground wasn't too even. The sun was low in the sky by now and it would be dark soon or at least as dark as the full moon would allow.

"You okay Nis?" Mac sounded concerned as he noticed her features etched with worry.

"Yeah. Well no not really I just got a bad feeling that's all." Her green eyes looked troubled as she took in their surroundings trying to calculate the best route of evacuation should they be tracked down. Eve had made her way to the blanket at seeing it laid out as she opened one eye and lay down, Canova was already seated there and was rummaging through what remained of the supplies when Nisa and Mac finally joined them.

"Hey guys what's happening?" Canova asked as he looked up his examination of the hold alls contents pausing momentarily as he took in their worried faces.

"It's probably nothing I just don't like being out in the open like this. I'll be far more relaxed when we make it into the forest in that mountain valley." She was looking ahead to where the dark green of the forest ahead split the mountain range in two forming the valley which they were aiming for.

"Only take us half a day or so to get there but we gotta rest up first even if we just hole up here for a few hours we could probably cover the distance tonight, with the full moon out it's gonna be like travelling in daylight anyway." Mac suggested looking from Nisa to Canova.

"Yeah that sounds good to me I just don't feel safe here," Nisa voiced. Canova looked over at Eve who had already

The Hand Of God

dozed off before adding his own opinion.

"Sounds good to me too but we gotta let her get some rest just in case we run into trouble and need to get outta there fast if you know what I mean?" He looked meaningfully at the others, Mac nodded understanding what Canova meant.

"Okay agreed then, we rest up here for a few hours then we head off and if we time it right we could probably make it before dawn." The other two nodded in accord and they made themselves comfortable as they laid out some provisions in preparation to eat.

12

The rest of Aleshia's journey through the desolate city had passed quickly enough the silence within the vehicle between the occupants was palpable and she couldn't wait to escape their company. The vehicle finally reached its destination now caked in mud and off loaded its occupants on arriving at the open plaza. The operations tent still remained on site and a helicopter sat prepped and ready to go, no time was to be wasted on this mission. Two teams had been assigned to this operation, one was to follow on foot the other, led by Aleshia, were to board the helicopter and sight and engage the fugitives from the air. The weapons were summarily issued from the back of the now stationary van, a dart rifle replaced the usual semi-automatic Aleshia usually carried her DNA encoded to the weapon via a small pad to the right of the trigger enabling her the sole use of the gun. Only the side arm she still carried in her holster offered her a little comfort at least, the tranquiliser darts she carried in a pouch attached to her belt, twelve in all, would take approximately twenty to thirty seconds to render her targets unconscious she was informed. Finally her team boarded the helicopter, the pilot and co-pilot already on board. Once strapped in and the door secured the rotar blades hummed into life gathering momentum. Well this was it Aleshia thought to herself and as yet she had no idea how to handle the situation ahead. Should she attempt to make contact with the fugitives? But her present company would make that almost impossible, or did she bide her time and take out her colleagues and pursue them herself, at least she'd have several hours ahead of the ground team. Maybe she stood a chance if the pilot dropped them in the field, that'd just leave her the other three soldiers to deal with. She casually took in her comrades as the helicopter finally took off. She didn't know them, two burly looking males sat opposite eyeing her up and down, one smiled luridly at her and she averted her gaze. The Afro-American female beside her sat with her eyes shut her ma-

The Hand Of God

chine gun cradled in her lap which worried Aleshia further as the others also carried machine guns, she was the sole possessor of a dart gun. She was aware of the larger of the two males nudging his companion and laughing as they continued to check out their commanding officer. "Is there a problem soldier?" She coldly asked, her eyes narrowing into a cold stare her jaw clenched.

"No lieutenant no problem here," came the reply the smile still remaining on his dry cracked lips, his mate shook his head in agreement his mind also lingering on other things as he continued to stare unwaveringly in her direction. Well that was her mind made up she sure as hell wouldn't lose any sleep over taking those two idiots out and as for sleeping beauty beside her, Aleshia looked at her again out of the corner of her eye and she caught her doing the same slowly shutting it again as their gaze met returning to her dark thoughts. Well the end game was in sight now and what was one more life amidst the many she'd ended over the years. The atmosphere onboard was one of intimidation, the two letching grunts opposite and the ominous calm of her third team mate unnerved her somewhat. It was them or her she concluded, she wasn't making it back to Heaven alive unless she employed some drastic measures. She took her mind outside the oppressive confines of the helicopter and took in the scene that passed below through the small port-hole window. She craned her neck slightly to get a better view and took in the scene of stone and twisted metal of the once inhabited city eventually giving way to the invading vegetation, a distant mountain range dominated the view ahead. Aleshia scrutinised the scenery below, she had to get herself and her team onto solid ground and get rid of the chopper and its crew before she could make her move. The rolling greenery below became denser obscuring her vision and they soon passed over a large stretch of woodland, presumably the escape route the others had taken in their bid for freedom offering them cover from the ensuing hunt. Obviously the pilot had received his orders as he continued unfalteringly on his flight path, probably intending to drop them further ahead on the ground, her team covering the area between them and the team deployed on foot back at the plaza in case the fugitives remained hidden amongst the trees below. Crossing the woodlands in only a few minutes the trees thinning the land opened up into a large grassy savannah peppered with solitary or small groups of shrubs and trees and amidst this what appeared to be a trail of some kind. The crushed and broken grasses easily visible from this elevation as it wound further into the wilderness below. Could've been made by animals but her instincts told her otherwise. She unbuckled her seat belt and ignoring the lewd pair of guerillas leant forward and rapped her knuckles hard on the window that partitioned the cockpit from where they sat. The co-pilot turned around in response and Aleshia indicated the trail below and gestured that her team should disembark here. The co-pilot looked out of his side window at her request and he registered the trail below, he returned his attention to Aleshia and gave her a thumbs up and voiced something unintelligible to the pilot who slowed the progress of the helicopter in response until it hovered steadily above the ground the grasses below almost horizontal with the force of the downdraft. Aleshia pulled open the sliding door and fed a nylon rope through the opening from a reel attached to the ceiling there, its blue length quickly reaching ground level. She then attached a hand held alloy brake to the rope and secured it firmly before raising her voice above the beat of the rotar blades and shouted to her team mates.

"Well what the fuck are you waiting for? MOVE!" And with that she firmly grasped the straps on the brake and stepped from the confines of the helicopter, the hand held brake taking her gently to the ground where she hurriedly removed them discarding them in the long grass and unholstered her side arm as she stepped aside out of the immediate vicinity of the downdraft and awaited her team, at least now it was just them and her, she just had to be patient now and cautious she couldn't afford to give them the upper hand, they had her out numbered and they had more fire power. The sun wouldn't be long in setting she noted, she'd wait till then before making her move. Once on solid ground again Aleshia had taken command of the situation ordering the two guerillas up ahead of her one either side of the trail, she followed her fire arm primed and ready for use. The

The Hand Of God

third member of her team remained at her rear which unnerved her as they continued on in silence.

Mac had volunteered himself to take first watch after their light snack making sure they had enough provisions left for at least the following day and Eve who had slept on through their meal. Canova stretched out sleepily beside her while Nisa accompanied Mac, her mind too uneasy too rest. "Got a strong feelin' they're onto us," she voiced her fears as she stood at Mac's side out of earshot of the other two.

"Yeah for sure that trail we made is gonna lead those fuckers right to us, Canova an' Eve could probably get us out of a tight spot if we need to leave quick but the kids exhausted and I doubt whether she could 'port all four of us outta here."

"I know I thought the same. There's too much cover for them to hide in out here. Our best chance is to try stay one step ahead of them at least until we reach that valley, plenty of cover there for us to ambush them."

"Totally. Give 'em a couple more hours then I'd feel better if we got goin' as well." He looked over at Nisa and she could tell by the look in his pale grey eyes that he was just as anxious as she was. Suddenly Mac turned his head slightly his focus tuning to something unseen.

"What is it Mac?" Nisa was uneasy at his reaction, he held up his hand hushing her into silence as he strained his hearing, his eyes pierced the distance behind them that they'd recently covered until his evolved sight sought out that which his hearing had picked up.

"Can you see it Nis?" He whispered unnecessarily. "Right out there just above the woodland." He pointed, his fingertip touching the small fly speck dot that hovered in the darkening sky. Nisa screwed up her eyes and followed the line of Mac's chunky digit.

"Yeah just, gotta be a chopper, doesn't seem to be gettin' any bigger though."

"No its hovering, off loading a hunting party no doubt must've spotted our trail. We'd better wake the others an' get movin' we can't afford to let 'em catch up."

"Let's look at our options first." Nisa deliberated. "A chopper holds how many? Half a dozen max." Mac nodded in agreement. "We make our move for those mountains and we put ourselves in full view there's not much cover out there, or we sit an' wait on them arriving, ambush them here it'd be the last thing they'd expect right?" Mac was thoughtful for a moment as he considered their options.

"Okay you've got a point only thing is if that chopper continues on the same flight path the pilots gonna see our trail ends right here and then we're fucked!" He shrugged apologetically at his bluntness.

"Unless we make a fake trial leading outta here throw them off the scent a bit, what d'ya think?"

"Okay reckon that might work." Mac nodded slowly warming to the idea. "You wake the others an' I'll get stomping us a new trail 'cos that choppers gonna be over here in no time at all."

"Okay Mac but don't be long 'cos I'm gonna need you here."

"You got it!" And with a mischievous grin and a twinkle in his eye he set off at full pelt calling upon his inhuman stamina for the job at hand. Nisa watched as he entered the long grass on the other side of their hide out as his large bulk created a fake trail, his figure soon obscured by the mass of vegetation. Nisa returned to the sleeping pair, well their confrontation with the Hand of God was upon them sooner than they'd anticipated she just hoped their ruse would work.

13

The last Witch hunt had finally commenced. Stats, his second in command Szebrowski and half a dozen militia had been joined by three Nefarious that had later disembarked from the moored catamaran much to Stats' surprise, for them to venture abroad during daylight hours was a rare occurrence indeed and reiterated how important this mission was to Nekros and his horde. The three were smartly attired, as were all their kind but their physical appearance retained little of what was once human about them. The trio were ghostly pale and gaunt the solitary female still retained a few gossamer threads of hair on her scalp which in Stats's opinion made her appearance all the more frightful but the three of them all had Nekros's eyes, black and unforgiving, reflecting no sunlight they seemed to absorb any traces of light consuming it completely.

The Hand of God team all gave them a wide berth as they headed off into the forest, initially following a rutted partially overgrown track visible between the fallen leaves before it blended completely with its surroundings. Stats eased off his pace allowing the other militia to overtake him but Szebrowski slowed down as well keeping a close watch on him, annoyingly, disturbing his thoughts. He could've easily unslung his weapon and mown them all down in their tracks but the lightness of the weapon he'd been issued with had confirmed his worst fears, his machine gun was unloaded but he kept that knowledge to himself although he knew Szebrowski was aware of how defenceless he was, only his hand gun was fully loaded and operational as he carried it on his person at all times. The ground underfoot became a carpet of dead golden brown leaves and rotten wood, the musty scent of the decaying vegetation filled his nostrils as they continued to tramp through the undergrowth. The Nefarious led the way and had commenced to ascend a small incline that took them further into the valley, the sound of rushing water now reached his ears, the river indicated on the map couldn't be far away now. Stats was aware of his second in command holding a two-way radio which was attached to his breast pocket and pulling it closer to his mouth he depressed the communication button. "Pack two this is pack one are you receiving me? Over." He released the button and a few seconds of static broke the silence before the crackling reply came through the small speaker.

"Pack one this is pack two receiving you loud and clear over," came the disembodied reply.

"Pack two report your current position over."

"About ten minutes from designated location site over."

"Roger that pack two continue on your current heading and await visual contact do you receive? Over."

"Affirmative will await visual contact over and out." Szebrowski released the radio and grinned maliciously over at Stats obviously enjoying the show of authority he put on for Stats who cheerily waved back much to his annoyance. "Is there a problem Stats?"

"No not at all just enjoying the scenery." He grinned back.

"Well if that's the way you feel maybe it's about time to let some young blood get a bit of the action if you know what I mean?" He held his grin as he marched past Stats shouldering him out of the way. Stats was so tempted to shoot him there and then, his fingers toyed with his still holstered side arm but he was still in close proximity to the rest of the team who would clearly hear his gunshot. Instead he followed in Szebrowski's tracks, he'd just have to bide his time until he was nearer the Witch's location then he could make his move at least half of the militias contingent lay on the other side of the river he just hoped this elusive blue-skinned liberator was holed-up on his side of the water course or that could prove to be a major problem, although he was sure that the leading presence of the Nefarious on this side indicated that they were onto her scent so for now he'd just have to tag along. Several minutes later they caught up with the now regrouped team, the Nefarious were spread out a little distance ahead scanning the forest for any psychic residue left by the Witch. The river was clearly visible now and its waters churned into a white froth as it cascaded down

The Hand Of God

a series of rocky outcrops and visible on the other bank between the trunks of the trees was a pack of two which consisted of another half a dozen militia and two Nefarious their ghoulish countenance clearly visible in the forests shadows. Well that confirmed his theory he thought, only one of them over there so they must be positive the Witch was hiding out on this side of the river. Szebrowski made an exaggerated wave to the other team affirming visual contact which was received and reflected back by one of the soldiers. He then radioed further orders. "Okay pack two spread out and move upstream maintain radio silence unless you spot anything over."

"Roger that over and out." The short communication finished the two teams spread out in a line about thirty yards separating each soldier so they covered a wide area, there was no way she was going to slip this net Stats thought unless she had a good couple of tricks up her sleeve. Stats had taken the lead at this point following the Nefarious knowing his only chance would be if he positioned himself at the furthest point at the end of the line which he managed surreptitiously, Szebrowski falling in immediately to his left. The Nefarious had formed a wide arc ahead of the military line, nothing stood to his right except open woodland. He felt a bit more comfortable now he wasn't hemmed in and he had a good view from here as the ground sloped downwards towards the river bank, the slope to his right leading into the mountains above. The ground here was also a lot firmer underfoot the majority of the leaf litter and other debris having been washed further down the slope onto the flatter ground below by the rain allowing him the freedom to move more quickly if it was required of him. He glanced over at Szebrowski and gave him a mock salute, smiling. His second in command scowled back briefly before returning his attention to the task at hand just as his booted foot snagged a protruding tree root causing him to stumble before regaining his footing again. Stats smiled to himself.

"That'll teach ya prick!" He muttered under his breath.

Some time had passed by the two lines of soldiers continuing unfalteringly on their course. Stats had calculated they must've covered at least three to four miles but their passage was slowing now as the ground underfoot became more and more uneven. The tree species slowly changed, pines becoming the dominant inhabitants here, their roots clearly visible in places, pushed out into the open by the rocky ground that made up the valley. Stats had had to climb his way over several outcroppings of rock determined not to relinquish his advantage over the others and maintain his distance. Very little was apparent in the way of animal life here no doubt they'd hidden themselves away at the sight and sound of their presence or perhaps they sensed the loathsome Nefarious that headed their troupe, could probably smell them from a mile away that'd explain why they hadn't seen or heard even a bird since they'd entered the forest. He came to a standstill at a large slab of rock that protruded from the earth, its surface deeply fissured, eroded by years of rain and wind, the wall of stone split the forest in two, now was his chance. To the left the gentler slopes that led to the river's edge and the Hand of God and to the right a rocky obstacle course that led into the foot slopes of the mountain range. He quickly checked the status of his team their attention was focused ahead including Szebrowski's, his interest in Stats had faded somewhat as they'd trudged for miles through the forest. He hastily made a quick decision and dodged out of sight using the slab of rock to shield himself from the others. He removed the unloaded weapon from his shoulder and tossed it aside, the extra weight would only tire him out besides it was useless to him anyway. Then he deftly lept up onto a small ledge etched out of the rock and rapidly scaled the unearthed stone, its fractured surface allowing him good purchase as he urgently increased the distance between himself and pack one. Now if he could only overtake the hunters and locate the hunted before they did. He fixed his mind on that thought as he continued over the rocky landscape that unfolded before him.

14

Mac had returned to the others about forty minutes later having had to tunnel into the undisturbed shrubbery aside the trail he had created hiding himself from view as the helicopter passed overhead. He waited until the noise of its rotor blades were barely audible before finally breaking cover and making his way back to the relative safety of the canopy of trees. Nisa had woken Canova and Eve and hurriedly explained to them what was happening. Mac barely out of breath after his excursion squatted down beside the others. "Okay what's the plan then?" His excitement at the unavoidable clash was plainly obvious.

"Well..." She paused briefly as she looked at Canova for approval before continuing. "We thought the best thing to do would be to hide either side of that new trail you made Mac an' ambush them as they pass, not much of a plan I know but with our talents it shouldn't be too much of a problem."

"Reckon I can take 'em out as long as there ain't too many of 'em." Canova continued, Eve sat quietly at his side listening intently.

"Sounds good to me." Mac affirmed, he always liked the simple approach to any situation and with that he left the others and made his way to the edge of the clearing remaining crouched as he did so in case they detected his movements. Once in position his mutated vision refocused as he checked on the progress of the hunting party at their rear. He remained unmoved for several minutes before reporting back to his friends. "Looks like we're in luck, can only make out four of 'em, heavily armed though but they've made good progress they ain't too far away now. How close do you need to be before you can zap 'em?" He directed the question at Canova referring to his psychic abilities.

"Well as long as I can touch on their minds I don't think distance matters too much, visual contact definitely makes it easier though."

"Good at least we don't need to get too close then. Better

lettin' them pass through here first and we'll nail 'em on the other side of this clearing, we don't want any stragglers escaping eh?" He laughed amiably slapping Canova on the back sending him stumbling forward.

"Hey darlin' you okay?" Nisa crouched down beside Eve and put a comforting arm around her shoulders. "Everything'll be fine I promise." She smiled at the scared child flashing her chipped tooth and Eve grinned back encouraged.

"I know it'll be okay it's just that they're going to die that's all I just wish they didn't have to that's all it makes me sad." Her dark brown eyes looked deep into Nisa's own green ones and she drew her closer and gave her a big hug.

"I know darlin' and maybe one day all the fightin' and killin' will stop but until then we gotta be strong 'cos it's more than just our lives at stake." Nisa felt her nod as she buried her head into her chest and still hugging Eve she turned to Mac. "Well what's the set up an' how long we got?"

"Right Nis an' I we'll flank this fake trail. Canova, you an' Eve hide out in the grass just beyond this clearing an' keep your eye out for stragglers, if your covers blown I'm sure Eve can get the two of you out of trouble quick time. Once they've passed through and continued on the trail do your mind thing an' take out the rear two Nis an' I got the leaders covered, Okay?"

"Okay." Nisa and Canova voiced in unison, Eve silently nodded now resurfaced from Nisa's embrace.

"Okay people let's get into position, I reckon they'll be here in no more than twenty minutes at the rate they were covering ground." Mac informed them. Himself and Nisa then followed the recently made trail a short distance before secreting themselves in the undisturbed grasses on either side and lay silently in wait. Canova and Eve had taken cover behind a large leafy shrub, its green oval leaves tinged yellow, being careful not to disturb the grasses too much as they went, which was situated about twenty feet from the previous trail and the clearing. Canova had a good view from between the leaves of the bush as they patiently awaited the arrival of the Hand of God.

Aleshia and her team had made swift progress as they

The Hand Of God

jogged along the readymade trail and as they approached the clearing ahead she signaled to the others to slow up. She had to split them up if she was to stand a chance so thinking fast she silently gesticulated to the two guerillas ahead that they should circumnavigate the small copse ahead and meet up on the other side. The two soldiers signaled their understanding and headed off in two separate directions, surprisingly quietly considering their size. Aleshia then unslung her tranquiliser gun and removed a red feathered dart from the pouch at her belt, broke open the gun and removed the protective cover from the hypodermic needle on the dart and loaded it firmly in place. She watched as the two soldiers slowly disappeared from view as they skirted the clearing ahead before turning round to confront the female who'd shadowed her since leaving the confines of the helicopter. Fortunately her attention had been detracted as she followed the progress of her two companions taking her a few seconds to realise what had happened the surprise registering on her face as she pulled out the dart that had lodged itself in her chest, its liquid cargo now deployed. The dart slipped from her fingers as the drug took affect her free hand attempting to brandish her own weapon in Aleshia's direction but it was too late as the butt of Aleshia's own gun struck her firmly in the face sending her drugged team mate to the ground. She raised her head briefly trying desperately to fight the effects of the drug but to no avail, blood oozed from the cut to her forehead as she slumped back unconscious, her eyes flickered momentarily before they came to rest. Right one down two to go she thought and hurriedly reloaded her dart gun before continuing down the trail into the clearing ahead.

Canova wasn't quite sure what he'd just witnessed from his leafy hide out although the moon was fully out now the scene that had unfolded before him was partially obscured by the long grass. Himself and Eve had held their breath as the other militia had skirted past their hiding place as they made their way around the clearing, once they were at a safe distance Canova had returned is attention to the two remaining figures, a sound like compressed air escaping had broken the silence and then it seemed as if one of the soldiers had struck the other one who went down and didn't come back into view. Strange he thought his eyes fixed unwaveringly on the remaining female soldier as she resumed her course.

Mac and Nisa were now aware of the approaching two guerillas as they rounded the copse, not as they had predicted through the clearing but through the long grasses that surrounded it. The two friends began to crawl commando style through the vegetation careful not to disturb the long stalks too much and give away their position. Once better positioned to intercept the unwary militia they stilled their movements once more. The unsuspecting soldiers passed close by to their hidden assailants by only a few feet and when they could see their backs Mac and Nisa sprung from where they lay almost simultaneously. Nisa's organic stilettos protruded before she plunged one set deeply into the man's neck the other set found his heart. Mac had grabbed the other in a massive bear hug before he could bear arms and with a large intake of breath Mac tensed his muscles and exerted his steel like grip on the trapped man, the guerillas strength was no match against Mac's evolved biology. Mac's veins bulged in his neck as he squeezed the life out of the soldier as he tried to wriggle free in vain. His struggles became weaker succumbing to the greater strength, slowly constricted his strength finally sapped and an internal cracking indicated the breaking of his ribcage. Mac finally released him from his deadly embrace as he felt his enemy go limp and he toppled forward, dead. Nisa reached Mac's side and punched him playfully on the arm. "When your quite finished cuddling up we'd better check on the others." She peered down at the crushed remains of the soldier huddled up in the grass.

Canova had whispered to Eve to remain where she was as he tailed the remaining militia member, his stalking skills left a lot to be desired and Aleshia aware of his presence swung round suddenly covering him with the dart gun its muzzle aimed directly at his chest. "Whoa don't shoot!" He blurted out trying to gain himself a vital few seconds in which to conjure up a psychic energy bolt.

"Don't move!" She commanded. Canova complied his hands raised in surrender as he felt the swirl of energy build in his head but much to his dismay he witnessed her finger

The Hand Of God

pulling back on the trigger as she pulled the gun slightly to his right. He flinched involuntarily at the sound of compressed air escaping before realising that she hadn't been aiming at him at all. She lowered her weapon as he lowered his arms and made her way over to where he stood. "You alright?" She asked.

"Eh yeah I'm okay," he replied somewhat confused, "who the hell are you an' what the fuck was that all about?" He'd regained his composure and could feel his anger building.

"My colleague over there turned out to be a tough little bitch, thought one dart would be enough to put her out, you were lucky I noticed the grass moving behind you 'cos the weapon she's carrying ain't as forgiving as this one." She smiled at Canova patting the dart gun she still brandished. "I'm Aleshia by the way."

"Canova," he introduced himself still bewildered at the events that had just unfolded. He waved to someone who was approaching from Aleshia's rear. "It's okay," he called out, "we're fine she saved my life seems like she's on our side." His dark grey eyes examined Aleshia. "You are on our side aren't you?" He asked still suspicious.

"I am now," she answered turning to see who was approaching from behind and by the looks of Mac and Nisa she had no need to worry about the remaining two militia. She turned back to Canova to find Eve standing close by his side her brown eyes staring up at her. "And you must be what all the fuss is about, I got to admit I never expected a child though!."

15

"Stats you son of a bitch!" Szebrowski spat through clenched teeth, a few strands of saliva escaped his quivering lips and lay glistening on his chin. He gestured with an upraised arm to the soldier immediately to his left. The signal was then passed down the line until each member of the team had halted. Captain Kochev Szebrowski, a twenty seven year old power hungry individual of Polish descent, whose servitude to the Hand of God and the Nefarious knew no bounds. He'd harbored a deep rooted hatred of Stats for many years, jealous of his position within the Hand of God and the respect that he commanded over his fellow soldiers. This hadn't gone unnoticed by Nekros and he had been the obvious choice to lead the current mission, to seek and destroy the Witch and "retire" Stats, who had managed to slip the net much to Szebrowski's annoyance, his complexion flushed red with anger his eyes squeezed tightly shut as he attempted to control his rage. He steadied himself with several deep calming breaths before slowly speaking into his two way radio. "Pack two this is pack one do you receive me? Over."

"Pack two receiving you over." Came the staccato response.

"Take five pack two until you receive further orders we've encountered a slight problem over here."

"Roger that over an out." The message conveyed Szebrowski clenched both his fists tightly, several of his finger joints cracking loudly as he did so. Stats hadn't escaped him yet but he'd better let the Nefarious know the situation, unless they were already aware of the missing officer. He reluctantly made his way towards the three spooks who had unerringly halted a little distance ahead as his men held their line. He aimed for the nearest of the trio, the female, typically the one that freaked him out the most. Once within about ten feet of his target she spun around suddenly her quick movement stopped him in his tracks. A cold invisible hand touched his mind and he instantly recoiled but the psychic fingers were persistent and they grasped him tighter in their grip, their icy chill numbing his senses. Her head cocked to one side like a hound tuning into some high pitched frequency inaudible to human ears. She appeared to be smiling her broken teeth showing between thin, cracked lips. Her loathsome mind continued its exploration of his memories her psychic touch like that of some diseased, sick pathologist. Suddenly he felt her relinquish her embrace, his heaving mind gasping for breath once released his brow beaded with sweat. He noticed her attention was now directed toward the other two Nefarious who held their position further ahead to her left in the dark forest, the pale luminosity of their death head faces easily discernable in the gloom. They remained that way unmoving for several minutes communicating silently amongst themselves before the female broke the contact and nonchalantly walked past him completely oblivious to his presence. Szebrowski having now regained his poise stood aside as she passed closely by, her footfalls so light she barely left an imprint amongst the litter in her wake. He watched her progress as she returned from the direction from which they'd just come, ordered to pick up on Stats' scent and hunt him down no doubt.

Progress had been good, the rugged terrain he'd navigated had put him in mind of his years of training when he'd first been enrolled into the Hand of God. He'd enjoyed those times, the only thing that marred those memories now was the realisation of what he was being trained for. He'd been on the run now for about an hour or so, it was dark now and if he hadn't already been missed then surely they would miss his company any time now. Szebrowski was probably on his tail right now hoping for a clear shot at his back down the sights of his rifle. This thought spurred him on faster. The rocky ground leveled out up ahead forming a plateau that overlooked the valley below. From there he'd have a bird's eye view of the river, not massive in breadth but wide enough to require a boat or bridge to reach the opposite bank safely. The drop from the plateau was steep, the incline studded with pine trees and occasional boulders. He squatted down, resting for a moment deciding on his next plan of action. He must've covered a couple of miles by now. So he must be nearing his goal he thought she couldn't be far away now. Well if these Witches did possess supernatural powers then maybe she could sense him and could maybe help guide him in. He formed the thought clearly in his mind hoping that she'd pick up on his thoughts because right now he didn't know what else to do. He stood up invigorated by a second wind and he popped the cap on a small rubber tube that protruded from his right breast pocket and sucked up a little liquid from the pouch there moistening his dry mouth. He resealed the tube before continuing onwards at a more leisurely pace conserving his energy. He had to reach her first, he knew she was close by now he could feel it.

16

Nekros's clawed hand stroked the sparse soft down on the head of the cuddly toy belonging to Eve in mock affection. His mind seethed, his rancid breath ragged and labored. Not only had Field Commander Kars Station abandoned his post but contact had been lost with the team assigned to the retrieval of the Porter. His hold on the bear intensified as did his wrath, its one remaining eye stared unflinchingly into his own bottomless sockets, mocking him. Grey bubbles of saliva bubbled at the corners of his mouth. The hive mind had reported the disappearance of Field Commander Station only minutes earlier and the Nefarious had felt his fury in repose, the mind of the Nefarious spreading his disappointment infecting them all with his ire. Nekros floated towards the elevator doors situated to the rear of his darkened office, the shadows there hiding it from view. The doors allowed him immediate access and he floated into the dark coffin like interior still clutching the stuffed toy, the door sealing itself shut once again as the lift descended. Yes someone would have to pay for this incompetence, someone always had to pay. He had an uncontrollable need to vent his anger, the darkness that dwelt in his heart burst forth expanding within him, consuming him completely. His body began to twitch spasmodically as the feeling seeped forth. The elevator doors opened onto a long corridor dimly lit by subdued red lighting. As soon as the first chink appeared between the elevator doors the screams of the damned could be heard, at the sound of their suffering Nekros's deathly visage lit up at the pitiful cries for help. Eve's Charley bear fell forgotten to the floor of the lift freed from Nekros's clawed hand, an evil smile played on his death mask face as he glided free of the elevator. He tapped his broken, blackened nails together as he held his hands together as if in prayer as he selected a door. It opened obediently and the screams that emanated from within increased in volume as the cretinous phantom entered the cell, the door closing silently behind him leaving Nekros and his play thing isolated in the blinding darkness.

17

Stats stopped abruptly and turned his head to the side positioning his ear as best he could to listen behind him. He held his breath for several seconds as he listened intently. No, nothing but he was sure he'd heard a noise, probably some night creature he tried to convince himself but a cold shiver ran up his spine followed by a feeling of dread as the feeling reached his skull. The Nefarious, it had to be nothing else on earth could make him feel like that but so soon how the fuck had it caught up with him so fast. He increased his pace aware now that keeping quiet wouldn't aid his escape now that they'd picked up on his scent. The silvery full moon illuminated his pathway keeping him safe from unseen obstacles. He followed his instincts blindly almost as if some other intelligence was guiding him on his way. He was fully aware of the vile presence hunting him down now, he could almost feel the grabbing of spectral hands at his back grasping for purchase. Stats concentrated harder at the task at hand as he leapt over rocks, dodged trees and ducked under low branches. He could feel something else now, a warm pleasant sensation had pulsed into life within his chest, beating in time with his own heart. It had to be her she had to be really close now. He altered his course periodically as the pulse faded homing in on it again and adjusting his direction as the warm beat gained strength once more. Just follow your heart Stats he reiterated to himself, just follow your heart.

The two remaining Nefarious heading pack one had received some sort of psychic communication. They turned as one and stared up at a point in the mountains not too far ahead, the other of their kind must have located its quarry as Szebrowski and his team had continued further into the forest. Now they were moving again their delicate airy movements eerie in the moonlight. They had now altered their course and were heading in the direction their attention had been drawn too further up the slope. They'd obviously detected the missing Stats or possibly located the Witch but Szebrowski wasn't interested in her he had a score to settle with Stats. Field Commander Kochev Szebrowski, now that had a certain ring to it. He grinned to himself malevolently as he signaled to his men the change in direction before pursuing the Nefarious himself eager not to miss out on his bloody reunion with his old rival.

Aleshia had hurriedly explained her reason for being in her present situation to her cynical audience. She related her own and her friend Stats' position and their concerns reguarding the Hand of God and of their fears concerning humankinds future on this planet at the hands of the Nefarious. The others listening in silence Mac standing impassively his arms folded firmly across his chest unwilling to accept this strangers truths. The full moon had past its zenith now and time ticked by as Aleshia reiterated how important it was for them all that they join forces and find the Witch before the Hand of God hunted her down. Mac still remained unconvinced the scars he carried inside from the massacre Nisa and himself had escaped ran deep and as a result he found it hard putting his trust in others, especially the militia. It was Canova who spoke to the outsider first. "Well that's kinda what we already planned to do." And Canova related to Aleshia his recent dreams in which the mysterious Thalia had spoken to him which had led, in turn, to himself and his companions present set of circumstances. He felt he could trust her he could sense her honesty in her mind.

"So you know where she is? Don't you?" Aleshia asked of him excitedly.

"No not really I've mainly been workin' on instinct," he replied rather self consciously, "but what we do know is that she's hiding out in that mountain valley on the other side of these grasslands."

"Do you think we should be telling her all this? She could be a spy after all." Mac joined in the exchange still wary of the new comer, he'd already relinquished Aleshia of her side arm and had jammed it in his belt. Nisa voiced her concerns also.

"I'm with Mac how do we know we can trust you? Could be a trap set up by Nekros himself an' you the bait, know what I mean?" Nisa leant forward intending to intimidate Aleshia who remained unmoved by her act noticing as she did so her own height was about equal with that of her would be aggressor.

"As I've already explained, we, Stats and I, agreed that our only hope was to make contact with you, form an alliance, together we stand a chance against Nekros, however slim that chance might be but we've got to try." Aleshia paused turning from one face to the next, "or we're all fucked!" She concluded unable to find the right words that would convince the small assembly of her integrity. Mac rubbed his chin thoughtfully before asking.

"An' where's this Stats then?"

"He's out there right now in that mountain valley as we speak leading the Witch hunt but he knows that our only hope of survival is to protect that Witch from the Hand of God and he needs our help if he's to have any chance at all, we can't afford for the Nefarious to get there first." The urgency in her tone didn't go unnoticed by Canova who was slowly coming round to her.

"Hey guys I think she's telling the truth and besides an extra team member wouldn't go amiss it's not like we'd be going out of our way or anything." He looked to his companions awaiting the outcome.

"Yeah an' another mouth to feed." Mac muttered to himself, adding, "I don't know I still don't trust her." He curled up his lip as he gave Aleshia a sideways glance.

"Hey why would I take out a member of my own team? Doesn't that prove something at least?"

"Proves to me that you'd be willin' to do anything to win the approval of your real masters." Mac's eyes narrowed this time and the look on his face chilled Aleshia to the bone. During the exchange between Aleshia and Mac, Nisa had returned from her brief examination of the fallen soldier that lay on the trail. The female lay flat on her back, a red tail of cotton fibres protruded from a point between her eyes indicating where the tranquiliser dart had lodged itself, her eyes were wide and staring.

"Good shootin'." Nisa commented to Aleshia, "you're team mate ain't gonna be a threat to us no more that's for sure. Well we ain't got time to stand about all night arguing but...," she turned to Aleshia meaningfully, "if you put one foot outta place..." Nisa extended the digits on her right hand and drew one of the deadly blades across her own throat making quite sure Aleshia was perfectly aware of what would happen to her should she double-cross them.

"Fine, fine," Aleshia agreed relieved of at least achieving some sort of truce between them. "But we've got to move now, there's a militia squad further back on foot following your trail they can only be a couple of hours away at most."

"Okay then." Nisa picked up, "but if you're in with us," she bent forward her fingers still extended and teased at the silver Hand of God insignia attached to Aleshia's breast pocket, "then this has got to go!" And with one quick swipe she tore off the pocket and tossed it aside. "Okay?" She added slowly retracting her organic blades in full view of Aleshia making her fully aware of what she was capable of.

"Okay can we go now? Now that we're all friends!" Canova interrupted the show of intimidation, "and what do you think Eve? You've not said a word all this time, you think we can trust her?"

"Sure," she shrugged as she looked Aleshia up and down. Why did she get a cold feeling in the pit of her stomach that she knew this women from somewhere?

"Okay let's go then." Mac was getting agitated now, eager to be on the move again. "Ladies first!" He waved Aleshia ahead of him in mock politeness. Aleshia just shook her head and without rising to the bait she took the lead through the small copse and headed for the trail Mac had forged earlier. Mac quickly grabbed the hold all that contained the blanket and the last of their supplies before rejoining Nisa at Aleshia's back, followed by Eve and then Canova covering their rear. Aleshia turned to Mac as they entered the grassy savannah.

"Where are the bodies of the other two?" She asked.

"Why do you wanna know?" Was his gruff unhelpful reply.

"Because one of them was carrying a couple of grenades, could come in handy." Acting instantly on this information Mac quickly located the two dead militia, the second body giving up his prize.

"Got 'em," he called over brandishing the two grenades like two golden eggs. He dropped one into his own pocket before casually tossing the other over to Nisa who deftly caught it one handed and similarly stashed it on her person.

"I don't think we're going to make it in time." Aleshia voiced her fears as she scrutinised the panorama of grasslands that stretched out ahead of them before they even reached the forests that marked the beginning of the valley for which they sought. "Stats left this morning to join his team out in the field, they've had a good few hours head start, we need to be there now!" She scanned the faces of the others her eyes settling on Eve for a few seconds before finally remaining fixed on Canova's grey irises her dark eyes pleading.

"I don't know that's a helluva jump! An' there's five of us." He chewed his bottom lip anxiously as he spoke aware of the importance of Aleshia's silent request. He crouched down in front of Eve. "Hey what do you think? Think you can teleport us all the way over there? I know it's a lot to ask..." He tailed off reluctant to push the exhausted Eve beyond what she was capable of. She first looked up at Aleshia and then back at Canova, his dark grey eyes were full of concern and worry.

"Well I can at least try, if it means saving the Witch then I've got to try." She smiled at them both and took Canova's hand. "We have to join hands so I can pull you all through with me, that's how it worked the last time anyway." Eve made to sit down on the trail and one by one the others followed her lead forming a circle, each holding the hand of the person seated on either side. Aleshia finally completed the ring by taking Eve's small hand in her own, Eve shuddered involuntarily at her touch. Eve paused momentarily before taking a deep breath and closing her eyes. She immediately felt her spirit soar into the night sky, maybe it was the recent practice she'd had or the high emotional state she'd been in recently since the death of her parents that lent her talents power, either way she had found this disembodied state easier and easier to achieve each time. She sailed high above the grasslands towards the forested slopes of the mountain range. Her incorporeal self swooping low again as she reached the first of the great trees growing on the lower slopes, searching...

Mac tentatively opened one eye and cast it over his companions. He could distinctly make out Eve's eyes moving rapidly beneath her closed lids. Canova and Nisa sat cross-legged their eyes tightly shut. Aleshia's remained open and she cast Mac a sideways glance aware of his piercing gaze, he just winked at her playfully but was then distracted by a faint vibration passing through his massive frame like the distant tremors of an earthquake.

Eve's spirit was now passing through the forest itself, dodging the many tree trunks that blocked her passage, skillfully turning this way and that expertly finding her way like a hawk hot the heels of its prey. A passing thought occurred to Eve, could she just pass right through the solid wood of the towering pines themselves in her present ghost like state? She thought better of it and considering the importance of her mission decided not to take the chance. So she continued onwards through the forest avoiding the obstacles as she went. She sped up the incline and up and over the plateau re-entering the forest once again and there, at last, a figure just ahead, no she was sure she could make out two the distance between them closing rapidly. She was almost upon the nearest of the two, her shadow self slowing as she caught up with the first of them her feet touching the mat of browned pine needles underfoot. She gasped in shock as she recognised a member of the Nefarious, its thin haunting physique stopped suddenly in its tracks and spun around in her direction sensing her presence. Eve's eyes widened in response to her evil toothy grin, her arms outstretched as she bore down on her new quarry. Eve drew in another deep breath, her physical self condensing further as she did so, as did the hands she still held drawing her friends to the spot on which she now stood. The female ghoul stopped only feet away from Eve as she became aware of the four adults materialising before her the surprise evident on her cadaverous features. On fully solidifying Nisa released her hands from the grips of her fellow travellers and covered the distance between herself and the lone Nefarious in two strides and in one swift action raised her scarred right hand and extended her killing blades as she aimed straight for the spectral visage before her. The razored tips pierced its skull effortlessly, her black blood oozed and bubbled from the puncture wounds when Nisa hastily withdrew her digits. The Nefarious twitched and jerked a few times, the vile black blood trailed down her face in thick globules as it exited the perforations in her face, one ebony eye foamed as its putrid contents leaked out burst by one of Nisa's lethal points. Finally the creature went rigid and fell forward lifeless, Nisa stepped nimbly aside avoiding the ghoul as she fell. She then stooped over the Nefarious and wiped the foul residue that clung to her fingertips on the dead things suit, the disgust on her face evident as she did so. Standing again she gave the carcass a solid kick and stepped back into line with the others, Canova breaking the ensuing silence.

"Well one thing's for sure we ain't gonna get back out of here in a hurry!" He looked down at the unconscious Eve as she lay slumped in his arms caught there by himself as she had passed out, the strain of the recent jump had obviously been too much for her. Mac voiced what Canova himself had been thinking.

"Shit must've been too much for her, poor kid, she is still alive right?"

"Yeah she's still alive," Aleshia reassured the others, "I can see the pulse in her neck but its weak from bringing us all through but we can't hang about 'cos we don't know how many more of those there are." She nodded towards the corpse stretched out before them.

Stats dared a backwards glance, his efforts increased as he saw the pale form of the Nefarious bearing down on him, he just couldn't seem to outrun it and the gap was closing fast. Dare he risk firing a shot? But decided to leave that as a last resort he didn't want to alert the rest of the team as to his whereabouts and he didn't fancy his chances against seven heavily armed militia. So he focused all his energy on evading his tireless pursuer. The comforting feeling that inhabited his chest now was strong and looking ahead he spotted a rocky outcrop up ahead atop a slight incline, the darkness at the foot of the rocky protuberance above suggested that of a hidden cave, that had to be it, the warm pulse in his chest glowed in confirmation of his speculation and he sped in that direction. He cast a quick glance back trying to keep track of his demonic stalker. Strange he thought, it looked like his hunter had stopped as the distance between itself and Stats had increased, still whatever reason had distracted the Nefarious it was to his advantage and without slowing his pace he pushed himself up the incline towards the rocky cliff above.

18

Mac had alleviated Canova of the still unconscious Eve, swapping him for the two hold alls he carried, Canova slinging one over each shoulder, Mac taking the lead as they ran through the forest. The brightness of the full moon combined with his own excellent night vision gave Mac a massive advantage over the others who pursued him single file through the grove. Nisa ensuring that their new addition remained in front of her in plain sight, Aleshia hadn't gained her trust yet. "There's someone up ahead." Mac called back clutching Eve tightly to his chest protecting her from being shaken up too badly in her current state. Aleshia who was right at his back answered first.

"Who? Can you make them out?"

"Wearin' a black uniform if that helps? They're headin' up that incline up ahead on the left, looks like there might be a cave up there."

"She's gotta be hiding out in there, shit they've found her!." Even Aleshia was impressed by Mac's seemingly undiminishable stamina as he pulled away from her and began pounding up the slope ahead, the gap between him and the soldier dwindling with each step. Nisa had slowed her pace keeping Canova close by, aware of her actions he breathlessly voiced as much.

"Hey Nisa don't hang back on my account you gotta make sure they don't get to Thalia first, you gotta protect her I can take care of myself," and he tapped his head with a forefinger his grey eyes glinting magically. Realising that he could do just that she gave him a thumbs up and sprinted ahead her long athletic legs covering the ground twice as quickly as Canova could've managed. Realising also that the fate of Thalia now rested in the hands of his new friends, relying on them to protect her from the enclosing Hand of God he slowed his gait regaining his breath as he did so.

Mac continued to thunder up the small hill, Aleshia had fallen some way back the soft ground of the incline slowing

The Hand Of God

her down, Nisa finally catching her up as she advanced up the slope. Mac confirmed the location of the cave as he rounded the top of the incline just in time to see the figure of the militia member being swallowed up by the shadows that lay there. Mac reached the entrance only moments later and kept to one side of the cave in case the soldier was armed. He carefully propped up the still unconscious Eve against the cold rock wall and was about to enter the dark confines of the cave and hunt down his prey when Nisa's head appeared over the crest, Aleshia several seconds behind her. As the two stepped onto the flat ground in front of the caves entrance a muffled voice emanated from the dark recesses of the cavern. Mac, eyebrows lowered into a frown, carefully peered around the corner his mutating retinas cutting through the darkness within but before he could locate the source of the voice it called out again louder this time.

"Aleshia? Is that you?" The call from within was far more coherent this time. Mac at once turned his attention to the teams latest addition suspicion etched into his features once again.

"Stats? That you?" Relief flooded over Aleshia as she recognised her friends voice. "It's okay he's my friend, the one I was telling you about," she called out to Mac before walking toward the entrance to the cave, running the short distance left between them as Stats, grimy and exhausted, re-emerged to greet her, his smile wide at the sight of her.

"Shit it's good to see you're okay!" He held her tightly, it had seemed like he hadn't seen his friend for weeks more than the day it actually had been, she returning the hug before they released each other, Stats aware of the strangers eyes watching him intently. "And your friends are?" He looked first from Nisa to Mac and back to Aleshia awaiting an introduction.

"That there's Mac and that's Nisa and this little girl is Eve, our elusive Porter."

"Wow I'd've never have thought it, she's just a kid," he exclaimed shocked before adding. "Is she okay?"

"I hope so she ported all five of us in here, the strain was too much for her weakened state. Reckon she just needs some rest and some food." Nisa spoke up from her position behind Aeshia.

"I hope so too," Stats agreed. "I take it I got one of you two to thank for getting that Nefarious fucker off my back?" He asked of Mac and Nisa.

"Yeah Nis did her good," Mac chortled proud to volunteer his companions deed.

"Well thanks for that, really thought that was gonna be the end of me!" He grinned amiably at his rescuers relieved at the sudden turn of events before frowning to himself as a thought occurred to him, "but you said there were five of you?" His query went unanswered as a gunshot rang out, the proximity of which sent them all sprawling into the dirt, the echo of the ricochet resounded in their ears as the bullet missed its target and struck the rock wall behind them. "Fucker!" Stats expleted.

"How many?" Mac asked calmly.

"Seven militia plus two more Nefarious."

"Better takin' cover inside the cave." Nisa suggested and stooping as to avoid becoming a target retrieved Eve and disappeared into the relative safety of the cave the others close on her heels.

"Where's Canova?" Mac asked once inside the cave.

"Don't worry 'bout him he can take care of himself," Nisa spoke to the gloom her vision now obscured. It was pitch inside and the fugitives remained relatively close to the entrance just out of reach of the illuminating moonlight and the snipers rifle. "Mac what can you see back there?" Knowing with Mac's genetic enhancements he could see just as well as if the cavern was lit by an electric light.

"Whoa! You ain't gonna believe this but I think we just found her." Mac answered incredulous.

"Yeah it's her alright." Stats confirmed, "I felt her presence as soon as I entered the cave before, but she's very weak." Another shot ricocheted on the rock that framed the entrance to the cave forcing them all to hunker down presenting themselves as less of a target, they all moved closer to the walls of the cave Nisa cradling Eve protectively.

Canova had watched Nisa bound into the distance marveling at her agility yet again. Shit that women had a sprinters genes in her somewhere he was sure of that. He main-

The Hand Of God

tained a fast walk as he attempted to slow his breathing when he noticed movement out of the corner of his eye over to his left, shit they had company. Spotting a large boulder just up ahead at the base of the incline he crept forward dodging from tree to tree until he was safely behind the lichen yellowed rock. He didn't have to wait long until the footfalls of the militia passed close by his hiding place and he also sensed the creeping putrescence that was the Nefarious's calling card seep briefly into his mind before he shut out the brooding darkness. Fortunately they were too focused on discovering the elusive Witch and the loathsome feeling soon passed him by. A gun shot rang out, he needed to act now his friends required his talent and fast. Taking a deep steadying breath he peered over the top of the rock and performed a quick head count, five or six militia and two Nefarious. Canova instantly called upon the fire that dwelt in his head, stirring it up into a crackling ball of energy. He rapidly pin pointed the positions of the soldiers, easily discernable in the moonlight and the two Nefarious, who moments before Canova released the force in his head had turned in unison their spooky, pale faces unerringly seeking out his position but all too late, with a gasp that left his head reeling the stored energy left his mind and found its victims and in perfect synchronicity they fell to the forest floor like disguarded puppets.

The others, still huddled in the cave, started to become restless and somewhat unnerved at the absence of any further attacks from outside. Aleshia had retrieved her dart gun, Mac had let her hold onto the weapon as it was encoded for her sole use only, deeming its presence as no real threat but he still retained her side arm. She loaded another dart from the pouch at her belt and trained the sights firmly on the caves entrance awaiting on the emergence of the enemy.

Captain Szebrowski had been unaware of the silent eradication of his team as he continued to scale the slope his mind fixated on bloody revenge on the one who had escaped him earlier. "Nowhere to run now Stats!" He muttered to himself. He shouldered his rifle and unholstered his side arm as he neared the brow of the hill and released the safety catch before taking cover behind a large pine tree situated at the very top of the incline in front of the cave. "Stats!" He shouted. "I know you're in there, give it up now or your fucked! We got you outnumbered." He frowned to himself as it dawned on him that his team were nowhere in sight. With his back to the tree he scoured the forested slope he had just scaled, no-one!"What the fuck!" He exclaimed under his breath. "You son of a bitch Stats!" He roared, his anger finally boiling over and throwing caution to the wind he broke cover, his pistol held firmly in both hands the muzzle trained at the dark entrance to the cave but before he could squeeze the trigger Szebrowski felt a sting in his chest. He looked down his eyes focusing on the red dart that hung there. Shocked at the darts sudden appearance he released his tight grip on the pistol and removed the dart with his left hand staring at it unbelievably before letting it fall to the ground. The tranquiliser was now beginning to take effect, his arm wavered under the weight of the gun he still held at arm's length. He blinked rapidly trying to focus, his blurry eyes trying to aim the gun but the metal was heavy in his hand, pulling his arm down. His strength left him leaving him unable to pull back on the trigger, his knees trembled as his eyesight faded to black and he fell back comatose and slid down the slope a little way before coming to a standstill amidst the needles and pine cones just as Canova reached the summit of the slope.

"You guys in there?" He called out in the direction of the cave. Stats appeared first much to Canova's dismay, the sight of this strange face wearing a militia uniform left him disconcerted until Aleshia close on Stats' heels informed him,

"It's alright he's with us." Mac and Nisa were close behind, Nisa still holding Eve close to her chest.

"She okay?" He asked Nisa worried at Eve's reluctance to return to consciousness.

"Yeah I think so her heart beats stronger now at least probably nothing a good meal and a good sleep won't cure." Nisa answered positively.

"And what about Thalia? You find her?"

"Yeah she's in there but she's very weak." At hearing this Canova ignored the others and entered the cave, slowly feeling his way around the rough wall allowing his pupils to ad-

The Hand Of God

just as best they could in the darkness.

Meanwhile Aleshia and Nisa awaited the return of Mac and Stats as they located Canova's victims checking for signs of life, they certainly didn't want any of them regaining consciousness when their backs were turned. Canova had performed well only one soldier remained alive, Mac dealt him a wicked blow to the neck cracking his spine and ending his life. Job done they returned to the cave Mac dragging the drugged Szebrowski unceremoniously by the ankle at Stats' request, he had a few questions for his nemesis yet.

In the cave Canova had traced his way to the rear of the hollowed out mountain of rock, some twenty feet or so in. As dark as it was he could just distinguish a darker shadow lying on the sandy floor there. He knelt beside the silent form his arm outstretched trying to recognise what lay beneath his touch. Her skin was deathly cold to his touch as he ran his fingers along the length of her arm until he met with her own cold fingers. He immediately clasped them within his own as he whispered her name gently. "Thalia? Can you hear me?" Her reply was faint but filled his mind and body with the warmth he'd grown accustomed to during their previous encounters.

"I knew you would come, even after all those years I had faith in you." Canova smiled with relief and clasped her cold hand to his heart his own body warmth spreading into her frozen fingers. He felt her fingers respond to his touch as they slowly found their own strength and clasped his own hand in return.

"Pack one this is pack two are you receiving me? Over." The small group of rebels all turned to look at the unconscious Szebrowski where Mac had dragged him to the mouth of the cave as his two-way radio burst into life. "Pack one are you receiving me, we heard gunfire are you okay? Over." Stats turned to Mac figuring his best chance would be to convince the big guy of his sincerity first.

"You gotta let me answer them Mac or they're gonna send in reinforcements."

"And how do I know you ain't gonna turn us over?"

Came Mac's expected reply.

"Your just gonna have to trust me on this one, please."

Stats pleaded with him turning to Aleshia for support.

"He's right Mac let him answer the call before it's too late." Aleshia agreed.

"Okay but you double cross us an' I'll snap your neck soldier, understand?" Mac stood aside allowing him to approach his second in command and the crackling radio. Stats quickly grabbed the two-way tearing it free from where it was attached to Szebrowski's lapel.

"Pack two this is pack one receiving you over."

"Pack one please confirm your status over."

"Everything's okay, one of my team got spooked by a deer and let off a couple of rounds, everything's under control, over."

"You sure pack one the Nefarious over here seem a bit agitated."

"Shit!" Stats muttered before once again depressing the communication button. "Yes I repeat pack two everything's under control please continue on your current route until you receive further instructions over."

"Roger that pack one over and out." The voice sounded unconvinced.

"That ain't gonna fool them for long." Stats commented, Mac grunted his approval at his handling of the situation all the same. "Those Nefarious fuckers'll cotton on quick enough so I suggest we get the hell outta here fast and put some distance between us," Stats suggested.

"Eh! And who put you in charge?" Mac growled.

"Mac reel it in he's right," Nisa acceded placing herself in between the two would be alpha males as she felt the tension building between them. Mac looked into Nisa's emerald eyes and reluctantly nodded.

"Yeah I suppose your right so what's your plan soldier boy?"

"We need to work together and get the Witch back to Heaven and the Hub."

"Oh is that all? And what about him?" Mac nodded at the seemingly lifeless Szebrowski prodding him with the toe of his scuffed boot as he did so.

"He might come in useful yet but don't worry if he causes any trouble I'll take care of him." Stats promised him.

The Hand Of God

"Friend of yours is he?" Nisa asked of him.

"Executioner more like." Stats informed her as he squatted at his side and slapped him hard in the face and a second time when he didn't respond.

"Hey what's going on?" Canova had emerged from the confines of the cave carrying the unconscious Thalia in his arms.

"Looks like we got a new recruit." Mac thumbed at Stats. "Wow I never thought I'd live to see the day." His attention now fully focused on the blue skinned beauty lying in Canova's arms.

"I know." He agreed. "She seems to be recovering fast too, touch seems to transmit life force directly into her so I think she's gonna be alright."

"Thank you all for your kindness I owe you all a great deal." Thalia spoke to them all, directly into their minds.

"Whoa! What the..." Mac exclaimed startled, taking a step back at the same time.

"It's alright." Canova reassured them, "that's how she communicates."

"Yeah most of their kind are mute or were mute." Aleshia informed them. Thalia smiled kindly at them as she opened her eyes spreading a feeling of peace and serenity amongst them as she slowly regained her strength. She cocked her head meaningfully at Canova and in response he lowered her bare feet to the ground. She took a couple of tentative steps forward placing herself at the centre of her circle of rescuers.

"Bring the little one to me," she asked psychically of Nisa who unquestioningly approached her the limp Eve still in her arms and held her before Thalia who closed her hypnotically beautiful eyes and placed the palm of one blue hand gently on her Eve' pale forehead. Moments later Eve's eyelids flickered and slowly opened as if awakening from a deep sleep. Thalia removed her hand and smiled sweetly at the now conscious child before her.

"Hi!" Eve spoke to Thalia and turned smiling up at Nisa. "It's okay you can put me down now." Nisa did as she asked. "What did you do to me?" She asked Thalia.

"Touch can convey many things little one, love, knowledge and healing. Silence is indeed golden."

"Can you also hear my thoughts?" Nisa found the courage to form the words in her mind.

"Yes I can if you desire me to." She thought back. Mac and Stats were captivated by Thalia's appearance taken aback by her stunning beauty and eloquence. Szebrowski propped up between them forgotten still firmly under the influence of the administered drugs delivered by the dart. The Witch's recovery had been remarkable already the blue colour had returned to her skin, her cheeks flushed with colour also. Her violet-blue eyes sparkled with an alien magical power, even her previously disheveled hair seemed to have regained some of its lustre as she stood tall amongst them clothed only in a long flowing black gown, closely fitting it complimented her lithe figure, only her delicate bare feet and ankles protruded. The sleeves long in the arm almost obscuring her slender hands and fingers. She tilted her head aware of the pairs interest in her appearance. "Does my appearance please you both?" Her words sounded softly in their minds causing them both to flush pink. Nisa elbowed Mac sharply in the ribs obviously annoyed.

"Hey what was that for?" He complained.

"Put your tongue back in your head idiot!" Aleshia also threw Stats a withering look, one of her shapely eyebrows raised. He raised his hands, palms outward in mock surrender and smiled amiably.

"Hey I'm sorry I've just never been this close to a Witch before."

"Yeah me neither." Mac hurriedly agreed the two men embarrassed at the sudden attention.

"See that's all it is." Stats backed him up.

"Yeah Nis that's all." Mac drew his attention away from Thalia to prove his point as he nodded in agreement with Stats. Nisa and Aleshia just shook their heads. Eve tried to suppress a giggle behind her hand and Canova couldn't help but smile at the two hardened individuals as they stood sheepishly side by side like two errant school boys.

"Well I think we should formulate some sort of a plan don't you?" Canova asked the group changing the subject.

"Canova's right." Thalia's whisperings filled their minds. "Many years have passed by awaiting this moment in time.

The Hand Of God

The Creatrix Mother has called upon us all to finally restore the balance. The time of the Nefarious is almost at an end but at a cost, alas some of us will perish fulfilling our destinies, it has already been decided."

"Shit and I was kinda lookin' forward to choking the life outta Nekros as well!" Mac interrupted.

"Me and you both." Stats agreed.

"Hey guys a little respect please!" Nisa frowned over at them both before Thalia continued.

"It's okay," she smiled, "their strength and courage is ours also for we all have our parts to play in this the end game, mine is to return once again to Heaven and seek out the Creatrix Mother."

"Creatrix Mother? Who or what is that?" Aleshia asked confused.

"She is the Mother of all that has ever been and all that will ever be." Thalia answered rather cryptically.

"That must be who Nekros answers to in the lower levels of the Hub but the power he wields is dark, evil, maybe its too late, maybe she's corrupted beyond redemption." Stats ventured.

"No. Her heart and soul are pure. Nekros draws his power from her mind and body for his own dark purpose. Like the weapons you carry." She turned and spoke to Aleshia, Stats and Mac. "The weapons themselves aren't evil merely the hand that wields them for the wrong purpose." The three exchanged glances somewhat embarrassed before Thalia continued with her internal narrative. "The Creatrix Mother's true purpose was to spread love and peace amongst the Sensitive humans on your planet and in turn prepare your species for its next level of existence."

"So the Nefarious were always meant to be the good guys they've just been led astray so to speak?" Aleshia asked.

"Yes. A black heart has led them down a dark path against their will which will in turn inevitably lead you all to your own end." Her eyes welled with tears at the thought of the bleak future that awaited them if they failed.

"So what can we do?" Stats asked her in turn.

"I am your last hope of redemption, the last of my kind I must return to my place of birth and return to Mother's side so that all our souls can be freed from the dark hell that awaits us all."

"Shit doesn't sound too good does it Nis?" Mac commented.

"No it doesn't." She agreed. "So our next move would be to get us all back to the Hub?" Thalia nodded. "Well that sounds like a job for you two." Nisa turned to Stats and Aleshia. "So what you got in mind?"

"Well then Stats it looks like it's up to you." Aleshia turned to him putting him on the spot. "There's no way I can get us back via the route I took."

"Yeah I had a feelin' that is was gonna be down to me. Looks like our only hope is to backtrack from here to the militia camp and steal a chopper or a catamaran."

"An' how do we pilot it from there? Kidnap the pilot?" Queried Nisa.

"I can take care of that leave it to me." Canova proffered. "Just need them alive so I can draw on his knowledge and experience. I'll get you back to Heaven."

"Sure you can manage that?" Mac seemed impressed.

"Yeah positive."

"Okay then we'd better make tracks before they realise what's going on. Unless they already do." Nisa pointed out.

"Unfortunately they already do. The Nefarious hive mind felt the loss of their kind and as we speak the others are searching for a way to cross the river." Thalia informed them telepathically.

"Right then let's move out." Stats ordered. "Just one last thing to take care of before we go." Referring to the now recovering Szebrowski.

"Thought you said he could come in useful?" Mac responded aware of the infliction in Stats' tone.

"Well what more help do we need he's only going to hinder us and we've no time to waste."

"Okay then that gets my vote." Nisa agreed coldly. Canova nodded in agreement but before enquiring of Thalia she answered them her head bowed solemnly.

"As much as I abhor violence and killing we can't afford for our mission to be compromised in any way and this ones heart is filled with hatred and revenge." She turned away

The Hand Of God

from the moaning soldier as he came to unable to watch what was to follow.

"Well it's unanimous then, I'll take care of him." Nisa offered. "Shut your eyes darlin'." She told Eve who went to stand at Thalia's side her eyes averted and before anybody could react she stooped beside Szebrowski and placed a single digit against his temple. His eyes opened widely for a second before his orbs rolled back in their sockets. Nisa removed her finger and his head slumped forward onto his chest, several spurts of blood escaped the wound the residue trailing down the side of his face and dripped onto his uniform. "Well that's him taken care of."

"Well that was quick and efficient. I like your style." Stats complimented her. "Although I gotta admit I was looking forward to dispatching him myself."

"Me an' you both." Mac added somewhat put out at Nisa's rapid intervention at dealing with their prisoner. The deed done the ex-Hand of God militia, the evolved humans and the last remaining Witch began to retrace Stats route back through the forest led by himself, to the encampment.

"Hey guys shouldn't we hide the bodies?" Canova asked as they made their way down the slope passing the corpses strewn there. Thalia shook her head sadly at the sight of the dead militia and Nefarious.

"Our time is running out and the Nefarious will be on to our scent soon enough, it would be far more advantageous for us to leave this place now and conserve all our energies for the confrontation yet to come." Her silent words eased his troubled mind like the gentle ripples of some distant lake lapping softly on some peaceful shore.

"Thalia's right." Eve agreed having remained silent during the adults earlier decision making and she smiled up at him although her eyes remained sad. "It'll all be over soon." She promised automatically touching the silver locket that hung at her neck as she spoke.

"Hey everything's going to be okay." He tried to reassure Eve, her sadness having a profound effect upon him.

"Yes I know it will." She answered following the others as they continued down the slope catching up with Thalia and taking her hand. Somewhat perplexed at her response

Canova scratched at his head and followed her lead bringing up the rear.

19

Nekros stood before his power source. The unlit room revealed only small glimpses of what hung before him. The figure was suspended mid-way between the cold stone of the floor and the high ceiling, her body splayed out as if crucified. A myriad of tubes snaked out from her seemingly lifeless form connecting her to a stack of electrical machinery and computers that dominated the large room. The twinkling flashing lights reflected back off the tubes and cables that entered her body at strategic points drawing upon her alien energies feeding off her very life force. His face was filled with rapture, his jaw slack, his mouth gaping, grey rivulets of saliva ran freely over his decayed teeth dripping unchecked onto his now blood soaked shirt. His head tilted back as he gazed up at his captive rocking slightly on his heels as he fed upon her. She was naked, her physical form emaciated, the flashing white, green and red lights revealing her bone structure periodically beneath her taught skin. Her chin rested on her chest, her eyes closed. Her breasts hung low on her torso, deflated and withered. Her flesh looked raw at the points at which the numerous tubes pierced her alien flesh as they pulsed rhythmically in the gloom. A shudder passed through her wasted body and Nekros's cracked, cruel lips turned upwards at the corners forming a smile in response. He felt his own black blood course through his veins with renewed strength, the visible veins under his thin scalp pulsed and expanded like the movement of some sick burrowing invertebrate that inhabited the space between his skull and his paper thin skin. The suspended figure above shuddered once again and let out a long sigh of breath before falling silent once again. Nekros averted his dead eyes and levitated into the air turning around in mid-air as he did so and exited the room in which she was incarcerated, kept alive for decades. Once free of the room he paused in the blank space outside, only the door behind him and the ones opposite that marked the site of the elevator interrupted the square blank room. He tuned his thoughts into the hive mind of the Nefarious and instantly his ecstatic expression changed to one of boiling, seething anger, the pulsing in his head increasing in strength and rapidity as they informed him of his prey's escape yet again. Unable to control his anger as it welled up from within he threw his head back his mouth gaping wide and emitted a blood curdling inhuman scream of pure rage that echoed back at him in the empty space. "Draw them to us, let us feed upon their fear for the time is upon us my children. Our playthings have ceased to be useful to us, indulge yourselves, feed upon their despair, consume them completely and be as one!" He mentally screamed touching the minds of the Nefarious horde simultaneously.

20

Canova trudged wearily behind the others feeling somewhat left out, kicking at the fallen leaves with his scuffed boots unearthing as he did so a rather surprised looking toad as it searched for food amongst the leaf litter, its large liquid eyes blinking at him several times before it hopped rather languidly into shelter once again. Mac and Stats had taken the lead closely followed by Aleshia and Nisa, the four seemed to have bonded already as they laughed and joked amongst themselves despite the gravity of their situation but that was probably how they were coping with the heavy weight that they all burdened firmly upon their shoulders. Funny he thought he'd never have guessed that only a few days ago he'd be in this scenario accompanied by two ex-Hand of God militia, two Shifters, a juvenile Porter and the last living Witch on Earth as they headed off into the unknown preparing to save the world and humankind itself. Thalia walked together hand in hand mid-way between the path makers and himself, their conversation private, unheard by himself and the others. He wondered curiously what they were discussing, did they both know what the outcome would be? And if they were aware of their futures perhaps the fact that they kept their thoughts to themselves meant that their prospects were bleak, their lives ended by the Hand of God as they undertook their seemingly futile attempt to save their own souls and that of the planets remaining inhabitants. Thalia threw him a comforting look, her thoughts reaching out to him touching his perturbed mind. "Be strong my love for you have yet a big part to play in what events are yet to unfold. Remember some souls don't die Canova they just evolve." And with that her soft psychic touch withdrew as the party of seven continued onwards. Grey clouds had formed in the night sky partially obscuring the moon throwing the forest into shadow and putting him further ill at ease. Only the bright star that was Venus continued to radiate her light upon them. His mind scoured the surrounding woodlands searching for unwanted company but he detected nothing, at least for now. "I conjured a "spell" as your kind would call it, that will throw them off our scent for a little while but the Nefarious are many and their will is strong the most that we can hope for is that we reach the encampment before they locate us. Have faith though Canova and we will achieve our goal." Thalia didn't look directly at him this time but a warm glow settled within his chest which lifted his spirits and filled him with a new sense of positivity.

"I hope your right," he whispered.

The militia encampment from which Stats had commenced the hunt was in darkness when they approached, silence prevailed in the few remaining hours before dawn, even the insect life here was hushed the deciduous forest giving way to an evergreen jungle. A small team of five soldiers remained within the camps proximity, no Nefarious were stationed there Canova confirmed. Two of the soldiers remained alert patrolling the area whilst the other three slept on in the tent on folding camp beds that had been erected. One soldier remained stationed outside the tent whilst the other, presumably the pilot as his uniform was of a dark green, lent idly against the helicopter in the other clearing, obviously bored. "Pack two calling base come in over!" The harsh radio voice cut through the deathly silence jolting the unsuspecting pilot into action as he hastily straightened himself up from his leaning post responding to the call.

"Base to pack two receiving you loud and clear over."

"We have a problem base it appears pack one may have been eliminated and on finding no safe place to ford the river to investigate are on a return course back to you, so stay alert we may well have intruders in the vicinity over."

"Roger that and what are our orders if we spot anything? Over."

"Shoot any unidentified individuals on sight over." The conversation at an end. The flustered pilot left his post and made his way over to the adjacent clearing the second soldier meeting him half way having been aware of the radio communication.

"What the fuck's goin' on?" He asked frowning.

"Intruders in the vicinity so keep alert I'll go wake up the

The Hand Of God

others and get them to cover the perimeter."

"Okay, did they find the Witch?"

"Fuck knows, maybe the Witch found them! All I know is pack two's headin' back to base so there must've been a major fuck up! Anyway better get those sleeping beauties outta their kip before they're on us." The soldier returned and entered the tent then systematically kicked each of the camp beds in turn as his comrade returned to the helicopter. "Come on you lot get the fuck up we got a situation here." He whispered as loudly as he dared for all he knew the enemy could be lying in wait watching them right now.

They were. Mac and Stats had stealthily crept through the undergrowth so as they could assess the situation and formulate a plan of attack just in time to witness the soldier at the helicopter jump to attention alerted by the radio. "Shit!" The two whispered simultaneously raising their eyebrows. Stats inclined his head indicating that they should retreat and rejoin the others. Quietly they crawled back the way they had come through the ferns regrouping with their friends who were hidden behind a large boulder not too far away.

"So what's the deal?" Nisa whispered.

"Not great," Stats began.

"Yeah they just got alerted to our imminent arrival and put the rest of those fuckers on alert." Mac finished for him.

"Well we need to do this quickly before the others get back, Mac how many we got?" Canova took over the situation. Mac dodged from behind the rock and repositioned himself behind the nearest tree trunk and peered around its perimeter utilising his mutated vision to scan the clearings ahead. By now the three soldiers had emerged from the tent and had taken up positions around the perimeter of the clearing, weapons at the ready. Mac ducked back into cover and crouching down he scrambled back to the cover of the rock.

"We got three in one clearing an' another two guarding the chopper." He reported.

"Okay we gotta do this fast. I'll take out the three, I can't manage the other two there's too much distance between them." Canova once again took control of the operation. "Aleshia think you can dart the pilot from here? I need him alive."

"Yeah no worries what about his buddy?"

"Leave him to me." Mac volunteered himself not wanting to be left out. "Just let me get into position first."

"Okay Mac you got five minutes then we hit 'em." Mac immediately set off at Canova's instructions on his hands and knees, surprisingly quickly for a man of his size.

"We all gonna get onboard this chopper or what?" Nisa asked.

"I think we'd stand a better chance if we split up." Stats ventured. "What if Thalia, Canova and Eve take the chopper and the rest of us got ourselves a catamaran back to Heaven? Double our chances don't want to put all our eggs in the same basket so to speak." He looked round at the rest of them who all nodded in agreement. "Okay then Aleshia you'd better get a bead on that pilot. Canova you ready?" Canova repositioned himself allowing him visual contact with the three militia and at once conjured up a psychic bolt allowing it to swirl within his mind awaiting the right opportunity. "Okay Aleshia we've given Mac enough time, take him out when you've got a clear shot." Mac had managed to crawl within a dozen feet or so of the unsuspecting soldier and the pilot right on the periphery of the clearing and waited until a red tipped dart embedded itself in the pilots neck. Good shot Aleshia, he thought to himself, and with that he launched himself from his position like a panther springing upon its unwary prey. The pilot had pulled the dart from his neck and stared at it aghast for a second, the drug taking affect quickly, his already blurring vision taking in Mac as he toppled to the ground sedated. The remaining soldier barely had time to register what had happened before Mac was upon him, one hard punch to the face and it was all over.

"Nice." Mac congratulated himself smiling and looked over to see the others already making their way through the undergrowth to join him. On their arrival Canova immediately knelt beside the drugged pilot and held his head between the palms of his hands and closed his eyes. He entered his mind searching for the memories that would allow him to pilot the helicopter.

"There got it!" He exclaimed jubilantly. "Let's go."

Stats ushered Thalia and Eve onboard as Canova climbed

into the cockpit.

"You three get goin' I never much cared for flying anyway." Stats grinned.

"Okay till we meet again." Canova shook hands with the remaining four. "And good luck." He added. He smiled sadly at having to part ways so soon but he knew it was the sensible thing to do. He closed the door and began to prepare for takeoff as Stats slid the other door closed. Canova instinctually flicked the appropriate switches the information required absorbed from the unconscious pilot. At the sound of the electric motor coming to life the rotar blades slowly began their revolution and with that the remainder of the group backed away to a safe distance.

"You take care kid!" Mac called to Eve who waved back at him smiling through the small window.

"Don't worry I'll take care of her." Thalia reassured him telepathically, waving also as the momentum of the blades built up.

"Come on this way." Stats pointed towards the rutted track that led into the forest. Unfortunately for them no off road vehicle was parked in the clearing so they'd have to cover the distance to the coast on foot. "It's gonna take us about half an hour on foot." And without another word Stats, Aleshia, Mac and Nisa headed off as the helicopter finally left the ground and began to ascend into the sky, now streaked with oranges and reds as the sun climbed towards the horizon.

"You two alright back there?" Canova shouted back over the noise of the engine forgetting he had no need to.

"Yes we're fine, no need to shout silly we can hear you." Canova realising that she'd spoken directly into his mind as Thalia had.

"How?" Was all he managed to think in surprise.

"We're all evolving. The evolved beings on this planet will lead the way into a new state of being, a new dimension of existence where we will coexist in peace. The time of crossing is almost upon us, the dawn of the new age will lead others like us into a parallel world of the mind and of the heart."Thalia tried to explain to him her soothing words once again filling him with hope.

"I always thought there was something more to this life than what the eye saw." He thought back already getting used to this new form of communication and checking the array of dials before him he set a course for Heaven where their futures awaited.

Meanwhile back on terra firma the four uniformed rebels had continued onwards down the track in silence. Mac checking over his shoulder periodically making sure they didn't have unwanted guests. Their progress had been unrelenting led by Stats and soon the forest began to thin up ahead and the ocean could be glimpsed beyond through the undergrowth in the light of the dawning sun. Stats held his hand up and slowed his pace. "Don't know what to expect here," he began, his attention momentarily distracted at the sight of Mac returning Aleshia's pistol to her, she accepted it smiling her gratitude and placed it back in her holster. "Well at least we got them safely on their way that's the main thing our only priority now as to create as much havoc as possible." Mac grinned at the implications.

"Yeah I'm up for some of that."

"Good man," Stats grinned back. The two had bonded well in the short time they'd spent together.

"If I could just interrupt for a second." Aleshia butted in. "I suggest from here on in we bring you two in at gun point," meaning Mac and Nisa, "and when we're close enough just shoot the guards, simple, I don't think we need to be stealthy anymore do you?" She asked.

"Yeah true. What about piloting the boat?" Nisa asked.

"How hard can it be? We'll figure it out." Stats was filled with a new feeling of positivity, he was even beginning to enjoy himself.

"Okay then let's do this." Mac was eager to get going again and he winked at Nisa who smiled in return. The two Shifters in front, Stats at the rear covering them with his hand gun, checking it was primed and ready for use and with that they marched around the corner and into view of the Hand of God who awaited them. Aleshia walked alongside the "captives" conveying the situation ahead back to Stats who's view was obscured somewhat by Mac's wide shoulders.

The Hand Of God

"Got two armed guards to the rear of the catamaran. The ramps lowered, can't see anyone inside 'cept three vehicles, could be someone further in so be alert people."

"Okay," he acknowledged lowering his voice, the guards were aware of them now and had raised their weapons in response.

"Halt! Stay where you are!" One of them shouted over, he sounded nervous.

"It's okay!" Aleshia shouted back raising her hands as she did so showing she was unarmed. "I'm Lieutenant Kulak and that's Field Commander Station, we got two prisoners here, we've been requested to bring them in." A short dialogue ensued between the two soldiers before the one who had spoken waved them forward lowering their weapons.

"Okay Mac, Nisa once we cover this distance just stand aside an' I'll take care of them." Stats ordered. The jetty was only about forty or fifty feet in length and the four covered the distance in no time. Aleshia noticed the guards looked really jumpy as they approached, had they been made aware of the fugitives? Either way it was too late now to retreat. The guards frowned as they noticed Mac and Nisa's grins as they drew nearer and stepping aside they revealed Stats brandishing his hand gun, aiming it straight at them. "Sorry guys." He apologised as he squeezed off two rounds, a bullet for each man, both fell back at the impact, one of the guards toppling over the edge of the jetty and plunged into the water with a splash. "Okay Mac I'm probably gonna need your strength to get through the door into the cabin. Aleshia, Nisa get that ramp up and keep an eye out for company. Here," he handed Nisa his hand gun. "I take it you know how to use one of these? Don't worry for some reason higher ranking officers personal side arms aren't encoded to their users, don't ask me why." She nodded her approval taking the weapon.

"Shit if I'd've known that." Mac exclaimed and with that the two men made their way up the ramp and entered the hull of the catamaran and headed for the steps that led to the cabin door. Nisa took cover behind the first off roader and kept watch for the enemy. Aleshia had already found the emergency ramp over ride switch, normally the ramp was controlled from within the cockpit. She smashed the glass casing that housed it with the butt of her hand gun and punched the button, instantly the electric motor hummed into life and the ramp began its slow ascent, just in time.

"We've got company." Nisa informed her from her own position aside the vehicle. Aleshia drew back from the gaping entrance and took up position on the other side of the vehicle and trained her sights on the group that had appeared from within the cover of the forest where the dirt track disappeared from view. Six Hand of God militia in all and they were closing the gap between them fast, two Nefarious were now also emerging to the rear of the troop of soldiers.

Mac had made short work of the cabin door. With a grunt the sole of his booted foot slammed into the locked door taking it clean off its hinges and slamming into one of the two-man crew inside, both of them alerted to the commotion by the gunshots. Stats was closest to the remaining man and he deftly kicked the weapon from his hand leaving him defenseless, he stood terrified unable to react further. "You got two choices, you either do as we say or my friend here will squash you, do you understand?" Stats offered him his choice and Mac's menacing grin convinced the soldier to comply and he nodded eagerly as he took in the shattered body of his former comrade. The solid steel door lay firmly on top of him, a small pool of blood had emerged from underneath, he wasn't going to come to his rescue that was for sure. Gunfire suddenly sounded from the rear of the catamaran. "Shit they've caught up with us. Mac you wanna keep an eye on our friend here?"

"With pleasure." Mac took a step closer and leered menacingly at the soldier who looked about ready to soil himself.

"Now get us the fuck outta here!" Stats bellowed at the pilot and with that he bolted through the doorway and down the stairs into the hold.

"You heard the man." Mac added."Let's get this thing movin'."

The ramp was closing painfully slowly, the attacking soldiers had flung themselves onto the wooden boards presenting less of a target as the shooting commenced, one of them dead before he hit the deck dispatched by a well aimed bullet

The Hand Of God

from Aleshia's gun. "Move back!" She called over to Nisa and the two backed up off loading shots as they went. A stray bullet from the Hand of God ricocheted off the four by four nearest the tail of the catamaran and grazed Nisa on the temple. She cried out in shock more than pain and dropped to the floor of the craft holding the side arm with both hands and rapidly squeezing the trigger in response, emptying the magazine at the five remaining soldiers, wounding one as he caught a bullet in the shoulder dropping his weapon as he clutched at the bloody wound. Another took a bullet in the head spraying his closet comrade with blood and bone. The Nefarious who had held their position further back until this point suddenly sprang into motion covering the distance between themselves and the catamaran in an unnaturally short time considering their slow fluid movements.

"Shit I'm out of ammo!" Nisa shouted out, by now Stats had joined them.

"Hey you okay?" He asked Nisa seeing the blood running down the side of her face.

"Yeah I'll be fine barely touched me."

"Better move back from here."

"What about Aleshia?"

"Don't worry I can take care of myself," she called over from the other side of the bullet riddled vehicle. By now the ramp had reached its half way point obscuring the militia from view and taking advantage of this they retreated further into the hold out of range. The two Nefarious had overtaken the soldiers on the jetty. They were going to reach the boat before the ramp had fully closed into position. The engines finally burst into life, the pilot completing his task under the watchful eye of Mac. The water churned into white froth as the massive propellers began their rotation. Aleshia could feel the close proximity of the two ghouls as they reached the jetties end, like a cold enveloping slime oozing into her mind. She shook herself free of their icy clutches and aimed at the one nearest her straight between its ebony eyes and pulled back on the trigger. Throwing its head back as the bullet made contact, a spray of black blood arced over its head as its emaciated body lifted clear off the platform before landing several feet behind its companion who howled an inhuman cry of frustration and anger. Aleshia shuddered at the sound, the vibrations of which passed through her very core leaving her feeling cold and sick. Finally the catamaran lurched slightly as it pulled away from the dock much to her relief and she stood and watched as the ramp finally closed the gap with a metallic clang that shut out the dawn light from outside. She exhaled a sigh of relief and joined the others in the cabin. Mac had retrieved the first aid kit from one of the hold alls he'd retained and was wiping away the blood on Nisa's face with a surgical wipe.

"You'll live babe, might leave a bit of a scar though." Nisa winced at the stinging swab.

"Hey careful!." She pulled away from his heavy hand. Once the blood had been cleared away from the wound it revealed itself to be no more than a two inch graze, the flow already stemmed. "Yeah another one for the collection," she grinned, Mac laughing aloud relieved it hadn't been worse.

"Okay sailor boy open this baby up." Mac prodded the quivering, pale pilot seated at the controls.

"You heard him let's go." Stats waved the man's gun in his direction after he'd reclaimed it from the floor where it had fallen on his return to the cockpit not knowing whether it would work for him but the show itself was enough for the pilot. He nodded and pushed forward the throttle the craft responded and picked up speed. Stats pondered for a second before removing the ammunition clip from the pilots gun and signaled that Nisa should return his own empty pistol, she did so and he replaced the empty clip with the pilots own full one, smiling he restored it into Nisa's care.

"An' no funny stuff or you'll be joining your mate." Mac promised him. Aleshia collapsed into the empty co-pilots seat, shaking a little as a direct result of her encounter with the Nefarious.

"Fuck that was close!"

"You okay?" Stats asked her.

"Yeah that was a little too close for comfort that's all, I can't bare those Nefarious gettin' close to me, they give me the creeps and worse." She smiled up at him. "But we made it, good work guys." She congratulated the others who smiled in return also elated at their escape from the Hand of

The Hand Of God

God, but the hard part was yet to come and deep down they all knew they wouldn't be as lucky next time.

21

Canova was gradually getting accustomed to the internal psychic dialogue between himself, Thalia and Eve as he sat at the flight controls of the helicopter making small adjustments periodically to their course, the motions perfectly natural to him now as if he'd been flying for years, as had the previous pilot his experience now Canova's own. He took in the scenario before him, a vast seemingly endless expanse of ocean stretched out as far as he could see, the sun now fully risen behind them reflected back off the water in places creating a mirror like effect, his mind wandered to his friends, wondering how they'd fared in their own escape attempt from the outlands, he hoped they had. "I sense a great shift of consciousness amongst the Nefarious they swarm like a plague of locusts, their mind is filled with rage at the escape of what they seek. I feel in my heart that our friends eluded capture and are now on route to Heaven as are we." Thalia's words offered him some comfort and he relaxed a little, for now at least they were out of reach from the Hand of God. His attention strayed beyond the confines of the helicopter once again and a smile played on his lips as he spotted a group of torpedo shaped shadows just below the waters surface. His time living within the coastal community many years ago had educated him in many things and he knew what they were, a pod of whales, safely living out their lives now freed from man kinds years of persecution.

"How long do you think before we reach Heaven?" It was Eve that refocused his attention, also using her mind to communicate, it had rapidly become second nature to them both. Eve in particular becoming close to Thalia accepting her into her life as an almost surrogate parental figure.

"Well according to the instruments we should be able to see the island in about three hours if all goes well."

"Thalia you've been to Heaven before what's it like?" She asked.

"That was a very long time ago, long before you were

born. A time in my life that I care not to remember, except what I need to. Alas my time there was as a prisoner and my view of Heaven is clouded by the atrocities that occurred within the Hub."

"I'm sorry, I forgot it must've been terrible." Thalia only smiled and smoothed Eve's dark hair but her eyes reflected the pain of what few memories she still retained.

Meanwhile aboard the catamaran Stats, Aleshia and Mac were rifling through the contents of the three off roaders. Nisa had volunteered to keep an eye on the pilot in case he attempted to sabotage their mission and threw them off course, which she'd been following on the radar screen set amongst the dials and switches. The vehicles hadn't revealed much, a few food supplies, which they added to their stash in the hold all, a couple of medi-packs, which they discarded, half a dozen two-way radios which were also of no good to them but they did find something of use, a sniper rifle fitted with telescopic sights and a full clip of ammunition. The weapon hadn't been issued and therefore hadn't been genetically encoded. They'd placed all the useful items on the back seat of the four by four nearest the exit, the rifle placed in the foot well there. "Well not much else here worth taking." Stats said shutting the rear door firmly after checking the keys were present, they were, he caught a glint of silver hanging from the ignition. "Let's just hope they keep our reception down to a minimum, don't want them making too much of a fuss over us."

"Ain't there anywhere else we could dock this thing?" Mac scratched at the growth on his chin, the coarse hair growing there making him itch.

"'Fraid not the coast's all cliff faces and even if there was somewhere they'd track our location from the Hub anyway. The ports the only way in or out by sea so we're just gonna have to hit them head on." Aleshia informed him.

"Shit! An' all we got are a couple of hand guns an' that sniper rifle. Oh yeah almost forgot about those grenades Nis an' I got."

"Well it's better than nothing, might be at least more than their suspecting, might just give us the advantage." Stats furrowed his brow thoughtfully. "Once there though there's only one way off this boat and back to the Hub." He patted the wing of the vehicle beside him. "We just need to be prepared."

22

Some time had passed by since leaving the outlands and they'd ascended skywards. The psychic conversation had been replaced by a warm, soothing feeling that enveloped the three passengers onboard, their words unspoken their shared emotions conveyed what they felt. Like being pleasantly sedated and sat out in the warmth of the sun, all their worries and anxieties dissipated for the present. Canova glanced over his shoulder, Eve was cosied into Thalia, her head resting on her lap, her feet drawn up onto the padded seat. Her eyes were closed. Thalia also sat with her eyes shut but not in sleep, her posture reflected that of meditation, a small smile played on her perfect lips her breathing relaxed. One of her blue-violet eyes opened aware of his attention and looked directly at him and her smile widened revealing her white teeth. "Thank you." Her sweet words of gratitude tingled warmly in his mind and he turned about embarrassed at his own admiration of her beauty. "It's okay for we were always destined to meet you and I, you're aware of the origins of your name?"

"My mother told me I was named after a famous artist who died many centuries ago, that's all I know."

"Yes indeed, a great Italian sculptor in fact, his greatest and most famous creation that of the Three Graces, representing the three hand maidens to Venus, the goddess of love, of who Thalia was but one, she who brings flowers." She educated him.

"So what happened to the other two?"

"The task at hand fell into the care of myself and two of my sisters our names adopted us and so our paths were chosen. Alas Aglaia and Euphrosyne were hunted down and murdered by the Hand of God during the Witch hunts many years ago I being the sole survivor. Since then I have remained in isolation awaiting the one who bore his name."

"Canova." He repeated his name to himself. "So everything that's unfolded, us all meeting, even my name was all a part of this, it was all meant to be?"

"Nothing is coincidental everything happens for a reason."

"Even Nekros and the Nefarious?"

"Yes even them for how would we see the light if there was no darkness for it to shine forth from."

"And your sisters? Others of your kind did they look like you?"

"We were similar in appearance but as with your race our features differed."

"If we do defeat Nekros what then? The Nefarious have amassed a large army and their power increases daily."

"Ah my love, without the loathsome one the Nefarious are no more, only the truely corrupted will perish, many still retain the vital spark within their hearts that make them human. These evolved beings, Sensitives, will awaken as if from a terrible nightmare and once again set foot upon the path they were always destined to tread, to once again spread love, peace and understanding amongst the people and lead them into a new world as foretold by the Creatrix Mother."

"And who is the Creatrix Mother?"

"She is a traveller of other worlds the last of her kind also, from a place you cannot yet conceive, she came here to save your species and continue her own line, a true goddess from another dimension. Your scientists experimented upon her cruelly for many years, her suffering was ours also, Witches, as we were called, but ironically without their foolish meddling the fate of the human race would've already been decided, condemned to exist in a world filled with fear, greed and hatred as would the spirits of our ancestors."

"So by creating you and others like you they inadvertently gave us a fighting chance, a secret weapon so to speak?" Her gentle laughter touched his mind softly.

"Ah yes how little they knew, what they tampered with they did not understand and what the eye does not see the mind and heart can manipulate." She added somewhat puzzlingly. "Nothing is coincidental all things happen for a reason only those souls filled with compassion would pass the test and cross over from this biosphere we exist in now into the noosphere."

The Hand Of God

"The noosphere?"

"A parallel existence on the mental plane an evolutionary step beyond this biological, physical world we currently experience."

"So kinda like how we're communicating now?"

"Yes in a way that is part of it but you will soon understand, our time draws near but first we must complete our task at hand."

"And what about Eve?"

"Ah the little one." Thalia looked down upon the sleeping child lovingly and stroked her hair gently so as not to disturb her. "She still has a big part to play, without her none of this would've been possible, without any of us it would already be over." Canova nodded his acceptance of her words for now satisfied his mind quietened and at peace.

23

The ocean crossing aboard the catamaran had been smoother than the outward journey only occasionally had the craft lifted free of the waters below sending the passengers reeling as they clutched at the dashboard steadying themselves. They'd all partaken in something to eat and drink having to resort to the military fare once again now the fresh produce they had gathered earlier had been consumed. "How long till we reach Heaven?" Nisa asked the pilot, who had calmed considerably since being convinced they wouldn't kill him as long as he cooperated.

"Approximately an hour. In fact you can just see the island up ahead on the horizon there." He pointed and on closer inspection an as yet tiny land mass had indeed materialisd faintly in the distance.

"Right then guys what's our plan of action?" Nisa asked, their meal finished, the wound to her head had now fully congealed leaving a dark red streak.

"Well..." Stats began pausing as the others centred their attention on him. "We lower the ramp when we approach our destination so it extends like a platform, reverse this boat towards the dock and when we're close enough we jump that four by four sittin' at the exit, it's our only hope, it'll at least offer us some cover I just can't guarantee that we're all gonna make it out alive this time. Those off roaders aren't reinforced in anyway and it would've been better if it was facing the other way. It's a chance but one we've got to take I just hope they haven't got a small army waiting for us or we're fucked!" Everybody silently agreed.

"An' what about him?" Mac motioned to the pilot who visibly stiffened at being mentioned.

"Don't worry 'bout him he'll be takin' a nap." Aleshia patted the pouch she still carried on her belt that held the remaining tranquiliser darts.

"I think we should just kill him." Mac disagreed enjoying the pilots obvious discomfort.

The Hand Of God

"Na not this time Mac he's kept up to his part of the bargain let him be." Nisa rested her hand on his bulky shoulder her touch quelling his bloodlust.

"Yeah okay Nis fair enough. You just got lucky bud."

The island was also visible from the windows in the helicopter, their time of arrival was closer to ten minutes though, the chopper covering the distance far quicker. "Hey we're almost there." Canova informed his passengers telepathically, it had now become a completely natural way to communicate and he barely gave it a second thought. Thalia roused Eve from her sleep and pointed out of the small window with her delicate blue hand at the cliffs of Heaven as they loomed into view. Stretching as she sat upright she peered through the glass rubbing her eyes as she did so. She seemed disappointed at the sight that greeted her.

"Oh I thought it'd be different somehow it's not how I saw it in my dreams." She thought. Thalia cocked her head lightly.

"And what did you expect angel?"

"Oh I don't know it's just not what I expected." She shrugged and seated herself back down again. "Maybe it'll be nicer when we fly over it."

"Well we'll find out soon enough." Canova thought. "I was gonna put us down somewhere on the fringes of the gardens away from the Hub itself, there's too much of a military presence there. I gained a little knowledge of the layout of the area when I learned how to fly, thought it might help." He grinned back at them over his shoulder. "At least that way we'll have a better chance of breaking in unnoticed, gonna have to rely on your talent again Eve, you up to it?"

"Sure," came her confident reply. The helicopter was now clearing the towering cliff below, beyond lay the vast lush expanse of jungle vegetation. Canova scanned the scene as it unfolded looking for an open space in which to land. He continued onwards for several minutes before a large square clearing appeared amongst the seemingly endless greenery. The area looked well tended, obviously looked after by the civilians that presumably dwelt nearby in a large glass housing complex that nestled among the botanical paradise, he hoped the locals were friendly but it was a chance they'd have to take. At least the reception they'd receive couldn't be any worse than if they'd landed directly at the Hub.

"Okay I've located a sight just up ahead, once I've set her down we're gonna have to move fast and we'll have to cover the rest of the distance on foot unless we can commandeer some transport." The enormous cables anchoring the solar towers were clearly visible now and Eve had returned to the window in awe of this new sight and judging by the close proximity of them he estimated the journey there would only take them a few hours.

"We're prepared aren't we Eve?" Thalia thought, Eve just shook her head her attention still on the sight ahead.

"Okay then we're descending now." He shifted the controls and the helicopter slowly altered its course as it approached the manicured lawn below.

The catamaran an hour or so later also approached the final leg of its journey, the pilot having powered down as they'd entered the islands inlet that would channel them towards the military port. Mac and Stats entered the hold and unchained the vehicle in which they would attempt their disembarkation as soon as they'd left the choppier waters of the open ocean behind them. Returning to the operations room, their job done, they could make out a relatively small island situated in the near distance the towering cliffs of Heaven hemming them in on each side. Once they'd navigated the rocky pillar on which a multitude of diving birds nested on its vertical walls and peppered the ocean surrounding them as they plunged into the water seeking food, the military port would be visible. "So this is it!" Well in case we don't get outta this one in one piece it's been a pleasure." Stats offered his hand to Mac who grasped it in his own shovel like hand and shook it vigorously.

"The pleasures been all mine mate, although I gotta admit I thought they woulda blown us outta the water by now with everything they got!."

"They never prepared for anything like this Mac, only a minimal store of weaponry was ever imported to Heaven before the shift, reckoned that'd be all they'd need to quell any uprisings. That was my father's theory at least but one I tend to agree with, the Hand of God never had any need to manufacture any really heavy artillery." Stats proffered his own and his father's opinion, which would explain the lack of military power during their journey.

"Yeah an' I bet they wish they had now, didn't expect us to come knockin' at their door did they," Mac replied. Hugs were then swapped between the other members of the team before a pervading atmosphere of tension fell over the four friends as they prepared themselves for this next clash with the Hand of God.

24

"Right men you've received your orders. Shoot on sight, no prisoners, is that clear?" Sergeant Callows bellowed to the gathered troops at the dock side.

"Yes sir!" Came the shouted response in perfect unison. The two dozen heavily armed soldiers stood to attention awaiting further instructions from their ranking officer. Callows checked on the progress of the catamaran, it was about forty feet away from the dock and closing, the boarding ramp had been lowered to about a thirty degree angle and the water frothed beneath it as the engines brought it closer by the second.

"Okay take positions and prepare arms." He returned his attention to the squad he'd been assigned to. He was a barrel of a man and he puffed his chest out filled with his own self importance. Rest assured, he promised himself, he wouldn't fail as had that idiot Szebrowski. He unholstered his own hand gun and thumbed back the safety catch.

Mac and Nisa were now strapped into the rear of the four by four, Stats sat behind the wheel awaiting Aleshia's return, who still kept a close watch over the pilot. The military dock had been blockaded at strategic points, Mac had no need for binoculars as he relayed the distant scenario to his accomplices as they rounded the solitary island that protruded from the waters of the ocean inlet. This allowed them little alternative as to where they could disembark, the trap was set. "How far away are we from the dock now?" Aleshia asked the pilot, unable to decipher the display he was reading.

"Twenty feet and closing." He reported checking the dials.

"Okay maintain your speed and hold your course."

"No problem the systems in automatic now the computer takes over at this point so it doesn't allow for human error." At hearing this Aleshia casually removed two darts from the pouch and detached the protective covers.

"Well thanks for your help and maybe we'll meet again

The Hand Of God

sometime under better circumstances. Sweet dreams." And with that she stuck both into the back of his neck and took a step back. The double dosage had an almost immediate effect as he gradually slid from his position on the chair onto the floor unconscious. Once she was sure he was out cold she left the cabin to join the others. Jumping into the empty front seat and strapping in. Stats immediately turned the key in the ignition and fired up the engine.

"And the pilot?" Nisa asked from the back seat as Aleshia rejoined them.

"Sleeping," she smiled.

"Okay everyone ready then?" Stats asked.

"No!" Came the unanimous response.

"Good then let's do this." Releasing the hand brake he slowly edged the vehicle forwards until its chromed bumper touched that of the vehicle in front. "Right just a few more seconds." He craned his head around from his position behind the wheel to look through the rear window and after selecting reverse gear he revved the engine hard and slipped the clutch.

Callows stood proudly in front of the soldiers he commanded awaiting his moment of glory, come on, he thought to himself, show yourselves. The catamarans ramp was feet from the dock, the interior dark revealing little, when an engine from one of the vehicles housed inside roared into life, the noise loud within the confines of the metal hold and without any further warning the rear of a four by four emerged from the gloom and took off from the ramp, clearing the remaining gap between it and the dock, coming straight for him. "Oh fuck!" Was all Callows could manage before diving out of the way, his soldiers scattering behind him as the vehicle crashed onto solid ground, sparks flying as the suspension compressed on impact, the exhaust and rear bumper scraping the concrete. Stats continued to keep his foot on the accelerator before yanking on the hand brake and pulling down on the steering wheel hard. The vehicle swung round and he banged it into first gear pushing the throttle to the floor, the tyres squealing noisily before gaining traction and accelerating away in a cloud of dense smoke accompanied by the sound of machine gun fire. Callows having regained his self esteem had picked himself up off the concrete and taking aim at the escaping vehicle emptied his weapons magazine. "Open fire!" He roared unnecessarily the soldiers drowning out his order with their own gun fire, spent cartridge shells bouncing off the ground around their feet. Magazines emptied the smell of cordite heavy in the air. The smoke slowly clearing to reveal the vehicle disappearing fast up the road that would take them directly to the Hub. "After them! Move!" Callows screamed at them as he ran for the nearest military vehicle, the catamaran forgotten about as it crunched into the dock side its propellers eating at the concrete before, with a protesting groan and a cloud of black smoke, the engines finally died.

On board the escaping vehicle the whoops of elation soon died down as Aleshia interrupted their celebrations. "I'm hit."

"What?!" Stats chanced a quick glance, his attention focused on the road ahead as their speed climbed steadily. Aleshia clutched at her left thigh with both hands, blood welled up from between her fingers, she looked in a lot of pain. A bullet had punctured the door membrane as the vehicle had careened from left to right during their escape and embedded itself in her leg. "Fuck! Where's the medi-pack?" Stats panicked. Nisa had already located it and was removing a bandage and swab.

"It's all we've got that's any use." She apologised handing them forward.

"It's okay it'll have to do." Aleshia removed her bloodied hands and accepted the offering, then tore open the bullet hole in her uniform a little and ripped open the swab packaging with her teeth and placed it over the open wound, her face contorted with pain. "Shit that hurts!" Clenching her teeth she shook the bandage open and lifting her wounded leg with a grunt began winding the bandage around tightly.

"Shit!" Stats swore again out of frustration. "You'll be okay Aleshia we'll get you to the medical centre."

"Hey I'm okay you got us the hell outta there, that went better than I ever imagined it would." She finished binding her wound and tied off the bandage.

"Yeah that was some cool driving man." Mac slapped the

driver on the shoulder appreciatively. "Looks like there on our ass though." Stats looked in the rear view mirror and sure enough through the haze of orange dust in their wake he could just make out the shapes of the pursuing vehicles.

25

The helicopter landed safely but not unsurprisingly hadn't gone unnoticed. They'd lingered in the beautiful gardens longer than they should have, Canova and Eve overwhelmed at the psychedelic abundance of exotic flowers and vividly coloured hummingbirds that called upon them, sipping at their sweet nectars. The unfamiliar sounds of monkeys filled their ears as they tried to locate the perpetrators of these wondrous new sounds their present predicament temporarily forgotten. Finally at Thalia's behest they left the gardens reluctantly and followed a pathway bordered with colourful flowering plants that wound lazily through this garden of Eden further into the heart of Heaven. Bees ambled from one delicate flower to another collecting pollen. "Ooh! What are those Thalia?" Eve's joy at the sight of the tiny furry insects made Thalia and Canova smile, her happy thoughts infectious.

"Their called bees, they're very special darling, without them your species couldn't survive, you see they pollinate the plants here in Heaven which in turn produce fruits and cereals so you can eat?"

"Don't you eat?" Eve's interest was once again back on Thalia.

"Yes of course although you know that warm glow you feel inside?" Eve nodded. "Well that..." Her mind fell silent and her attention went to the pathway up ahead. "Someone comes." Canova looked up his attention had also been attracted by the sight of the bees, he couldn't see anybody as yet but stopped awaiting their arrival trusting Thalia's judgment.

"How many?" He prepared himself in case the visitors proved to be hostile.

"Only one, they are old of years, their time is close at hand." They stood together silently for a few minutes, the only noise the buzzing of the insect life around them and the calls of the undiscovered primates. As predicted a lone fig-

The Hand Of God

ure appeared ahead in short time and the three companions continued up the path to meet them.

"Well, well, well." The stranger exclaimed out loud as they approached each other. "Who'd've thought it after all these years the last of the Witches! What kept you? I waited long enough, decided to come down an' look for you myself, thought you might of ran into some trouble." His eyes were firmly fixed on the blue-skinned Thalia taking in her alien appearance before acknowledging her two companions. As Thalia had foretold he was old, at least seventy or eighty Canova thought. He still retained most of his hair, now white with age although he was still spritely considering his years, no walking stick had aided him on his journey down the path to investigate the arrival of the helicopter and a humouress sparkle twinkled in his dark blue eyes. He wore lose fitting black jeans and white trainers and t shirt, a small logo embroidered on the front and a word, NASA. "Anyway no time for explanations. I think introductions are in order though don't you? I'm Ray." And he extended his hand, Canova was the first to shake it.

"I'm Canova, this here's Eve," he placed a hand on her head. "And of course, Thalia," before realising he'd spoken internally and repeated himself openly much to the bemusement of Ray.

"Well Canova, Eve and Thalia you'd better follow me quick because they know exactly where their missing helicopter is and we don't want to be out in the open when they arrive do we?," and trusting his visitors would comply to his suggestion he turned about without a further word and set off at a surprisingly quick walk back the way he'd come, they did, hastening in his tracks.

"How's the leg babe?" Stats' voice was with filled with concern, the strain was beginning to show on his face now as he drove as fast as he dared on the uneven road surface. Aleshia forced a smile.

"I've felt better."

"They're gaining." Nisa interrupted. "Can't you go any faster?"

"Doin' the best I can this ain't a particularly powerful model an' we got a little extra weight in the back. No offence

Mac."

"None taken. They're gonna have to get real close anyway before they can take a pop at us, we're kicking up a lot of dust. Nis go and hand me up that rifle." He asked her as he peered through the glass of the rear window. She pulled it from under their feet in the foot well and handed it over. "Now how do I get this thing to work?"

"Just place your thumb over that smooth panel next to the trigger an' wait till the red light turns green and your good to go." Aleshia instructed him from the front seat. "You think you can hit them at this distance through that dust?" She added. He just smiled his eyes twinkled mischievously. He did as Aleshia had instructed and waited until the tiny L.E.D. turned green then positioned himself as best he could as the vehicle bumped and lurched. He removed the protective lens covers and shouldered the weapon, loading a bullet into the chamber. Then closing one eye he looked down the telescopic sight with the other. The pursuing vehicles consisted of three four by fours and two vans, which were some distance behind. Mac aimed at the driver of one of the off roaders and concentrated. His retinas altered and the drivers determined face filled the lens of the sight. Mac grinned to himself and holding his breath squeezed the trigger. A loud crack filled the cab at the same time a small round hole appeared in the rear window. Through the sights Mac saw the drivers head kick back with the force of the high velocity bullets impact and the whole scene slew to one side as the driver slumped to the right pulling on the steering wheel as he did so. "Got 'im!"

"Good shootin'." Aleshia congratulated him impressed. Nisa could just make out the faint black shape of one of the following vehicles tumbling across the road, partially obscured by the lingering dust, as it collided with one of the other four by fours sending it careering off the road into the forest beyond.

"Now that's what I call an off roader." Mac smirked amused at his own attempt at a joke, Nisa just shook her head unamused. "Hey just havin' a little fun." He defended himself.

"Hey guys heads up we got a chopper bearin' down on

The Hand Of God

us." Stats had spotted it a little way ahead but it was gaining size fast. "You think you can bring that down Mac?"

"Yeah no worries." He repositioned himself aiming through the windscreen this time. The chopper was real close now and Mac had a good bead on the crew. "Shit they got a fuckin' rocket launcher, now that's just not playin' fair." He took aim resting the barrel on Stats' shoulder. "Don't mind do you bud?"

"Lean away." The pilots head filled his sights and he fired just as the helicopters crew launched a rocket. The chopper pitched forward the pilot collapsing over the controls. "They got one launched hang on guys this might get a bit rough." Stats swung the vehicle to one side his ears buzzing with the proximity of the gun shots, getting as close to the bordering vegetation as he dared dropping a gear as he did so. The rocket soared over the roof missing them by several feet before impacting into the compacted red dirt behind them in an explosion of yellow fire and black smoke. The force of the explosion fragmented the rear window and lifted the rear wheels from the ground with the resulting shock wave. "It ain't over yet!" He warned and on a head on collision came the out of control chopper spinning erratically towards them. Stats was close enough now to see Mac had taken out pilot and co-pilot alike with the same bullet their lifeless bodies shaken about like rag dolls within cockpit. He pulled down hard on the steering wheel again and veered in the opposite direction. The rotar blade caught the corner of the roof as he desperately tried to evade the collision and it seared the gleaming metal clean off before the helicopter crashed into the ground just to the rear of the four by four. It hit the ground hard in a tumble of metal, the rotar blades shattering sending deadly shrapnel in all directions, the crew smashed into the ground as they were flung from within, the trashed chopper bounced down the road before finally coming to a halt, twisted and broken. The four by four barely held the road, Stats grounding all four wheels skillfully regaining control after their collision with the chopper had sliced through the roof, he changed up a gear and steered them back on course, his face was glistening with sweat at the effort. Mac looked somewhat disappointed.

"Hey what's wrong?" Nisa noticed her companions frown.

"It didn't blow up! Thought it was gonna blow up." She shook her head despairingly.

"We gettin' any nearer to the Hub?" Nisa asked the pair up front.

"Yeah not much farther and it's what's waitin' for us at the other end that's worryin' me." Stats answered.

"Yeah me too." Aleshia looked very pale now and a red stain had appeared through the dressing on her leg, which hadn't gone unnoticed by Stats. If he couldn't get her to the medical facility within the Hub soon she was going to bleed to death.

The trio had kept their minds silent as they'd followed Ray along the path. Canova could see the trees and ferns thinning further ahead as it opened up into a smaller but equally well looked after garden. The whole scene dominated by the smoked glass panels that made up the housing complex beyond. Ray eventually slowed and the others caught up with him at the edge of the clearing. "Hurry please they can't be very far away now."

"Why are you helping us?" Eve thought. Ray turned to look at her and winked before answering her telepathically.

"Because that's why I'm still here. I have only a small part to play in all this but I'd like to think an important part none the less, one that will save you from the Hand of God I hope. My only role was to hasten yourselves on your journey, every second counts eh?" And he beamed widely at the friends before hastening across the lawn.

"You're a Sensitive?" Thalia asked surprised.

"Yes I am, a few of us still remain hidden from THEM, we learnt to shield our minds and resist absorption by the Nefarious."

"You mask your abilities well. Please forgive me my ignorance lately my abilities have been somewhat weakened." Thalia apologised.

"Don't be for it was my purpose to guide you on your way, you need to conserve your energy for what is to come, all of you." By now they'd reached a door set within the smoked glass of the building, almost imperceptible until up close. Ray stood before it, once scanned and identified the door granted him entry and it slid silently upwards revealing a minimalistic but opulent interior. "Come, come no time to waste I can hear them approaching." Ushering them inside Ray remained where he stood. Canova felt suddenly ill at ease and in response the old man smiled at him warmly. "Your powers are evolving yet Canova, you wield more power than you realise, believe in yourself and in others, it's okay to trust." The feeling lifted and was replaced by a warm glow within.

"Aren't you coming too? What about the others that live here? Are there other Sensitives on Heaven?" Canova was suddenly filled with numerous unanswered questions for this mysterious Ray.

"No I can't come with you, my job is done now. Eve it's up to you now, I'll try and hold them up long enough for you to find you way, there's a map on that table over there use that to guide you." Eve nodded solemnly her eyes were misty. "Now I've got to go they're almost here." He turned to Canova. "I'm not aware of any Sensitives other than myself on Heaven but we agreed long ago to never to seek each other out, we decided we'd be safer that way. As for the occupants of this building I am but the sole tenant." Canova looked surprised. "Few survivors lived to see this new Heaven and the ones that did... Well you won't find any children here only the militia repopulated this land or at least as long as the Nefarious deemed it necessary. Anyway that's a tale for another time my friends."

"Well thanks Ray, thanks for helping and I suppose it's goodbye then?" Canova shook his hand in gratitude his head still full of questions.

"Oh don't worry I'm sure we'll meet again," and the last thing Canova saw as the door descended was a star like sparkle in the old man's eye.

"Over here you two." Eve called them over with her mind. She'd found the map and was examining it intently, it showed the island of Heaven. The Hub was clearly marked just off centre of the land mass, a small cross marked their present position, standing in Ray's home. Canova marveled at the plush, elegantly decorated interior, a large dark brown leather sofa stretched across one side of the large room and on the opposite wall an oil painting depicting an unknown artists rendition of the three graces, the female forms masterfully captured on the large canvas.

"There's no such thing as coincidence," he murmured softly to himself before returning his attention to the map once more, the gravity of the situation and what lay in wait for them at the Hub undaunted him, they'd come this far now, he believed in his friends their combined determination would end Nekros's ordinance one way or the other.

"Aleshia come on don't give up now we're almost there." Stats removed one hand from the steering wheel and squeezed her other leg gently. Her eyes opened in response to his touch and she forced a smile. Her complexion was deathly white, strands of her black hair stuck to her perspiring forehead.

"Hey I'm still here babe." She gasped. Nisa reached around the seat and took her bloodied hand in her own.

"We ain't gonna let you go now, don't want you missin' out on all the fun."

"Yeah you can count me in we still got a job to do."

"Hell yeah!" Mac joined in his enthusiasm contagious filling everyone with a little courage and they were going to need it.

"We're here." Stats could see the jungle petering out about half a mile ahead, falling back to reveal the Hub its cylindrical curves rising above the last of the trees. The massive cables soaring into the sky above and as expected a military blockade.

"They got some pretty heavy duty stuff parked up ahead." Mac filled them in on what lay ahead his evolved vision picking out the details. "Aim for the far right of the line, they got a jeep stuck on the end might just scrape through there."

"Got ya." Stats followed Mac's advice and swerved aiming for the weakest point in the blockade. A hailstorm of bullets was unleashed as they closed and they all ducked down, Stats cautiously peering through the steering wheel aiming the four by four as it smashed the lighter vehicle out of the way. Everyone onboard was flung violently to one side as they collided with it, Stats expertly altering their course again leaving the road block behind and making for the main entrance to the Hub.

"We fuckin' made it!" Mac was the first to regain his poise and he punched the air jubilantly, his fist exiting the vehicle as he did so through the aperture the helicopter had made. The vehicle was well beaten up, a hole gaped in the roof, the front end and one side was crushed, several windows had been shot out and the once pristine paint work was riddled with small craters where the bullets had impacted. Stats rounded the corner and he spied the staircase that fanned out in front of the entrance. The Hand of God couldn't have expected them to make it through the road block as there was no military presence here only a few white jackets milled about, who at seeing the beat up four by four screech around the corner scurried for cover. He slowed the vehicle as they approached the entrance and stamping on the brakes hard they screeched to a halt at the foot of the stairs. Not waiting for any encouragement Mac and Nisa leapt out bringing their equipment with them and hurried up the stairs. Stats followed their lead and ran around to the passenger side opening the door, Aleshia toppled toward him still held in place by her seatbelt.

"Aleshia?" He placed two fingers on a point on her neck but he didn't feel a pulse. "Aleshia! Please no!" He leant into the cab and unclipped her belt, her full weight fell into his arms. He lifted her dead weight and ran up the steps to a point just inside where Mac had removed a nearby door that led into what appeared to be a small empty laboratory.

"Hurry in here." Nisa beckoned. He followed her inside where Mac was reloading the rifle ready for action.

"You still got that grenade Nis?"

"Sure do."

"We leave everything we don't need from here on in its guns an' fists." Mac finished talking and noticed Aleshia lifeless in Stats' arms as he lay her gently down on the floor. "Is she..?" He tailed off already knowing the truth.

"Fuck! Why did it have to be you Aleshia? Why?" Stats was overcome, she lay there her eyes shut, her face pale but beautiful none the less, at least he'd always thought so. Nisa touched him gently on the shoulder.

"I'm so sorry Stats but we've gotta move don't let her die in vain it's not what she would've wanted, you know that, it was her time." She squatted beside him and pointed out a bullet wound to the side of her chest Stats hadn't previously noticed. "Must've been when we came through that road block."

"She was one of a kind Nis, one of a kind." He looked her in the eyes his own red with grief.

"And she always will be." She squeezed his shoulder. "Now let's go and show this Nekros who's the new boss around here and I can hear the sound of vehicles approaching." Mac grim faced stood waiting for them at the open doorway, nodding in affirmation with Nisa, the military were almost here, adding.

"I'd say a couple of minutes, maybe less." Stats pulled himself together the need to avenge his friends death surpassing his grief for the moment. He unholstered Aleshia's gun and stood up, Nisa still retained his own, her knife held firmly in her other hand. His heart pounded, he readied himself, Nisa at his side Mac waiting sniper rifle at the ready. He looked from one to the other and nodded.

"Let's do this."

"Hey old man!" Ray took his time standing up from the weeding he was doing amongst some larger shrubs, an enquiring look on his face.

"Yes can I help you gentlemen?" He offered as a dozen soldiers rounded the corner of the building and approached him.

"A helicopter landed not far from here, the fugitives on board are highly dangerous and for your own safety we're requiring everybody in the vicinity to remain indoors. Have you seen anybody?"

"No nobody," he looked around, "as you can see I'm all alone out here."

"LIAR!" A cold hiss invaded his mind instantaneously. Bile rose in Ray's throat as a member of the Nefarious emerged joining the soldiers to confront him. "Where are they? Tell me now." The creeping cold stabbed at his thoughts but Ray resisted utilising his own talents, forcing back the invading cloying mind that tried to overpower him.

The Hand Of God

"Fuck off you vile, putrid piece of shit!" Ray shouted back into the mind of the Nefarious who took a step back visibly shocked at his rebuttal.

"Kill him!" It screeched. "Kill him now!" Its black eyes wide with rage, they had no need for this old fool his attempt at subterfuge would not alter the course of what was to come, his death was inevitable. The leading ranked soldier cocked his gun and took aim. Ray just smiled back at him lovingly.

Canova, Eve and Thalia stood around the small wooden table that the map lay upon holding hands seance like. Eve focused on the centre of the Hub that was marked on the map. A single gunshot sounded from outside. They all jumped at the sickening noise for they all knew what it signified. "We must leave this place at once." Thalia's thoughts relaxed and soothed Eve, who they both relied upon at this conjecture and taking a deep breath she closed her eyes. Eve's heart pounded and her head began to swim instantly. Her powers evolving each time she used them, there was no need to leave her body and seek out her destination this time, now she knew where they were going and she could take herself and her friends straight there...

Outside the door to Ray's home the single Nefarious stood in raging silence, whether already programmed to allow their kind access anywhere they wished to go or whether it simply over rode the security system somehow using the hive mind the door began to slide upwards. The soldiers responded and gathered behind the suited ghoul their weapons aimed towards the dark opening, which as it increased revealed nothing but a luxuriant living room at the centre of which sat a small wooden table the ephemeral visitors gone.

26

The atmosphere within the Hub was thick and satiating, like that of an old abattoir as the overpowering hive mind of the Nefarious permeated the upper level from below. Nisa's stomach churned as she sniffed at the air as they entered the corridor beyond the small room. "Can't you smell that?" She asked her nose wrinkling in disgust.

"Sure can Nis like death an' decay, there's something real bad goin' on in here." Mac spat, his heightened senses picking up on the sickly odour and magnifying it. "Where to Stats? Lead the way."

"We need to head for the operations room, from there we can take the elevator down to the lower levels that's where that foul bastard'll be hiding out." And they set off, disorientated white-coated scientists and medical staff alike stepped aside letting the determined looking trio past unhindered the sickly ambience affecting them also. As yet they'd encountered no military presence since entering the Hub, presumably the majority of the recruits had been deployed at the barricade and the dock and were hot on their heels. They continued to jog along the chaotic corridor towards their destination and the elevator that would lead them to Nekros's lair, Mac growling in the direction of any staff members that paid them a little too much attention along the way. Unhindered they covered the distance in short time led by Stats. "Okay as soon as we round this bend we're gonna be there so be alert and get those weapons ready 'cos this is gonna get hot." Sure enough as soon as they rounded the corner a squad of militia lay in wait at the entrance to the room of operations, they ducked back into cover amongst a hail of bullets. A nearby technicians white jacket turned red where a bullet caught him unawares, his body spinning with the impact before he dropped to the corridor floor, the sheath of documents he was grasping raining down upon him. "Mac I'm gonna need that doorway cleared can you roll a grenade amongst them? Then we storm the room on the left."

The Hand Of God

"You got it, at last some action." He grunted his approval and with his free hand removed the matt green metallic sphere from his tunic pocket. A small metal hoop protruded from its surface which he grasped between stained teeth and pulled hard spitting the pin to the floor. He took a couple of steps forward and using an under arm bowling technique rolled the explosive along the corridor towards the Hand of God. A few seconds ticked by followed by a surprisingly loud crack which was quickly followed by the screams of the wounded militia. The three didn't waste a second, taking advantage of the chaos ahead and leaving their cover they sprinted forward headed by Stats The grenade had been well placed by Mac and the soldiers lay broken and bleeding, the area surrounding them charred and blackened, a small pall of smoke spread out from the bomb site conveniently assisting their entry. The gunfight that followed was short and bloody. Wasting no time on the wounded soldiers who now presented no threat as they lay sprawled at the open doorway. Together they charged the room opening fire before emerging from the dissipating smoke, the depleted militia inside presenting no great threat, the trio having the element of surprise, they quickly took control of the situation making each bullet count as they felled one after another. Nisa and Stats ducked behind a nearby control console in answer to the returning fire. Mac, on the other hand, stood out in the open roaring his battle cry his high velocity rifle blowing holes the size of his fist in the bodies of his targets. He took one then a second bullet in the shoulder and chest respectively, both lodging in the muscle there, he continued unimpeded, it'd take more than that to put him down. The others taking careful aim from behind the cover of the electrical equipment, sparks showering the air as the militia's bullets pierced its metallic casing. Nisa used her throwing arm to firmly embed her knife in the back of a soldier who'd managed to creep up on Mac's blind side. In less than five minutes the shooting ceased, Mac's rifle was spent and he threw it directly at the last standing soldier taking him clean off his feet as it smashed into his face his final spray of ammunition going wide, he wouldn't be getting up again.

"Nisa cover the doorway keep an eye out for reinforcements." At Stats' request she left her position and headed for the door they'd just entered through the masking vapours now diffused.

"Mac you okay?" She called over as she relocated herself.

"Yeah just caught me some lead, just a couple of flesh wounds don't worry 'bout it." Stats moved over towards the elevator doors. He just hoped the retinal scan system would still grant him access. It did, or so he thought as the doors slid open silently to reveal Nekros in all his detestable glory.

Eve had learnt to utilise her talent well in the short time she'd had to develop it. The three had experienced a swirling of tingling energy that built up steadily within them, the feeling increased in strength until it enveloped them completely and just as quickly the feeling began to fade. Canova opened one eye tentatively, revealing a dark corridor dimly lit by overhead red bulbs. A series of doors permeated the solid wall opposite them. "Well I presume we're in the Hub then." He thought turning to Thalia for confirmation.

"Yes, I remember the feeling." He felt her shudder through their still clasped hands. "We are on a level below the surface, the Creatrix Mother lies incarcerated below us." Canova looked about and spotted what appeared to be elevator doors behind them. The rank atmosphere seeped into his mind as he hunted for a way to access the lift. "Allow me the system requires a retinal scan I should be able to over ride the system." Thalia joined him at the doors, he noticed her strained features, understandably considering the conditions she'd endured during her years incarcerated within these subterranean depths, combined with the debilitating ambience that crept and slithered into their rationality it was a miracle they could still function at all.

"Are you okay?" He noticed Thalia touch her brow with one graceful hand.

"Yes I can hold them at bay for a short time but Nekros is very aware of my presence here, the dark one will do anything to prevent our escape now. The feeling is almost overpowering we must reach her quickly before it's too late."

"Canova." Eve whispered her voice almost imperceptible. "They're here." He turned around leaving Thalia to crack the

The Hand Of God

security system alone. All along the darkened corridor the doors were opening in silence spewing out the Nefarious, their sickly, pallid features tinged red by the dim lighting above, the spectral visages seemed to hover bodiless in the gloom as their soulless eyes fell upon the intruders in their midst and as one they grinned insanely as they homed in on their prey.

Stats stumbled back from the doors the choking stench of Nekros's diseased mind sent his own senses reeling rendering him incapable of forming a coherent thought as the psychic vampire floated free of the elevator. "At last Field Commander we meet again, for the last time," and with a casual flick of his withered, taloned hand Stats was bodily lifted off his feet by some unseen force and was sent flying into a bank of computers, rolling noisily over the top he crashed to the floor behind them. A wild cry unexpectedly filled the room and Nekros's attention was directed toward the source of the roar to behold Mac closing the gap between them bellowing his rage, his features contorted his heart filled with retribution. Nekros made to send this new assailant crashing to the floor also but the proximity of the enraged Shifter made the action impossible.

"Time... to die... fucker!" Mac forced out the words as his mind competed with the superior psychic grasp that tried to hold him at bay, his size and momentum made sure he found his target regardless. Nisa raised her weapon from her position at the doorway but held fire afraid she might shoot her friend instead. Stats had also clambered onto his feet once more, still somewhat dazed. He shook his head which hurt from where he had hit the equipment hard, he also felt nauseous from Nekros's presence. His vision cleared just in time to witness Mac leaping toward Nekros, his features filled with loathing for the suited demon that stood before him, the reason for the persecution and murder of his fellow Shifters over the years. Then with an audible crack, that made Stats wince, Mac head butted the skeletal Nekros full in the face his withered, frail physique succumbing instantly to the powerful attack. The two of them went down simultaneously, falling in opposite directions.

"Mac! Mac!" Nisa screamed his name in disbelief and

came running to his aid, Stats reaching his prone body at the same time, his mind now recovering from the attack, he looked down at the ghoul his eyes were wide and his mouth was slack, a large dent was clearly discernable in the middle of his forehead. His body twitched into stillness, his death throes complete.

"I don't believe it Mac I think you've done it! I think you've killed him." He turned to Nisa who was kneeling at Mac's side holding one of his stout hands in her own, his body also twitched spasmodically but the random spasms seemed to be increasing in strength. "Nisa get back I don't like the look of this." She ignored him still trying to raise her friend back to consciousness. "Nisa get back now!" Stats roared as he noticed Mac's eyes opening his once mischievous grey irises replaced by two dark pits, a wicked smile played on his fleshy lips.

"Oh fuck!" Nisa had also noticed the sudden change in his appearance and leapt back shocked, Stats catching her arm to steady her as she did so. He turned his head toward the doorway, the unmistakable resonance of military boots reached his ears from the corridor beyond, the previously evaded soldiers had finally caught up with them.

"Quick get in the elevator!." He shouted at her, the figure that had once been her friend sat up glowering at them saliva running down his chin sticking to his beard. Stats had to literally drag Nisa bodily into the confines of the lift and he punched the button that would send them deeper into the heart of the Hub. Mac had risen eerily to his feet as if controlled with invisible strings by some unseen puppeteer and floated towards them, accompanied now by the appearance of the Hand of God as they invaded the room behind him. Nisa aghast watched transfixed as Mac approached the elevator, the doors closing just in the nick of time, his mad features thankfully disappearing from her line of sight, the militia seconds too late to redeem themselves. A frustrated bang sounded on the sealed doors above the echo of which followed them as they slowly descended.

27

No words were communicated between himself, Thalia and Eve, who now stood behind him terrified as Thalia continued to work her magic on the security system. The rancid stench filled their minds and their nostrils, icy claws caressed at their thoughts sucking at their memories. Canova powered himself up automatically pushing the cold slime from his mind as he did so but as more and more Nefarious emptied into the corridor he doubted he had a chance at all against the creeping hive mind of the horde before him. They were almost upon them when he heard an almost imperceptible hiss from behind him. She'd done it! Their means of escape had thankfully materialised. He instinctually turned around to see with his own eyes, relieved to see the interior of the lift revealing itself his mind distracted just for a second by the sight of a child's stuffed toy discarded on the floor inside but it was all the powerful mind of the Nefarious needed. Instantaneously the combined might of their growing numbers took advantage and threw him forcibly against the wall adjacent to the now open elevator. Thalia likewise had been caught off guard and was thrown by the psychic tidal wave crashing into the lift, the impact rendering her unconscious. Canova on the other hand had a certain amount of protection built up around him and regaining his senses fast he sat up, for now forgotten by the Nefarious, they had other things on their mind. "Canova!" She screamed aloud this time as they reached her, petrified she remained rooted to the spot, the Nefarious held onto her mind tightly preventing her from teleporting herself to safety. The amassed horde filled the corridor now and the nearest creature grasped her arm and lifted her casually off the ground like a doll and with a powerful flick threw her across the corridor where she smacked into the wall with a sickening thud, cutting off her piercing scream. Canova's rage new no bounds now and a scream, a power he'd never experienced before exploded into his mind and unable to contain the pain and anger he'd felt at witnessing Eve's body as she lay crumpled on the floor any longer, released the mind bomb. The scream within escaped his lips also, his vocal chords vibrating filling the underground space and the Nefarious mind. A psychic wave penetrated their black mind, the resulting shock wave reached far and as one they fell back like toppled dominoes. At once the nightmarish atmosphere lifted and Canova too keeled over where he still sat, a trickle of blood dripped from his nose and pooled on the cold stone floor beside him.

"Mac! What the fuck?!" Nisa was still in shock, her green eyes wild, tears streamed down her face, the first time Stats had seen any real emotion escape her steely exterior since he'd met her. He put an arm around her and hugged her.

"I'm sorry." Was all he could think of to say in the way of comfort.

"It's... it's okay, but what? How?"

"There's no way Nekros would've survived that impact, he must've known that and sent his consciousness into Mac and absorbed him, taken over his body."

"But Mac wouldn't let that happen."

"Remember they have a collective mind even Mac couldn't have withstood that." Before she could reply the doors opened once again this time to reveal Nekros's lair.

Canova stirred, his faculties returning and as he remembered their current dilemma he sat up quickly. His head thumped and he winced at the pain, then dabbed at his nose with the back of his hand noting the tacky red residue there and the small congealing pool on the floor next to him. "Eve!" Ignoring his hurting head he sprang to his feet and stepping between the prone Nefarious he approached her crumpled form, noting briefly the twitching limbs of the felled ghouls, the corridor now resembling some horrific tomb. Eve's body was limp, her head bloody, her chest still. He bit his lip hard as he fought back the tears and lifted her weightless body into his arms then made his way back to the elevator. Sill holding Eve he pressed the lowest button on the panel as Thalia stirred into life. Fortunately the elevator responded, apparently once accessed the security system no longer required further verification. He looked out at the morgue scene beyond as the doors slid shut. The last thing

The Hand Of God

he saw was one, then another, then several of the Nefarious sitting up their heads turning in their direction.

Meanwhile Stats and Nisa had located the elevator doors in the dark recesses in the office above. the doors remained tightly shut unresponsive to their presence. "What now?" She asked him hoping he had the answer but before he could reply they both turned about as the light emitted from the first lifts interior was shut out, the doors closing as the elevator was summoned.

"Shit! Well we ain't got much time so anything's worth a try." Stats waved Nisa back as he checked his pistol, he couldn't have much ammunition left. He shielded his eyes with one hand and aimed the barrel of the gun at the scanning device and squeezed the trigger. The sound of the resulting shot deafening in the confined space. The two friends waited expectantly for some kind of result. The scanning unit smoked and sparked where the bullet had shattered the disc and ruined its heart, but the door remained sealed.

"There's nothing happenin' Stats!" Nisa panicked, for once in her life she was scared.

By the time Canova felt the elevator coming to a standstill Thalia had fully recovered and pulled herself up, retrieving the toy bear discarded by Nekros earlier as she did so. Her eyes were filled with tears for of course she had experienced Eve's pain and fear as if it were her own. As the lift doors opened she placed a hand over Eve's bloody face. "Find your way little angel so others may follow you." Her whispered telepathy kissed Canova's mind and heart and he felt a warmth spread between them, a twinkling speck of energy sparkled and blinked out before his eyes. "Her soul is safe, they almost had her for their own." She smiled at him sadly, a single lilac tear rolled down one pale blue cheek, she leant forward and kissed him tenderly. "Come let us finish this," and together, Eve still in his arms they purposefully strode towards the final door, the cell in which imprisoned was the Mother of all.

The empty elevator was now ascending responding to the summons from above, the destroyed scanner unit rendering the security on that level useless. "Okay how much ammo do you think we got left?" Nisa struggled to focus her mind.

"Not much a few rounds at most."

"Must be about out too but I've still got this," she patted the pocket were the grenade sat.

"Let's hope it doesn't come to that just yet." Both of them knowing that an explosive of that size would kill them both if detonated in a room of this dimension. So side by side they aimed their pistols at the doors opposite. The elevator had reached the office and the doors began to slide open at the same time the one from below appeared. Mac, or at least the physical form that was still recognisable as him launched himself into the dingy office. Nekros's mind boiled and twisted within its new host, his ebony eyes bulged as he powered across the room suspended in mid air. Nisa and Stats had quickly entered the lift behind them Nisa frantically pressing the button that would send them to the lowest level and the door commenced closing. Mac was almost upon them his progress suddenly slowed as the companions emptied the magazines of their guns, firing on empty after only a few rounds as they'd predicted. The bullets punched into Mac's chest and delayed him long enough for the door to finish closing unhampered. Nekros hissed to himself through clenched teeth as he hovered before the door, the muscles in Mac's neck bulging his veins popping. "You have nowhere to run to now fools, all of you, here, together, a family reunited, oh how you will scream." Mac's possessed features contorted into a mask of shrieking insanity.

28

"Mother of all what have they done to you?" Thalia's empathy for the crucified woman before them touched him deeply also and they fell to their knees filled with reverence and compassion. Canova laid out Eve's body to rest before her, straightening out her silver necklace and placing the small heart directly over her own, now stilled. Thalia laid the dilapidated toy on her motionless chest and crossed her arms over the top, restoring Charley to Eve's charge once more. Breaking through their reverence the suspended female spoke out to them telepathically. "My child you have returned." The emaciated figure lifted her head to view them as best she could in the gloom and Canova was sure he saw a small glow of golden light pulse once within her chest, the brief glow showing through her frail physique. "At last this pain and suffering is almost at end but the threat is not over yet. Thalia, Canova and little Eve, her life ended all too soon, this is how I always knew it would be, I have dreamed of this moment for decades. The time is almost upon us when we must move beyond these realms and lead the others into the future. For close to a century now I have kept hidden what Nekros has searched for, delving deep into my memories but it lay protected by a "spell" that could only be broken with the knowledge of love, an alien concept to one as evil as HE. The knowledge of creation spirituality housed within a mind as corrupted and diseased as his would have infected the very fabric of creation and the universe itself." During this informative dialogue Canova and Thalia had both felt a beating within their chests which fell into time with their own hearts and dwelt there, the knowledge safe once again. "Now my children it is done."

Nisa and Stats stumbled into the basement room as soon as the doors opened which immediately closed again behind them. "Here we go again!" Nisa tried to joke and winked over at him trying to alleviate the situation and steady her own nerves.

"Any ideas?" Stats asked. She stood to her full height and took a deep steadying breath.

"Leave him to me." She moved to the side of the elevator flattening herself against the wall as much as she could, the ends of her fingers extending into lethal points the same length of her fingers again. "You've gotta keep him distracted." Stats didn't argue that cold look had returned to her green eyes once more and he just nodded his compliance. He positioned himself in line with the lift, his back pressed firmly against the opposing door just as it slid open behind him, Canova and Thalia standing on the other side. The two jumped back at the sight of Stats stumbling backwards towards them. He steadied himself and beamed widely at the sight of his friends and hugged them both, the smile disappearing as he noticed Eve, lifeless on the floor behind them her toy bear hugged to her chest and his jaw dropped when he made out the source of all Nekros's power suspended in the gloom.

"Not now." Canova vocalised aware of the many questions that had just entered Stats's head.

"Yeah, yeah sure." He nodded, his mind still reeling from shock and pulled himself together. "We still got a problem. A Mac sized problem to be exact," and he turned around just in time to see the lift doors opening. HE was here. Nekros burst forth his dark eyes homing in on Thalia and he paused for a second basking in her proximity. Sharp pains stabbed at his neck and ribcage puncturing his carotid artery and his heart. He swatted his attacker to one side, Nisa, sliding to the floor after hitting the wall with a smack. The body he inhabited was mortally wounded now, his was haemorrhaging a lot of blood from the bullet and stab wounds and the muscular heart beat it's last tune, his parasitic mind needed a new host. "The Witch! Ah yes the Witch!" His twisted mind pushed Mac's ruined body onwards his goal almost within his grasp.

"Now it is my time." Thalia's resolve was strong as her words sounded in their minds, she just smiled and spoke psychically once again. "You should all leave now while there is still time."

"Get Nisa outta here Stats, I'm staying." Canova ordered.

The Hand Of God

"You sure?" Stats checked on Mac's progress, less than twenty feet. Canova nodded, his mind made up.

"Thalia needs me." She smiled at his willingness to remain with her.

"You had to decide for yourself, thank you." Her love filled his being as she communicated her gratitude.

"Okay Stats you've gotta move now Nisa needs you." Stats saluted them both his military upbringing kicking in.

"You can count on me," and with that he rushed past the wounded Mac as he lurched towards them, Nekros no longer able to sustain levitation in this ruined body, a trail of dark red blood in his wake. Stats took a dive and rolled under Mac's desperate grasp at him but Nekros's reaction was too slow, his focus concentrated on Thalia. He rolled back onto his feet and ran over to where Nisa sat slumped against the wall and he shook her gently. "Come on Nis we gotta get outta here." She opened her eyes and in the periphery of her vision she noticed Mac was still upright, Nekros's powerful mind keeping his host alive.

"But what..." She began but Stats shushed her and grabbed her hands pulling her to her feet.

"Not now." He interrupted her. "They got it covered." He gave Canova and Thalia a final glance, Nisa following his gaze noticing her friends for the first time before Stats dragged her to the waiting elevator.

"Wait!" Nisa pulled on his hand to stop him just as he entered the lift. She delved into her pocket and retrieved the remaining grenade. "Heads up Canova!" She shouted and skillfully tossed the sphere over Mac's head. Canova heard her clearly and kept his eye on the metallic ball as it arced over the looming shape before them and right into the palm of his cupped hand.

"Good throw!" He called back.

"Anytime." She joined Stats in the elevator and hit the button.

Canova and Thalia backed further into the room. "You wouldn't dare destroy the one you love." Nekros spat into his mind, his words rasped at his brain leaving it raw and bruised. "You can't destroy me with your mind or your toys." He cackled at Canova's reliance on the grenade he clutched. Blood spilled from Mac's chest and bubbled from the puncture wounds in his neck that Nisa had dealt him, his massive bulk fell forward as Nekros's hold over his physical body lifted as his leech like mind sprang into Thalia's, taking hold and biting deep. At once she responded.

"You fool Nekros, you never did understand, your greed would always to be your downfall. The magic that was always an intrinsic part of our species, that of creation through the act of love would be your unmaking. Your accumulated power held us back for decades but we retained our faith. I, Thalia, was chosen to hold the "spell" that would finally unravel the evil you have committed and to dispel the darkness."

"Your will can't hold back the combined force of the Nefarious. I will inherit this body your mind is already ours." She could feel his grasp strengthen and her mind tried desperately to squirm free but no avail, he was right they were too powerful, they had no options left, the time had come.

"Be strong Canova, for both of us." Thalia communicated to him while she was still capable. Canova was held gripped in a tight psychic lock unable to move his limbs, paralysed, he focused hard trying to break free. "I love you." Was Thalia's final thought before the slimy darkness oozed into every lobe of her alien mind. Her final utterance gave him all the encouragement he needed. Nekros's hold had lessened slightly as he writhed in ecstasy exploring his new host but it was all he needed, Canova pulled the pin. Nekros realising what he had done looked at him through Thalia's eyes, the miasmic blues and violets slowly staining black like spilled ink blotting out her once beautiful orbs and she smiled horribly. Canova held out the grenade on the palm of his hand half way between them and an all consuming white light filled his mind as the grenade detonated.

Unfortunately for Nisa and Stats the Nefarious on the floor above had fully recovered and were amassed at the elevator doors awaiting its return. "Shit Stats we've stopped movin'!." He didn't reply as the space that slowly appeared before them was filled with a mass of skull like faces all grinning madly.

"Shit wrong floor!" Was all he could think of to say as

the Nefarious pushed their way into the confined space, the rank odour accompanying the Nefarious making them both retch. A powerful shock wave passed through the elevator shaft from the level below rattling the cubicle in which they both stood and a fraction of a second later the Nefarious dropped to the ground, the power that had sustained and motivated them gone, shattered by the seed of love and compassion Nekros had consumed on entering Thalia's mind. The combined will of Witch and Psych melting away any last residue of his lurking foulness.

"It's over." Nisa exclaimed, the fetid mood lifted as the Nefarious remained motionless were they lay. "They've done it!." Together they cautiously hauled the bodies that were jamming the doorway back out into the corridor reluctantly handling the corpses and boarded the lift once more, the doors shutting blocking out the morgue scene in the corridor beyond. They hugged each other closely as they ascended, the terror was over.

29

During the months that followed a great transformation had unfolded on Heaven. Nekros, now destroyed his army of Nefarious at last released from his servitude the threat finally eliminated. Many of their kind died, their black hearts and minds bursting as their master and nemesis was vapourised in the subterranean explosion. A few at least did survive, awakening from their horrific nightmare amongst the stiff bodies of those less fortunate souls.The remaining populace of Sensitives were quick and eager to fulfill their destinies and in return their human appearance began to resurface, their eyes once again regaining their true colour and humanity. Many, as they recovered, found comfort and solace communing with nature, enjoying the flora and fauna in the gardens and forests on Heaven, basking in the sunlight once more, their hearts now beating to a different tune. Stats and Nisa, his new second in command, had taken the lead following the demise of Nekros, having initially recruited a small group of willing followers on their triumphant return to the surface now that they were freed from the constant threat of Nekros and his horde. Their supporters quickly swelled in number and a new order was soon established. Transport was dispatched to the outlands to ferry the remaining survivors back to Heaven. At first they feared it was some new trick conjured up by the Hand of God but steadily a mutual trust was established and eventually even the handful of evolved humans that had hidden themselves away for so many years resurfaced, the last surviving Bioshifter's were the last to accept the hand that was proffered them. Civilians, military personnel and Hub staff alike joined forces and soon a new regime was born, one ruled by compassion. The lowest levels had been permanently sealed as a mark of respect for those who had sacrificed their lives for the greater good of all. The memory of the heroic part their friends had played living on in Nisas' and Stats' hearts.

The two remaining friends walked side by side in the af-

The Hand Of God

ternoon sun, which sat low in the sky, small blankets of cloud obscuring the golden orb dispelling its glare. Winter on Heaven was almost over the cooler winds would soon once again be replaced by the energy depleting ones of spring and summer soon enough. They continued in silence following the pathway underfoot deep in thought. Stats and Nisa had substituted their militia uniforms for civilian clothing. Nisa had grown her sleek black hair in and it now hung to her shoulders, swaying gently as she walked slightly ahead of him. The tight jeans she wore showed off her athletic figure as did the close fitting leather jacket she now wore. Sensing his attentions she turned and smiled at him, her front tooth still missing a corner but her smile shone and her beautiful emerald eyes found his own pale blue ones.
"Hey Stats what ya thinkin'?"

"Do you think there's life after death?" Nisa smiled sweetly knowing fine well what he'd been thinking about.

"You know years ago I would've said no, we live we die an' that's it, but now..." She paused staring up into the dusky sky, a lone raptor soared high above. "Yeah I do think there is something more, I get the feelin' sometimes that Mac an' the others are keepin' watch over us, you know what I mean? Or am I just being wishfully paranoid."

"I know what you mean, get that feeling too sometimes, like their waitin' on us."

"Yeah that's it exactly." Nisa nodded glad he had confirmed her own perception of recent occurrences and without another word they continued onwards down the trail eventually arriving at a small cemetery within the gardens of Eden. Only civilians and high ranking officers serving the Hand of God had previously been granted burial plots here, the other less fortunate inhabitants had been unceremoniously cremated in the underground furnaces, as had the bodies of the departed Nefarious, no Lord's prayer to ease them on their voyage home. Together Nisa and Stats wound their way toward a row of newly laid headstones, respective of the graves of their ancestors as they traversed this sacred place. Five gravestones in all, fashioned from black marble veined with white and silver, the names of their fallen friends carved skillfully into the stone. Aleshia, who was laid to rest beside her long dead parents, to Stats and Nisa's left were they stood heads bowed. The aged stones weathered now and tinged green with algae and moss. Mac's headstone was planted next, then Canova, Eve and Thalia. The graves below empty, their friends physical remains destroyed utterly in that deadly explosion that had altered the course of humanity but for Stats and Nisa their fallen comrades would always be with them in their thoughts and in their hearts, patiently awaiting their return home.

"Rest in peace guys." Stats whispered and took Nisa's hand in his own, she clasped it in response lacing her fingers with his and together they left the cemetery as the sun slowly set over Heaven and the gardens of Eden.

EPILOGUE

The flash of blinding white light obscured his vision and his thoughts. All was wiped clean, erased of all the hurt and pain he'd endured over the years. His disembodied mind floated aimlessly in a white haze unable to form a coherent thought as yet. "Canova return to me my love." Thalia's words slowly coaxed him back to reality but where was that? They were dead weren't they? Killed in the explosion? His mind trying to piece the recent events back together. "Only our physical shells perished our true essence lives on." Her warm words touched on his heart and he felt it beat inside his chest.

"I'm alive!" He gasped his eyes finally opening.

"Or to be more precise you're not dead." Mac winked at him his pale grey eyes twinkling as he proffered him a helping hand were he still lay. Canova accepted and Mac hauled him up to his feet effortlessly.

"Mac I don't believe it your okay."

"You better believe it," he grinned. Canova turned to Thalia who stood at his side, she looked radiant and he kissed her firmly on her perfect lips, her cheeks flushing a darker blue as she returned his affections. He lost himself for a time in her beautiful eyes as she held his gaze lovingly, their breathing synchronised.

"What about Nekros? Is he..?"

"Dead?," Mac finished for him. "For sure, he's toast, you an' your woman there did a good number on him."

"And at last the doors are finally open to the noosphere." She sighed softly in his mind and took his hand her slender fingers entwining with his own. He looked ahead as two more figures approached out of the foggy haze of this new realm of existence. Aleshia and Eve, who held her hand all past sins forgiven and absolved in this new world, she clutched at her Charley bear with her other hand who was now as new, its once missing eye returned, both his friends looked healthy and very much alive, Aleshia's white teeth flashing as she smiled at him her eyes filled with light.

"Come on you three the others are waiting." Eve informed them happily and beckoned them to follow herself and Aleshia back into the fog. Mac slapped his back gently and smiled following them. Canova turned back to his beautiful Thalia and smiled and hand in hand they followed their friends into a new dimension of evolution.